Suspicious River

Suspicious River

▼

Laura Kasischke

HOUGHTON MIFFLIN COMPANY

BOSTON • NEW YORK • 1996

For information about permission to reproduce
selections from this book, write to
Permissions, Houghton Mifflin Company,
215 Park Avenue South, New York,
New York 10003.

For information about this and other
Houghton Mifflin trade and reference books
and multimedia products, visit The Bookstore
at Houghton Mifflin on the World Wide Web
at http://www.hmco.com.trade/.

Library of Congress Cataloging-in-Publication Data
Kasischke, Laura, date.
Suspicious river / Laura Kasischke.
ISBN 0-395-77397-0
I. Title
PS3561.A6993S87   1996   95–46801
813'.54 — dc20   CIP

Printed in the United States of America

Book design by Robert Overholtzer

QUM 10 9 8 7 6 5 4 3 2 1

for B.A. —
Plan A

I would like to thank
Lisa Bankoff and Dawn Seferian
for their assistance
and support.

One
· · · · · · · · · · · ·

*T*HE FIRST TIME I had sex with a man for money, it was September — still like summer, but the heat in the motel room was on and it seemed to coat my throat with dust. The man was dull, small-eyed, no taller than myself, but he seemed afraid. He wouldn't look at me. When I asked him what he wanted me to do, he said, "That's your job."

There was a powdery film between us, the glare of the one lamp on the nightstand making haze of the artificial heat. I could see my own image through that haze, above the dresser, reflected in a mirror the length and width of a coffin — a silver one, lined with mercury and sterling, a stainless steel table in an operating room, or morgue, propped up against a wall:

That was my own body floating in that mirror, I thought, reflected in sharp triangles of light. My *body* in a closet of pure flat space, like a piece of bent sheet metal abandoned on a beach.

Still, I looked young. I had shiny black shoes on my feet and a clean, new blue cotton skirt, a white knit top with lace around the throat, and I saw myself glance sideways out of that glass, standing still and blank-faced in front of a man as thick-armed and short as an ogre, hairy — though the hair on his body was blond and nearly invisible, curling in tangles, white and sticky as the threads of a spider's web, pushing out of his black T-shirt, up his neck. Sickly tendrils climbing the post of a fence. His face was pink and square, a canned ham, and the skin of it was unlined, damp — a fresh baby's — though his teeth looked yellow and forty years old.

Already, the motel heater rattled, mechanical, and it blew moon dust between my knees — those two dead and bone-white satellites — and between my body and his.

Two total strangers in a motel room, in a mirror.

I got on my knees and unzipped him. It lasted no more than a minute. Finished, he just sat down heavy, steak-faced, and exhausted on the edge of the bed, his pants around his knees, shaking vaguely, and wouldn't look at me.

I'd gotten my sixty dollars up front, and afterward I went straight home.

But the next day, I did the same thing with someone else. Sixty dollars.

And the next with someone else, and someone else.

A hundred and twenty.

A hundred and eighty.

Two hundred and forty dollars by the end of the third day.

Three hundred and sixty by the evening of the fourth.

As I've said, it was September. One day would be muzzy, the sky white with haze, a weakening sun in the middle like a cool fried egg.

The next day there would be sheets of gray rain followed by a velvety purple light beyond the orange leaves.

Other than that, every day was the same:

I was making money, saving money.

I was saving money for something that glistened a bit in the distance — slippery mirage of water on the road ahead of me on a hot, dry day. Something that rose and fell in a fog, changed shape and size, something I might have glimpsed once from the corner of my eye as a child.

Sometimes that thing floated over me and spit out colored light — a mushroom cloud.

Sometimes it was just bright chrome, a hill of sugar, or a pillar of salt.

Sometimes it rose to the surface of my dreams like a second skin, a kind of foreskin floating to the top of a pan of scalded milk or dragging the snow in a long white robe.

I assumed I'd recognize the thing when I saw it.

I assumed I'd see it when I'd saved the money to buy it.

"Where have you been, Leila?" my young husband would ask when I came home a little late again. He had dark circles under his eyes:

He was getting thinner as I got richer — though there was still a snapshot of him pinned to the refrigerator's slick door with a black magnet, and in it he was forty pounds over-weight, smiling widely, a pliable white purse of belly hanging friendly over his belt.

"You know," I shrugged. But he didn't.

Though Rick made me a sandwich every morning to take to work every afternoon, he'd quit eating bread and butter himself in favor of raw vegetables months before. All that bushy color shoved into the crispers at the bottom of the fridge smelled fresh and stiff, smelled more like the white tissue they wrap your new shoes in than food, smelled like nothing; and that nothing was his only meal, as far as I could tell — all he ate all day. Even his breath had changed. Now it was like cold air and dry white rice mixed up in a plastic bowl.

All I wanted of the sack meals my husband made for me was the can of diet Coke, warm and stinging the roof of my mouth by early evening. But sometimes I'd eat a cheese sandwich

if there wasn't any butter on it. Occasionally a homemade
cookie tasted good after a cigarette.

The motel where I worked wasn't seedy. It was the kind of
place you'd like to take your wife, if you had one, and your
kids. There would be things for them to do — swing set and
picnic tables by the riverbank behind the motel and a miniature golf course across the street with a mini-waterfall and
greenish water that slapped the plastic rocks all day and night.
It was simple and easy to golf there. You could do it in your
sleep. From the front desk of the Swan Motel, I could hear
children screech every few minutes, their parents shouting
"Good one!" in triumph — voices sifted across the light traffic
of Riverside Drive.

But winning that game wasn't even a minor accomplish-
ment, not even a lucky break, it was just the way the course
had been laid by some intelligent out-of-towner who knew
that tourists always want to seem to win the games they pay
to play. Therefore, it was as if the holes just sucked those
golf balls into earth with a whoosh of wind and tongue.
Even when you'd barely grazed your ball with the club or sent
it rolling in the wrong direction, you'd end up with a hole
in one.

I imagined those white balls tunneling through cardboard
shafts underground like legless mice in a kind of dry, deaf hell.

And the Swan Motel across the street was fresh and clean —
starched sheets, beige carpet, decent white towels we sent to
Ottawa City in a pickup full of olive green trash bags to be
bleached twice a week. Out back, Suspicious River ran swirl-
ing and black, but the water looked clean, and there were
swans who congregated on the motel lawn like a tea party of
rich old women and movie stars, stretching and honking along
the river's clammy banks, a few lounge chairs scattered
around where you could recline with a bottle of Orange Crush
or beer and watch those long birds extend their subtle necks,

open and close their wings, slowly lift and lower their webbed and prehistoric feet as if they had somewhere to go — deciding once again not to go, pressing their feet back firmly into the damp mud and grass.

Those swans wanted desperately to be fed — anything — even stones, even styrofoam — and they watched the motel guests from the corners of their eyes, waiting for a soft flash of bread retrieved from a clear plastic bag, a glimpse of something tossed toward them, edible or not — a greasy palmful of old potato chips, a crumpled coffee cup. Always ravenous, they stood stiff as angelic soldiers, slick-eyeing the motel guests, feigning nonchalance. Then, fed, they'd slosh away, bread sloppy and calm in their orange beaks, slippery feet churning up the dark water of Suspicious River, quiet as death.

Still, you might never know by looking at the Swan Motel, with its blond bricks, white shutters, glassed-in office, pink neon (NO) VACANCY sign sputtering at the street. You might never know, as you stepped inside the office door, where the air conditioning would first hit you in summer, refrigerator-cool, a bit like ether or 7UP but mixed with canned air freshener, kiddy-cocktail sweet, or the buzz of electric heat making a gray towel of the air in winter:

You *couldn't* know, as you passed the rack of shiny postcards toward the front desk girl, you wouldn't even *suspect* what she was doing, or willing to do, for sixty dollars. You'd be tired from your drive up North. You'd be looking at the number on the plastic key she'd handed you, not at me.

But there are all kinds of people in this world, and they're not all like you. Some of them come to a small motel up North, and the front desk girl is the first thing they see.

There's a way to ask her what you want to know, and a way for her to answer.

The Swan Motel was a good place to spend a weekend, as I've said. Simple, and quiet. Its riverbank boasted the swans' only nesting ground along all sixty-four miles of Suspicious River. Between 1857 and 1859, seven hundred and seven swan skins had been snagged at that very spot, sold to Hudson's Bay Company, shipped to London where they'd been sewn into wedding dresses and spinsters' hats, pillows, pens, strippers' boas and tails:

Imagine. Hundreds and hundreds of white and muffled shipping trunks of dead feathers shifting around beneath a boat's wet deck as it crossed a choppy ocean.

But this was 1984, more than a century later, and the swans still came to town two by two each March, building their nests in cattails in the marshiest part of the water — that swollen lip of mud and river behind the Swan Motel. There, they'd float around slow as pleasure boats all summer, then rise up in October, listening to something in the distance, and fly off all at once — necks and wings stretched out, looking crucified against the sky, making one low bassoon noise together as they flew above our trailers and houses and Burger King, *oo-oo-oo.*

Behind the Swan Motel there was even a rickety dock with warped and splintered boards, slithering with deep green and weedy hair, where you could sit in the summer, dip your feet into the darkness of Suspicious River, see how lukewarm it was. But you wouldn't want your wife or children to swim in there. They'd come up covered with bloodsuckers, sticky as black scabs. You'd have to burn those off with a match while someone you loved squirmed and flinched beneath your hands.

Rick had been fatter when I married him, fatter even a few short months before, and I preferred that — preferred the way his belly had felt between us in the waterbed when it was there, familiar. The way he'd smelled a bit damp between his shoulder and his ear, a little like Wonder Bread, fresh from the plastic package — clean and soft. We'd been married for six years, and it had been his extra flesh I'd gotten used to feeling for in the dark across the rolling motion of our waterbed when I still thought he loved me, when I thought maybe I was the one who couldn't love.

But lately I'd find him at least once every day standing shirtless in front of the bathroom mirror, pinching the folds of his lost belly together with the fingers of both hands. He'd study that skin from three angles with something like love or fear on his face.

"You're not fat," I'd say, and he'd turn to look at me — the new, sharper bones of his face pulled back into a stranger's smile, faked. He was tall and dark-haired. When he was overweight, he'd looked charming, boyish, a high school football player gone soft the very afternoon he turned twenty-one. But, thin, he looked like a young salesman — a bit frantic, or hostile, new on the job, an angry Christian.

For lunch he might have a salad with just vinegar on it, no oil. For dinner he'd have carrots sliced onto Saltines and an apple cut up into wedges like miniature canoes. He'd eat those boats slow and one by one while they turned pale brown and glazed over like wounds just starting to heal. Then, at night, he'd toss around in the waterbed as if he were swimming laps at the Y. Slow at first, as if to save his energy, but faster as the night wore on — more like drowning than swimming by morning, more like swimming in a high and ice-cold river than swimming in the gray and murky pool at the Y.

After a while, I couldn't sleep with him anymore, so I slept on the couch. Still, in my dreams there would be that background noise of the waterbed splashing and rolling — just the way I could hear Suspicious River splash all afternoon and evening past the Swan Motel from the front desk there.

"Your room is just above the ice machine."

I handed him a key with 47 on one side and the imprint of a swan on the other.

This one was wearing plaid pants. A bright green golf shirt. He had a beer belly and a pink tan, a white belt on and white shoes. Fifty, I guessed. I guessed his mother hadn't warned him not to wear white shoes after Labor Day.

His fingertips touched mine when he reached for the key, and they felt moist and dry at the same time. He looked a little winded, like someone with high blood pressure who shouldn't drink beer, but did — maybe in secret, in his basement at night while his wife was asleep with a head full of tight pink curlers upstairs.

"Thank you, sweetheart," he said.

His teeth were small and smooth.

It was about four o'clock on a Tuesday in the twenty-fourth year of my life. I'd started my shift at three, and I had seven hours to go. September, it was bright and humid outside. I looked past his shoulder through the office glass to be sure no one was just that moment pulling into the semicircular drive with the hushed purr of a tourist's American motor, and a film of light like TV glare or wet glue painted the parking lot white in my eyes. I had to squint to see out there, and my own reflection in the window got in the way.

I wanted to think my hair was red, but maybe it was brown. In the window glass, all colors were gray. It was thick, though, and wavy, and it hung in three fat, knotted ropes — one on each side of my shoulders, one heavy down my back. I believed I was thin and pale enough to be pretty but too pale and thin to be beautiful, so I preferred clothes that made me look young, still or again like a little girl — lacy, with ribbons. I liked clothes, and even before there was so much money, I'd buy a new wardrobe every month at the skinny strip mall in Ottawa City:

One new skirt and one new shirt and maybe a pair of pantyhose or short white socks. I'd walk down the gray tunnel of that mall between J.C. Penney's and Sears and imagine one day I'd work at one of those department stores, when I got tired of the motel, or fired. Maybe I'd work in Lingerie. I'd imagine myself wrapping pink silklike slips in tissue paper and slipping them into my purse when the manager took her coffee break.

At that mall, I always felt dimly full of hope for the future. Someday, I thought, I'd get a job there, and the petty thieving would keep me from looking as bored as the girls behind those counters looked — bored as mannequins or topless dancers, pale under too much fluorescent light. Those girls were all born and raised in the blond skirts of field or the cleared forests around Suspicious River, Ottawa City, Fennville, and their snow boots sat lined up, panting and black, in hall closets all summer while they shivered in the mall's dry air-conditioned air. Their nipples stood out stiff against thin summer dresses as they waited for you behind their counters, arms in front of their chests. They stared toward the bright glass doors to the parking lot when they weren't smiling at customers or squinting at the braille numbers on your credit card, with a smirk.

The man in the green golf shirt took his time looking at me.

There was one reservation for that night, and he was it. The owner of the motel, Mrs. Elizabeth Briggs, came in only for emergencies during my shift because she trusted me. I'd worked there without incident for years, and Mrs. Briggs needed her rest. It was all too much for Mrs. Briggs. She suffered more than she let anyone know, she said.

There was the swish of lukewarm autumn wind through emptiness outside. The whole town had already closed down — boarded up, it seemed, for winter. Just me and this golfer, this paying guest, alone together in the glassed-in office of the Swan Motel like the plastic bride and groom knee-deep and stiff in stale cake behind the bakery window.

He let his eyes move over my shirt slowly, and the eyes were yellowish, but I could see they used to be bright-white blue. He set his elbow on the desk and sighed.

This is usual. If the front desk girl doesn't want to do anything next, she'll take a small step backward, maybe look down at the pen in her hand. But if she's willing, or willing to think about it at least, she'll look straight into your eyes. She'll lean forward a little. It might even surprise you to realize your hunch was right.

Then you think about what her breasts would look like bare. You might imagine that she is pushing them toward you, whether or not she is. She's wearing a white blouse, and you think maybe you can see a tuck of lace at the V of her bra — one of those glued-on rosebuds?

Maybe your heart speeds up if you haven't already done this a million times — a bloody nest in your chest, soggy, like something dredged out of a river: Your heart, you never want it to stop.

If she's not just considering, if she's done this a lot, she might tilt her head as if she's stretching her neck. Casual. Nothing's being said. She must be waiting for you to say something — so, perhaps you are clever, you say something funny like, "Sure is hot in here," tugging at your collar with an index finger or loosening your tie. But if you can't think of anything like that, or it's just not your style, you'll say, "I'd enjoy some company in Room 47. Meaning you," looking hard at her now.

"Is that right?" Flirting, and slow, "And what's good company worth to you?"

You smile. Maybe your palms are sweating or, if you're a different kind of man, maybe all this makes you mad but makes you want it even worse. "Name it. I'll see if I can scrape it up."

"Well." She's looking at your name in the guest register now and it makes you a little nervous, whether it's your real name or not. "Your room was sixty dollars. I think the company would be worth that, don't you?"

It's less than you expected. Or more. Maybe that makes you a little sad for her, or angry, but you don't want to think about that now. You wink, but don't smile. You say, "See you up there, sugar."

As you're walking out the office door you hear her humming high and light under her breath. You wonder if she's watching your back, wonder if she's noticed your limp, worried that she's taking down your license number, but you also think about her breasts. They looked good. Her lips were sweet. She's young, early twenties, petite and polite-looking with thick reddish hair, a small-town girl — but you know now she's a slut, too; she'll do whatever you want. By now you're so ready for it you can hardly stand to think about what's next.

What's next is oddly almost always the same. She knocks on your door, whether or not it's open. The room is small and smells like mildew and Pine Sol. The bedspread is thin and crisp, swirled with subdued colors — rust, gold, navy blue. The heat or the air conditioning has just kicked in, you've turned it on high because it was too hot or cold in your room, and it's rattling now. It's dark, even with the light on. You pulled the curtains already. Maybe you rinsed out your mouth. Maybe you used the toilet and it's still running in the bathroom behind you.

Now that she's out from behind the front desk, you see she's wearing a short skirt or semitight jeans — nothing special, but she has nice legs, little hips, small waist. She's thin and pale, especially under that messy red dredge of hair. But she looks healthy. When she holds her hand out for the cash, you have it for her, already counted and folded. She looks at it before she slips it in her shoe, under her heel.

Suddenly your heart is kicking like a big black boot in your chest, and it makes you either shy or angry, sometimes both.

You probably don't kiss her, you just put the palms of your hands on those breasts you've been thinking about, move your fingers around on her shirt, and you're breathing hard. But she just stands there like a closed white door.

You're touching someone who doesn't want to touch you back — all yours, like the room, the TV, the conservative bedspread for the night: You already paid. But she's so quiet, sort of smirking, you think. It makes you nervous. You can't help it that your hands are shaking, but you're a big man who worries a lot about his middle-aged heart — all those uncles lined up in coffins dead of heart attacks, predictable in Michigan as winter. In a flash you see yourself five years old in a little blue suit on tiptoes peering over the edge of a glossy trunk to get a look at one of those uncles as a powder-dusted corpse:

You realize, as you take her flesh in a handful, that you're the age of that corpse now.

Lately, you sweat in your sleep, wake up soaked and cold.

Dead, they smelled like women — talcum and old rose water.

You unbuckle your belt with one hand, you've pushed the other up under her shirt and bra. Her breast is cool and soft. If you are hurting her, grabbing it too hard, she won't let on. You wish she would. You grab it harder as you pull yourself out. You take your hand out of her shirt and put it on her shoulder. You're holding yourself with the other one. You push her down to her knees, put it in her mouth, and there's that warm parting of lips like sinking slowly into mud. You groan when you feel something soft and hot swim over the tip of it — and now you know she's a pro. You wanted it to last longer, do some other things to her, too, but she knows what she's doing, and you come.

Some sweet small-town thing: Right.

You barely last ten seconds.

Sixty fucking dollars.

She coughs, closes the door lightly behind her like a kind of apology, or a shrug.

That night you sleep badly in your motel room. Mold and river, even between the sheets. With the lights out it's so dark you think for a terrible moment that you've gone blind. Instead of dreaming, you turn on the TV, and when the sun comes up you blow your nose in a towel and leave.

There's another girl in the office when you check out. This one is pregnant, chatting on the phone. She doesn't look at you when you drop your key on the counter. Your mouth tastes mossy all day, and something pale films your tongue.

You drive on.

$\mathcal{T}$ HE WHITE FLASH of a sailboat, silver light on water, a high blanched sky, too bright. A woman in a navy blue striped bikini: She has long legs. She's holding a dented can of beer, stepping onto the boat. Her narrow foot, toenails painted red, is poised for a moment in shimmering air.

Wind billows the sail, the sound of sheets flapping on a line and the smell of bleach.

The woman holds her arms out in the air like wings, a dancer balancing herself onto an extravagant curtain of movement beneath her. She laughs, and a shirtless man, tanned, takes her hand, the hand that has no beer can in it, to help her onto the water. She stumbles, the boat rocks harder.

He doesn't embrace her when she falls into him, but their bodies meet.

They look, then, at me, and I see his hand flat in the small of her bare back. The hand is dark and large against her pale waist. Her shoulders are round and smooth as blank faces, gleaming.

"Bye-bye, Leila," she sings.

Red fingernails and flesh — she is drinking from the beer, cold and sweaty in her hand. Waving bye-bye baby with the other.

He waves bye-bye, too — my uncle, my father's younger

brother, a salesman like my father, but luckier, and also a magician who knows a card trick in which the Jack disappears into thin air, then reappears, fast and flashy, behind your ear.

They are carried away together by wind on my uncle's boat. The sail, a sharp knife of light then a bright blur receding.

When they are farther into the water, a fading image, overexposed in so much wild white clear as gin, she reaches behind her and unsnaps the back of her bikini top. It slips off fast — a quick yank of sexual gravity like a scream.

She holds the bikini top in the empty hand and waves it toward the shore back and forth in arcs above her head, as if in surrender.

Then the scene scintillates, glints, and a piece of bent metal on the boat blazes; I have to squint. I can't be much older than four or five. Her breasts are even brighter than the rest of her body and more pale than the glare all around her, but I can't stare into it any longer: a shock of skin like white milk spilled all over a wax-white tray.

They are shrinking, crumbling into the sheen, while their sail beats the air like a single, thrilled wing — a huge white bird with those two human captives smiling in its beak. And my uncle, whose looks, I know already, though I'm only a child myself, are handsome, more handsome than my father's, shrugs toward my father, who clears his throat apologetically behind me.

There's a foamy rolling of water between my uncle, the woman with her bare breasts under a beating wing now, and the place where my father and I stand with our eyes nearly closed to see it better. She turns her back to us, and what we can see of it is a blank slate, as they say. She is moving naked over water and moving away.

She's my mother, and then she dies.

"Rick," I said one of those first afternoons in October when I'd been doing what I was doing for more than a month, "I may be a little late tonight. I told Mrs. Briggs I'd do some accounting, and maybe I won't have time until after Samantha comes in."

I looked steadily into Rick's dark eyes to see what he might suspect, but in them I just saw myself, twice, miniaturized, wearing a jean jacket, clutching my red purse against my ribs. My image in each of those eyes was smaller than a half-moon rising in a fingernail, but exact.

"Well, O.K.," Rick said — only a dip of disappointment in it before he turned back to the game show he'd been watching.

A board of light bulbs zapped. Sirens. A woman shrieked, put her face in her hands, cried and cried and screamed as if she were being stabbed, over and over, with a dull knife. She was overwrought, overweight, and wearing a halter-top. Her arms looked moist, doughy, in the TV fuzz. Some of her skin rippled when she sobbed, but some stretched taut as too-tight bandages. She'd won a compact car, and the body of it was revealed to her slowly between two maroon curtains parting around the car like lips — something sporty, red, and sexy waiting for her in a wide, warm mouth. She gasped. The host of the show stood stiff beside her in his heavy dark suit. You could not see his arms or even his neck, but his face was open and round as a stopped clock. He put his hand on the woman's bare back and rubbed it up and down, numbly — smiling into the distance, which was us.

Rick looked back up at me. "Bye," he said.

Even under his T-shirt I could see the wide V of bone on his chest like a seagull's spread wings, thinned and rigid, caught between the rotors of his shoulders.

"Bye." I said it brightly, but my back was to him when I said it.

It was a short drive to the Swan Motel from our apartment because it was a small town. Still, a lot of people passed through the town every year, tossing candy bar wrappers out car windows. In the summer, they swept by on their way to the lake, staying a night or two on the river, which was also eternally sweeping toward the lake. In the fall, they came to see the leaves go bloody or gold before they fell, or to see the swans flock and rise up above us in October like a flying church choir in white robes, leaving, while the Michigan winter shuffled itself together on the horizon, ready to blow.

Then, the tourists came to ski down Soprano Hill — black pinpricks whipping through January blizzards. It wasn't much of a hill, but it was the only one around for miles, and we were lucky to have a hill at all, there in the flat part of the state — the western ridge of the Michigan mitten. At night it was illuminated, and it lit up the whole town like a rest stop above us — especially when it was blown with artificial snow, which shot furious into its bare face like long feather boas in the cold zero of a spotlight on a stage.

Finally, spring. The swans would come back, and they would build their nests outside the Swan Motel, drop their fist-sized eggs while the tourists stared, scratched their heads, used their hands like visors to look toward the sky, which would be blue in May and full of nothing. Soon enough their identical children would crack into the world, sticky wet and dirty white as dog-chewed tennis balls, and the tourists would creep closer through the damp grass on hands and knees to take blurred snapshots with expensive cameras of the new swans shaking off their eggs — broken and spermy with membrane, fresh birth mess.

When you saw the weather map on the news at night, you probably didn't think about us up there, living our lives on the pinkie of that fat Michigan hand — driving to work, boiling potatoes, digging graves. You were looking at your own edge of something and hearing *Eighty percent chance of rain, occasional sun, a storm system out of the West,* while the river just scrolled on, ink black, making a steady thrumming under us and, above us, a softer sound like lashing, slashing, clapping — or a child being lightly slapped, over and over, in a game.

The tourists liked to have their pictures taken together under the sign that said WELCOME TO SUSPICIOUS RIVER. They laughed about the name of the town, though the name didn't mean anything anymore to us, if it ever had — just assonance and syllables flagging up the vague image of a place we knew we lived.

When I got to the Swan Motel, Millie was in her jean jacket, ready to go. She had a pink tissue pressed to her forehead. "Oh," she said like a sound, not a word, "I've gotta get out of here."

"Go," I said, friendly, "get out of here," and I pushed my own jean jacket and my purse, a small red patent-leather oval like a stomach stuffed with Kleenex, under the counter. Both of them were damp.

It had begun to rain while I was driving to work, and the moisture made the air in the office smell like tin, or sulfur, murky as a dirty locker room. Guests would come in asking where the indoor pool was. "At the Holiday Inn," I'd want to say, but wouldn't: There was no pool at all.

But I could see why they asked — that odor, damp air, especially when it rained. The Swan Motel smelled of mold, chlorine, musk. The rooms were humid even in the driest, deadest dead of winter. I could smell the Swan Motel in my hair at night like formaldehyde, or copper, before I fell asleep.

Millie stood with her back to the glass door, buttoning her jacket. Her hair was long and frizzy in the humidity and so black it washed her eyes away until they were only the faint blue of a white eggshell. She said, "So everything O.K. these days, Leila?"

I shrugged, glanced at the clock. I could feel the wet rubber that lined the soles of my shoes seep dimly into my skin.

Millie was younger than I was, but she was plain and wispy as fatigue itself — a scarf of air and smoke, frayed, a shred of a yellowed lace dress left for a long time on a wire hanger. The tips of her teeth were pointed, and Millie used them to dig at the skin around her fingernails, to scrape her bottom lip until it paled, cracked, bled pink onto the smaller, lower teeth.

"Yeah, O.K., I guess," I said.

"Does Rick eat?"

"You know." I shrugged again. "Not much."

"God," she said, "I couldn't believe it when I saw him last week. He's like — nothing — now."

I bit my own lip, which tasted bitter, like iodine, and I nodded. Millie put the scaly tip of her left thumb between her teeth and said, "What does he act like at home? Weird?"

"Normal," I said, and I pictured Rick on the couch in boxer shorts watching the television blink. "He goes to work. He cooks." I held my hands up in front of me as if to show Millie there were no clues in them, or trouble.

"Wow." She shook her head as she pushed backward out the door.

In a casual flash, like tonguing your teeth quick and tasting something sour, I hated Millie for being so pale and inquisitive — a slow perplexed look even about her hair. But then she took her hand out of her mouth to wave good-bye, the tin bells on the glass door jangling as she stepped out, and I remembered she wasn't family, or a friend, just someone whose job I shared, who wouldn't bother to think too long or hard about the details of my life, and the bad feeling passed.

After Millie was gone, the shadow of her Pinto moving briefly over the wet parking lot tar like a phantom horse, the empty office hummed its familiar silence, and I heard an empty click in my ears like the hammer of a toy gun, fired, when I swallowed.

After a while, I opened the leather-bound guest register.

There were seven names penciled onto the weak red lines under Friday October 15. Six of them were in Millie's loopy handwriting, so I knew they were likely to be stuck under the wrong dates, wrong arrival times, last names misspelled or inaccurate altogether. Millie was a bad receptionist by any standards, and she'd most likely be fired soon, I thought — though she didn't seem to be aware of that herself, complaining daily about the job as though she'd always have it. But all Millie needed as far as I could tell was one more major blunder like Labor Day weekend: Not a vacancy in all of Suspicious River, and Millie'd given the same room to a family of four and a couple from Ohio within a few hours of each other.

It was an accident.

Millie had checked the family in first, but they'd gone to Grandma's house for dinner across town before taking their bags upstairs. The couple from Ohio came later, wearing matching polo shirts, purple, confirmation number for their reservation firmly in hand, but Millie couldn't find their names in the ledger.

Of course, the motel was packed, but it was impossible for Millie to know that since she hadn't bothered to do the paperwork for a crowd of couples and their kids who'd come in just as she was eating her sack lunch and talking to her mother on the phone. Millie just handed out keys and ran credit cards, eating, chewing her fingers, talking long distance the whole time.

Perhaps Millie simply panicked when the couple got articulate and angry, college-educated and exhausted from their drive, and asked Millie to produce a manager. Or, more likely, Millie knew she'd be out of there, at the drive-in necking or watching *Psycho II* with her boyfriend Ed before the trouble started. In any case, the Ohio couple waited, impatient and tapping their Nikes officially on the dull linoleum of the office floor while Millie wandered around the Swan Motel with her master key, knocking on doors, looking for an empty room to give them. When no one answered, Millie opened the door and peeked in to see if there were any bags, if the beds were mussed. Of course, one family's room was untouched: They were just that minute sitting down to pork chops on the other side of Suspicious River.

So Millie assigned that one to the couple, gave them the duplicate key, thinking, or so she said, that she'd just misplaced the original. And when the family of four came back to their room, the couple from Ohio was naked in it, sitting at the edge of one of the double beds, smoking a joint and watching a blank-eyed woman writhe on a leopard skin bedspread while a man stood over her, masturbating into her mouth.

For only six dollars you could have this film specially cabled into your color television set. If you'd paid for your room with a credit card, you didn't even have to tell the front desk girl what you wanted to watch. You just turned to the channel and the six dollars would automatically appear on your bill. Not another word about it.

Mrs. Briggs hadn't wanted to offer this special service at first, but then the cable company salesman appeared with his soft burgundy briefcase on a slow April afternoon of sleet and mud, and he showed Mrs. Briggs how much money she was likely to make. As it turned out, sixty percent of the guests were happy to have this entertainment option — though the televisions in their rooms were fifteen years old and the colors on the screen were brighter than life, hard to look at directly for very long. Lips turned flame red or hot pink, bleeding fuzzily into the screen, and each voice reverberated tinny through the sound grill, echoing like a loudspeaker in a cavern, turning all musical instruments to banjos.

The couple from Ohio was watching *Love Rides the Rails*. It would be the same film shown over and over every night after 8 P.M. until October 22 and *Hot Seat*, when the faces would change, but, of course, the plot would stay the same.

"Mommy, what are they *doing?*" their blond daughter screamed as if for her life when she opened the motel room door while Mom, Dad and Brother hauled their Samsonite from the station wagon up the long flight of concrete stairs behind her. Mrs. Briggs had to be called at home that night, and she'd been dead asleep. Her voice was full of phlegm when she answered the phone, and Millie's future at the Swan Motel had been in limbo ever since.

The phone rang then, and it was Rick.

"Hey," he said.

I said, "What's going on?"

"Nothing, I just thought you might want me to bring you some dinner over there. You forgot to take your sandwich."

His voice sounded far away — a bad connection. I could hear another conversation on the line taking place somewhere beyond his voice: a woman's singsong rising and falling, telling a story, and I remembered a TV show I'd seen once when I was a child — was it *Twilight Zone*? — in which a ham radio in a man's basement began one night to play a frantic wireless call for help from a soldier during the last bloody battle of a war that had ended forty years before.

I wanted to listen to the voice in the distance, but Rick spoke up louder as if to block it out. "I could bring pizza, or I could just drop off the sack if you want."

"No," I said. "I'll get a snack out of the vending machine and eat the sandwich when I get home."

"Sure?"

"Sure."

"See you soon."

"See you."

He hung up while I was still listening for the woman's singsong again. I heard a man laugh vaguely, and the woman, muffled, seem to say, "Jesus!" before the line was cut.

A PHOTOGRAPH taken of my mother before she died: She wears a sleeveless white dress. A trellis of pink roses, puffy and soft as pneumonia in the late summer haze, twists and struggles behind her. Her hair is dark and down to her shoulders. A slight breeze seems to sift the loose curls lightly. There's even a glimpse of the sky beyond her — muted blue, a fading Kodak color that looks nothing like real sky.

My mother has just opened her mouth to say a word, and her mouth is frozen in the shape of a spoon. Silence is all that comes out.

Over the years I come to believe, like a child, that my mother is saying my name in that aborted breath, her pink mouth matching the roses behind her:

"Leila."

There it is.

There it is, I want to believe for a long time: my name flashed forever on a glossy square of radium paper. My mother speaking to me from oblivion. But as I get older I imagine instead that what comes out of her open mouth in the moment of this snapshot is a long sweet howl like a hungry cat. Not interrupted. Even by death. A long, round sound like train brakes screeching into infinity.

But animal.

A hungry cat outside a white door about to be closed.

"Smith," he said, "Gary."

Sure enough, it wasn't in the ledger.

I looked up at him. His smile was a flinch on one side of his face — a smirk, a wink — sexy, I thought, experimental. He smoked a cigarette and the smoke weaved around his head like a web, the way an egg white, cracked, swirls and rises in a glass of water. Then he started to cough, rattling and wet, and he said through it, eyebrows raised in a question, "You don't got my reservation?"

"No," I apologized, "but it's O.K. We have plenty of empty rooms."

Luckily he didn't seem to care. Some people will get upset that you don't have their names even if the whole motel is empty. They'll stand around fretting long after you've checked them in, room key safely in their hands, wanting to know exactly what went wrong, looking as if some piece of themselves had been lost, like a greasy playing card disappeared from the deck without which the game could not go on. It seemed to be proof to them of an insecure universe, proof that they might barely even exist if they didn't insist on it. I'd want to comfort them, to say *It's just Millie, she writes nothing down*, but I couldn't.

"I called last Saturday," he said. "Morning."

His leather jacket was thin, a starched white shirt under it, and there was rain on the shoulders and the slick sleeves. He was small, but nice-looking. Thin. His hair was brown and short, wavy — sparse on top, and he had a scruffy beard that might have been new, accidental, or both. He scratched at that stubble as if to make sure it was still on his chin.

"Hmm," I said, looking at the open book again, though I knew his name wouldn't be in it — Saturday morning, Millie's shift. "Well," I said, trying to change the subject, "Fortunately it's not a problem at all. How many nights?"

"One for now," he said, and I noticed his accent then. East Texas. Or Tennessee. And thick. A little like humidity between us.

I took a check-in card out of the drawer under the adding machine and began writing the date on it, then *Smith, Gary.* He flipped his wallet open onto the counter and handed me his Visa — small slice of plastic silver like a homemade knife. But the name on it was Jensen, Gary.

I glanced back then at the guest book, still open on the counter. And there it was, in Millie's handwriting — Jensen, G.

He'd lit another cigarette and leaned, smoking it, with his elbow on the counter. He was watching me write. I picked his credit card up off the counter between us with fingernails painted shell pink, and ran it. A long string of numbers and Jensen, Gary — smudged and permanent imprint on a piece of paper.

I wrote $60.00 under Payment. $2.40 under Tax. $62.40 under Total. Then I turned the paper toward him and watched as he signed his name: Gary W. Jensen. Then he looked up.

"Forgot my own name," he laughed. "Forgot I wasn't gonna use the credit card, and then I forgot whether or not I'd put the reservation in my real name. Sneaky guy, huh?" He tugged on his shirt collar and smiled. "Guess you caught me," he said. His eyes were brown and clear. Forty, I guessed. He smelled like soap mixed up with smoke.

"Guess so," I said, and I held his eyes in silence until he started to look nervous.

It works every time. They think they're bigger than you, bigger than some girl behind a motel counter, that God made them that way. But if you don't flinch, and it's sex that's being negotiated, they wither under it like a hot light and start to sweat.

"Well." He looked behind him, and I could see the inch of neck exposed between his hair and the collar of his coat. The skin looked just shaved, a bit naked, scraped. There was no one behind him, and he looked back at me with his eyebrows raised and his face seeming younger for a moment than forty, with a teenage boy's shy deception, charming and inept, and he said, "Reason for all the shenanigans is I was looking for a girl my buddy told me about. In addition to needing a room, of course. You wouldn't happen to be her?"

I leaned forward, wrist close to his fingertips. "Might be," I said, singsong.

He cleared his throat and straightened a bit. His voice was scratched. "So, I guess you know where my room is, don't you?"

I reached under the counter then and took 42 off the rack of plastic hooks and tossed it to him gently across the counter. It landed at his elbow.

"42," I said.

Maybe he looked worried then, like a man in a restaurant who wasn't sure how to eat what he'd ordered for dinner.

Here's your flaming rack of lamb, sir, I might have said.

I could see him swallow. He had the cigarette burning a small orange eye in one hand and with the other he smoothed the thin brown hairs on top of his head.

"How much?" He opened his eyes wider when he asked it.

"Sixty."

"Now?"

"I'll give you some time to get settled in your room, Mr. Smith," I said, teasing him, feeling powerful and innocent as a child lying straight to your face.

He forced a smile, but it wasn't easy for him.

As he was leaving, I could see he was wearing blond cowboy boots, his nearly new blue jeans tight around the ankles. The boots made a sharp sound on the linoleum, and the bells on the office door jingled tinny and cheap as he stepped out.

There are different kinds of men, I thought then, but not many different kinds. There are men who aren't as strong as they think they are, trying all the time to prove something. And there are men who are stronger than they think they are, trying all the time to prove something. It all adds up to the same thing in the end, until all men seem the same. But, I thought, Gary W. Jensen Smith looked like a man who was stronger than he thought he was, though he would never find it out for himself. He had the body of a boy — and the boots, the leather jacket, the jeans. *Rascal,* I imagined his mother saying under her breath about him until he turned forty and was still a boy.

When I left, I set a plastic sign on the front desk that said RECEPTIONIST WILL BE RIGHT BACK.

The rain had stopped, but it was dark. Only five o'clock. But the days were getting shorter, and this one had been dark to start. The air was damp, and it gave me a chill that began in my hair and crept down my back as I stepped over the puddles of rain, which were shallow and swirled with peacock colors from old oil. They smelled like tarnish, like the inside of an empty tin can. Iodine, or was it indigo, in the dusk.

A cool steam rose ghostly from the hoods of the few parked cars, and I thought the silver Thunderbird must be his. Nice. Florida plates. I passed it on my way to 42 and touched the hood briefly with the palm of my hand. It was warmed from within, like an electric blanket, or a big cat.

The metal railing vibrated, and it felt solid, heavy, but hollow under my hand as I walked up the stairs. Mrs. Briggs had hired a blond high school boy the summer before to paint it aqua blue, and the paint had already begun to peel, leaving ovals of rust like elbow patches where the smooth gloss was gone. My shoes were red — they matched my purse, back in the office, but they looked too bright to me on my feet that evening against the gray slab stairs.

Gary Jensen's door was open about an inch.

This is common. Maybe they're afraid you won't wait if the door is closed tight and locked, but they don't want to leave it gaping open either, especially in the evening, especially if it's damp. I knocked.

The week before, I'd walked in, and the man was already naked. Hard. Pumping his thing with one hand, a little plastic glass of whiskey and ice in the other. A big celebration. He must have wanted to shock or impress me, I thought, but he did neither. I just wondered to myself how it was I hadn't noticed that he was fat back in the office, and bald. Maybe he'd been wearing a hat, I couldn't remember. I just looked at him, blank. His own expression was wide-eyed and full of crazy hope. When I sighed, he frowned and stopped pumping. He put his drink down on the chest of drawers. When I held out my hand for the money, he said, "What?"

"The money," I said.

His jaw dropped a bit and then he covered himself up with a towel — suddenly shy — while he fished through the pockets of his black pants, which were laid out carefully on the bed, to find the money for me.

"Here." He shoved the three twenties toward me like a disgruntled tenant. He wouldn't look at me.

I didn't ask him what he wanted, just got on my knees and took it in my mouth. He whimpered when he came but never touched me. His arms were straight down at his sides, fists gripping and ungripping nothing, and I kept the soft cash in my own left hand the whole time.

Remembering him, I wondered if that man might have been Gary W. Jensen's buddy, the one who'd told him about me.

Probably not.

Maybe the trucker from Milwaukee. He'd left real happy and said he'd send his friends.

"Come in." Friendly.

Gary W. wasn't undressed, though it seemed to me he'd changed his shirt. This shirt was starched stiff and light blue. Hadn't the other one been white? He was sitting on the edge of the bed, smiling, a bottle of Rolling Rock in his hand, and now that he had his leather jacket off, I could see that his shoulders were no wider than my own. He was only a few inches taller, couldn't even have weighed much more, but he looked solid, scrappy — a thin tough man.

"Here," he said, holding the green bottle toward me. I saw another one, then, between his knees, and I thought he must have mistaken this for some kind of date — strangers getting to know each other better, something like that. But that's not what this was about.

"I can't," I said, gesturing behind me, "I'm working."

He started to laugh at that. His eyes were true brown. "Oh," he said. "You can come up here and give blow jobs to total strangers, but they won't let you drink a beer."

It wasn't angry, the way he said it, just honest — pointing out a contradiction, sharing an absurdity. I wasn't offended. I laughed, too. I liked his smirk, his accent, which seemed sarcastic, consciously a little stupid.

"Well," he stood up and put the two bottles of beer on the dressing table, which was blond and shiny, made of wood pulp and sawdust pressed into boards — fake, like everything in the motel room. The drywall was smooth and freshly painted, and the partition that separated the bathroom from the rest of the room was covered with metallic wallpaper that reflected the light from the window. It all seemed identically, eternally, fresh and sterile from room to room.

He hadn't closed the curtains.

"Well, here." He fished through the pockets of his jeans and handed me the money politely, then stood facing me, seeming happy, not nervous at all, just excited in a shrugging, boyish way.

I looked at the money in my hand. Two twenties. Two tens. I slipped my foot out of my shoe and bent a bit to slip the bills in under my heel.

The slap surprised me as I was standing up again, lifting my eyes back toward him.

We were both still smiling.

Just the flat surface of his hand made contact with my face, and it knocked me off balance. He stood in the same place, looking.

I hadn't wanted to gasp, but I knew I had by the way he laughed, that smirk, at my shocked face. It stung. It must've gone very red, burning, or drywall white. Then he hit me again, leaning into it more deeply this time, taking a step toward me as if he were pitching a baseball game, and then he pulled me forward onto the floor, onto my back.

I closed my eyes and heard a jet pass over the Swan Motel. Someone going somewhere fast. It took him a long time, a lot of scrambling, to get my skirt up and himself between my legs, and after he did, he kept one hand pressed at my neck the whole time, one on my wrist. I opened my eyes, and he stared into them while I stared out. It didn't hurt at all, though I supposed from the look on his face that he was hoping it would.

Gary Jensen lowered himself over me until the side of his jaw was against my mouth, and I could feel the sparse dark beard, a bit of sweat beading between the whiskers. I could have bitten him then, but I closed my eyes again instead.

I supposed he was hoping I'd fight, or whimper. But I wouldn't: Smelling his neck I realized without surprise that I'd been wrong about what he was, completely wrong — the skin there smelled like boots. And whatever he'd expected of me, I wanted him to have the opposite of it, too. For instance, what's the point of hurting someone who doesn't mind being hurt?

I only worried about the curtains being open. I worried someone might be waiting at the front desk for me. There were six other guests on their way to the Swan Motel in the fog and tinny drizzle that night, if Millie's calculations were anything close to correct.

But the office was empty when I got back.

I slipped the sixty dollars out of my shoe and into my red purse behind the counter. The bills were warm and moist from my skin. Maybe I counted them one more time before I put the purse down again, beside my jacket.

*S*HE SOBS, "You don't love me."

My father turns his palms up helpless and empty toward her — a salesman with nothing to sell. "I do," he says. "Bonnie, I just don't like you flirting with my brother, that's all. What's wrong with me saying that one thing? I'm not even mad."

She buries her face in her hands, then turns to the wall.

"Bonnie, I love you." He presses up against her back, slips his arms around her waist, kisses her black hair. "Bonnie."

His hands shake when she's angry.

He's tall and thin as a scarecrow.

My mother turns on him fast, and I can see her lips are dead pale pink. "Get the hell away from me," she screams, going toward his face with her fingernails, "Get the fuck away from me," slapping, clawing.

He crosses his arms over his forehead and ducks — a man in a shirt with gray stripes like a prisoner's uniform, pursued by a large bird.

Feathers, claws, shadows.

We are in the kitchen, which smells warm and salty as a ham, and I'm still small enough to crawl into the cupboard under the sink.

I do. It's dark. Under the sink there is a coffee can half full of water that's leaked from the pipe, and I knock that can over when I crawl in next to it. A fat metal snake of drain presses cold against my cheek as the liquid soaks my plaid skirt and green tights — is that my kindergarten uniform? — with rust. The smell of old water, like thin blood.

Later, when the sound of scuffle and confusion stops, I come back out into the silence, like something just hatched, cool and damp, and we all sit down to dinner. The ham is candy pink on the kitchen table, and it's sticky with pineapple rings and maraschino cherries.

Through dinner, my mother's cheeks are flushed. Otherwise she's ashen and blue-eyed under her black hair. My father's eyes are army green, and his ears burn at the edges like meat. He has a crew cut, hair so short it isn't any color. My mother squeezes his hand and says "I'm sorry" when he reaches for the butter dish, while her other hand rests peacefully on her cold silverware, and my father smiles at the butter — a little shy, with small false teeth.

I went into the bathroom and closed the door behind me. The tile was pink, but dull, as if there were something gray seeping up under it, pushing itself into the Swan Motel from outside the Swan Motel, and the smell was sweet as ether — a basketful of small pink soaps, chemical fresh and clean. Next to the sink there was a full-length mirror, and I looked at myself in it:

Nothing had changed. My skirt was creased, but it wasn't torn. My hair was messy, long and copper, and I combed it then with a small black comb some former office girl had left behind. There was a ripping sound as I pulled the comb through my hair, but only a few strands tore out, and I shook those into the wicker wastebasket. On my neck — high, under my ear, as if I'd been playing a violin — there was a small red mark. Nothing more noticeable than that.

It had grown darker outside and begun to rain harder. I stepped out of the bathroom into the office and found the pack of cigarettes in my purse under the counter. I smacked one into my hand and it felt light and fragile when I took it between my fingers — combustible, and paper. Still, I had to strike three matches to light it, each match sputtering out fast in the air as I moved it toward my face.

When the cigarette was lit, I went to the window and stood with it, the smell of smoke cutting the damp, making me vaguely dizzy, making haze.

The office lights were too bright for me to see out into the darkness, so I looked at my own reflection in the window instead, watched myself blow smoke into the glass, imagined for a moment that I was someone else, someone I'd never met, when a pickup truck pulled into the semicircular drive outside, cutting my image in half with headlights.

A woman stepped out into the rain, leaving the pickup running, engine high and agitated, even leaving the driver's-side door open, the pale yellow dome lighting it up inside. I could see a string of red beads like bloody baby teeth swing gently below the rear-view mirror.

She opened the door to the office and the bells announced her like the right answer to a game show question.

Her hair was dirty blond, down over her shoulders. She wore an orange top, a jean jacket open over that. No bra. I could see her nipples under the orange cloth, stiff in the chill. The thin, slippery cloth. The woman had on tight jeans and looked tired, weathered, but pretty in a made-up way. "You work here?" she asked.

I nodded, put the cigarette down in the aluminum ashtray, cylindrical and sterile by the window, and started back toward the counter, toward the guest book to find the woman's name in it or not.

"Where's Gary Jensen?"

I stopped before I got there.

Ordinarily we didn't give out room numbers. Policy. Instead, we'd ring the room for guests and let them speak for themselves to whoever was looking for them at the Swan Motel. Mrs. Briggs believed this policy saved a few lives every year, or a few disruptions at least. Kept women from being kidnapped by their husbands. Kept men from being caught with their lovers by their wives.

"42," I said, not caring, in this case, about the policy.

The phone rang as the woman was leaving, and I didn't notice if she'd parked her pickup in the lot and gone up the concrete stairs to 42 or not, but she'd sped out of the drive too fast. I heard someone honk long and hard. A near collision, I imagined. It was slippery out there.

"Leila." It was Rick.

"Hey Rick," I said.

"Just checking again to see if you want me to bring you some dinner."

"No. Like I said."

"Everything O.K. there?"

"Yeah. Fine. Everything O.K. at home?"

"Fine."

"I'm tired," I offered into the silence.

"I'm tired, too." Silence again. "I tried to call awhile ago but there was no answer."

"I was in the bathroom," I said, "I heard it ring but it stopped before I got it."

"Well. I'll see you tonight."

"I'll see you tonight. Bye."

▼

Rick had fed me since the beginning. In the chaos of the high school cafeteria he would sit beside me, open a carton of chocolate milk, slip a straw into its beak and pass it to me, watch me sip, arm around me the whole time. He'd ask me afterward how it was, and it was always fine. There would be the sound of grease splattering behind us. The *sssss* of a metal fork, dropped or tossed, sliding across the linoleum floor.

But back then, Rick would eat, too. He liked extra cheese on anything. Every afternoon, before we left the cafeteria for class, a couple of candy bars from the vending machine would be tossed down to Rick by a hidden, mechanical hand.

"I love you," he said on our first date.

It was a Christmas dance in the gym. Outside, the snow had turned pewter blue under a blurred moon. The air was empty and sharp. I'd barely been able to breathe as we ran from his father's warm Ford into the sweaty heat of the dance, and my lungs still hurt, as if I'd been stabbed with oxygen — too pure and icy clean. My high heels were strapped around my ankles with leather laces, and my dress was burgundy as old blood, but Rick felt full and soft beside me, my hands on his shoulders as we danced. He moved his own hands up and down my back, and it was warm. I pressed against the dark wool of his suit, then looked up. "I love you." His face was as grim as a father's when he said it, and silver glitter from the decorations, hung with twine from the lights, had settled in his hair.

I didn't know what to say, so I said, "I love you too."

Rick played guitar and worked on cars. His father owned pinball and vending machines, and Rick would drive to forty-seven different bars all over the county once a week and empty coins from his father's machines into a big black velvet-lined briefcase. His father paid him ten percent when Rick was in high school — more after graduation, after we got married — and it was Mr. Schmidt's hope that he'd retire and Rick would take over the whole business then.

When his father talked to him about his future, Rick would nod absently, the same look he had on his face those days when he ate — cheerful, as if he didn't know he was eating, as if what other people ate was what he noticed — spooning and chewing the whole time, as if he weren't.

Rick's parents adored him. Like me, he was an only child,

but his parents had wanted him, had wanted a big, messy family — all its old bikes rusting with the smell of oiled revolvers in the garage. Though, not having had a big family made them even happier with what little they had. Even after Rick had grown to be six foot three, two hundred and twenty pounds, his father — himself a small bald man with an embarrassing green eagle tattooed on his chest like a battle scar, its head reared back ecstatically — would grab his son around the neck and rub a knuckle into his head, call him Sonny, or Loverboy. Even when Mr. Schmidt wore a tie, you could see a green beak peeking out of his shirt.

Though Rick's father's smile was all yellow teeth and a flash of gold from his molars, Rick's mother's smile was dazzling. She had been a beauty queen — a semifinalist, anyway, in a state competition in 1960 — and still had a sort of beehive, though it had loosened and grayed since then. But it was glistening. And those pearl teeth. She answered the telephone cheerfully, "This is Peggy Marie."

I liked their house. Busy wallpaper and flowered throw pillows. It smelled like meat loaf and talcum powder and didn't remind me of home.

"How can you stand it here?" Rick asked the first time he came over to the house where I lived with my father.

I just shrugged, but I could taste old carpet on the back of my throat when he said it. We had to whisper because my father was asleep in the other room.

"It's a place to live," I said. I tried to keep it clean, but I was never much good at cleaning.

"It's cold," was the only other thing Rick said.

▼

A man propped the glass door open with his foot and pulled a maroon suitcase through it. It seemed the suitcase was too heavy to lift. He dragged it to the counter, smiling the whole time.

"Hi," I said.

"Whew," he said, "Ain't you a pretty little thing."

"Pretty heavy suitcase there, looks like," I said. His bald spot was wet and white as a saucer of milk in the middle of a mess of jet-black hair. His upper lip was sweaty, and he wiped it with the sleeve of his suit coat, cheap and tweed.

"Man alive," he said, staring. "Wow. Woo-wee, look at you."

I could've asked him right away if he had a reservation, turned the conversation to business, but I just stood stone still so he could look. Then I smiled slightly with my lips closed over my teeth and let it sink into him for a minute that I might be available if that's what he was interested in, which he seemed to be. I licked my lips, stretched my neck in slow motion as if it were stiff. Finally I said, "Do you have a reservation?"

He seemed flustered, shook his head no.

"No problem," I said.

He was looking straight at my breasts. I took a deep breath and watched him watch them press a little tighter against my shirt — a thin white cotton one with a silver button at the neck. Then I took a check-in card out of the drawer. He exhaled, and the sound of it was like the tire of a tricycle, perforated, leaking slow. Whatever it was we weren't talking about now was slathered like shaving cream all over the silence.

"How many nights?"

"Just tonight."

I turned the guest card toward him. Showed him the total. "How will you be paying?"

"Cash," he said. When he looked back up at my face, I held his eyes longer than he expected, and he leaned toward me then, sounding out of breath, "Oh, baby," he said, "Uh."

"Maybe you need a back rub after lugging that enormous thing all over. Think?"

"Yeah. Oh yeah."

"Well," I put two fingers lightly on the top of his hand with the red pen in it, "it wouldn't cost any more than the room. Does that sound good?"

"Oh shit yes, sweetheart. Yes, yes." He signed his name fast on the check-in card then handed me two fifties, which were crisp and stuck together. "You just keep the extra," he said, "I'll give you the rest in a minute if that's okay," he pointed to his suitcase, "It's in there."

I handed him a key, 22 — right underneath Gary Jensen's room, I'd already thought about that — and said, "I'll be over in ten minutes."

He stared at me some more before he hauled his suitcase back out the door like a load of bricks. I tilted my head and waved a few fast fingers bye-bye at him, and after he was gone I made change for myself from the cash drawer and put the money — thirty-seven dollars and sixty cents — straight into my red purse, locked the cash drawer again and hid the key, put the plastic sign on the counter and, this time, took the phone off the hook before I left.

*M*Y MOTHER stands to the left of the choir, white robe glowing under the hot ceiling lights. Dust settles in long, rose-tinted boas of morning sun behind the stained glass in the church silence, and then her voice lifts through empty air above the pews and hymnals, the winded mailmen in their stiff Sunday suits, the young mothers with infants struggling red-faced in their laps.

My father has his hands pressed over his kneecaps as her voice rises above us all, an invisible bird — one perfect, earth-shattering note. High and cold, it is a needle taking a piece of white thread up to the ceiling like a stitch.

Ave — half breath, half pure steel scream — Maria.

Helium, the simplest and lightest of the elements.

All the women in the church touch their throats at that moment, afraid the sound has come from them. The men look away, ashamed. But the children look up to the ceiling, believing we might even be able to see that last note as it pierces the thin blue skin of the sky like a woman's wrist.

Then, it's Sunday night, and my mother sits at the edge of my bed and describes Spanish moss to me before I go to sleep — how it hangs in wet ropes over the branches of trees in Louisiana, matted as fur.

You can smell it like old blankets in the air, everywhere, even in the house.

"I hated it," she says — hated the whole damn state where she was born.

She wears a slippery nightgown, metallic baby blue shimmering sleek and dreamy in a crack of light that bleeds up white from the hall outside my bedroom door, and she's drinking something thick and minty from a coffee cup.

I can imagine the Spanish moss of my mother's childhood like corpse hair, or the dark ruined hair of my dead dolls — trees trapped under cloaks of it, bats and animals smothered and human in a turquoise veil of twilight in the state where she once lived.

And I imagine her being born into it — a baby sleeping in a cradle of clotted hair, a moon snagged in branches, like another mother's face, filling her cradle with silver light.

"Bonnie," my father calls, "Are you coming to bed?"

She kisses my cool forehead as she leaves.

I can hear them struggle through the thin wall between my room and theirs before I fall asleep.

"Jesus," my father says, and she sobs.

"Goddammit," my mother mumbles.

Then my father, "Bonnie, no."

Something broken. He says, "We'll clean it up tomorrow. Bonnie. Please. Come here. Come back here now."

I fall asleep when they go silent, and every morning the sound of yelping from the neighbors' back yard wakes me when the sun comes up, liquid and fast.

You might imagine Suspicious River as a small, friendly town if you'd never been there. One bowling alley. Seven churches. Ten motels. Fourteen bars. A 2,700-square-foot gift shop, its facade a cinderblock mural of Pocahontas emerging from a teepee, sprawling for a block along Main Street.

The sky was painted turquoise in that mural. Two white-tailed deer stood blinking at one another. An old Indian with red feathers in his headdress glared at his own empty hands while Pocahontas, dark skinned, with long black braids, smiled at a shirtless white man. Her breasts were enormous and barely covered with the deerskin she was wearing. Midriff exposed. Her thighs were fleshy and curved into a dark place hidden only by a half-inch of ripped skirt. The tourists liked it, took each other's photos from across the street, waving under the Indian princess.

Her eyes were blue.

Local legend was that the artist's Swedish mistress had posed for the painting, had stood half-naked every day for six weeks on Main Street even after the weather turned cold, while the artist painted her into Pocahontas.

But the mural was four decades old, and no one really remembered its genesis with any certainty at all. Still, it was a landmark in the town, perfectly preserved, something larger than life and twice as bright living right there beside us — though the Indians themselves, who'd found and named the town, who'd inspired the gift shop full of moccasins and plastic tom-toms, were gone now except for their graves mounding the river like three soft green bellies, inhaling and exhaling water.

Years earlier, a condominium developer had wanted to level those Indian mounds, had even started to, had taken a big yellow bulldozer to them like a huge and hungry bird. But he must've expected the dirt underneath the long, soft grass on the mounds to be solid, expected the mounds to just roll off the edge of the earth like guillotined heads. Instead, the earth under there turned out to be pitch and mud — half water — and in it, poking up here and there, floating in that dark soup, human bones — a length of spine, a skull, a shard of pottery with a stick figure buck painted on it in what looked like blood.

After that, the Indians came to Suspicious River from further north — looking exotic and poor in our town. They made a human chain in front of the bulldozer and stretched a white banner across themselves that said REST IN PEACE in big black letters.

All day for days, carloads of families streamed past, craning their necks to get a look at the Indians and the massacred mounds hacked open like corpses. It puzzled the newspaper reporters, this attachment to the old bones of people the Indians had never known, who'd lived and died before their own grandparents were even born — not to mention the other garbage under there. The Indians didn't want the bones, even to sell to a museum or a gift shop in Detroit. They just wanted it all buried back under mud and grass again.

Publicity, the paper speculated.

Pity, publicity, and cold hard cash.

Comparisons were made to try to convince us the Indians were sincere. *How would you feel if Sacred Heart Cemetery was dug up for condos and your grandma's bones were sold to a professor in New York?* Still, no one in Suspicious River really believed we'd care. Briefly, maybe, but they'd just be bones, and we'd be over it by August.

But the Supreme Court ordered the mounds to be re-mounded, and then that was over, too. Just now and again an arrowhead was found in the forest, which was no surprise. Anything could wait in that thick woods for a few hundred years to be found. That forest, surrounding the town, seemed to whisper all day and night to the condominium developers, *Surely there's plenty of room for condominiums and Indian mounds on this empty planet.* But the Indians couldn't hear it over the din of bulldozers and garbage trucks.

As I've said, you might imagine this was a small and friendly town. Like the swans, you might think it was a good place to build a little wet nest at the river's edge, hidden behind a wall of cattails and whistling reeds. Every March I'd watch them through the window in the office. Always in pairs. One of the big white birds would bring a beakful of uprooted river weeds to the other, who would stuff the weeds mechanically into the mud.

22. I knocked. The door was the usual half-inch open. The curtains had been closed.

He said, "Come in."

The room was cold. His maroon suitcase was open on the floor. Black socks and gray underwear spilled out of it. I said, "You could turn the heat on."

"Well," he said, shrugging, "I couldn't figure out how."

"Here," I said, going to the radiator under the window, turning the dial to ON. Twisting the knob in the direction of the red arrow pointing to WARM.

He looked over my shoulder as I did this. "Wow," he said, "great. Is that all? Hmm."

Then he handed me a twenty and a ten, which he'd already had in his hand. I leaned down to slip it in my shoe, and I could smell him. Old Spice and Listerine. He was standing close to me in his undershirt and blue polyester pants. I could see black hairs on his chest sprouting out of his T-shirt. His belly was soft behind his belt, and he was breathing hard.

I could hear country music drone above us. Someone singing O-O-O over and over. Twang and thump. Gary Jensen stomping in his cowboy boots over our heads while I undid the buckle of this man's belt, unsnapped his pants and pulled them down.

He was trembling, practically screaming, "Oh my god. Oh. Oh my god."

When it was over, he wanted more. I told him I had to go, but he held onto the sleeve of my blouse. "Please," he said, "just let me see your titties."

"No," I said.

•

When I got back to the office, Gary W. Jensen was leaning on one elbow with his back toward the counter, smoking a cigarette. He wasn't wearing the leather jacket, and he looked lean. His brown hair was combed now. The thin beard looked darker. He looked like someone vaguely familiar from a TV show — maybe the deputy on *Gunsmoke,* but sexy, clever.

I didn't look at him, just walked around the counter, took the money out of my shoe and reached under the cash drawer to put it in my purse, checking first to make sure the rest of my money was still where I'd left it. Then I stood back up and said, "Can I help you, Mr. Jensen?"

"You sure are a busy little beaver, ain't you?"

"Yes." I looked straight at him. "So what can I help you with now?" Not a hint of anything in it — sex, fear, anger, nothing.

"Well." He cleared his throat, which led to a long cough, and then he said, "To be honest, I wanted to apologize. I know I'm really a bastard. I should never've hit you."

"It didn't hurt," I said. It hadn't.

He looked surprised. "I'm glad of that, at least, but I still feel so damn bad about it." The Texas accent made him sound sincere, and his eyebrows were knitted together. His eyes were dark and sad. He dragged on his cigarette and looked hard at me, though he didn't look for long. My fingers felt cold and thin to each other.

"Forget about it," I said, and meant it. I'd gotten the money, he'd hit me, so what? It was just my body, and it was over.

"Thank you," he said. "You're real sweet, you know that? You shouldn't be doing what you're doing. I know it's none of my damn business, but you're real pretty and nice, and it's just wrong. It could be dangerous, too, with fools like me running around loose."

I felt my throat tighten, near the spot he'd held me down against the floor.

Here he was, someone else again, and what role was left for me to play?

I swallowed and said, quieter than I'd meant to, "Why'd you hit me then?"

He leaned across the counter and whispered, as if it were the most astonishing fact I'd ever hear, "Sweetheart, I have no idea." He shook his head and looked at his thumbnails lined up next to each other on the counter, then he looked up at me again with damp eyes. "That's the truth," he said. "I don't have the slightest damn idea. Just something sick in me, I guess."

"I guess you're right," I said, and my own eyes went stupidly damp. I felt myself step back a bit then, away from my body or out of it, and I could see myself as if in a mirror. Embarrassed, sentimental, blurred.

Gary Jensen began to fish for another cigarette in his shirt pocket and handed one to me, too. The flame was warm near my face when he lit it, and I didn't look up again.

Outside now it was deep blue, though the October sky had begun to clear with just a bruise of old light, the sun already sunk like a shipwreck to the west, where Lake Michigan sloshed sloppy with dead fish and weeds.

The office felt too small and hot, a dull fan scrambling the heat, blasting dust into the air, and I imagined the dry mummies of mice stuck in the electric furnace duct, crumbling and blowing mouse ash into the air. Us sucking it into our lungs. The cigarette smoke filled my mouth with soot.

"You saw that woman then, the one who came looking for me?" he asked.

"I guess so."

"She's got a good heart, too, and I've broke it to pieces. She's the mother of my child, for chrissakes, and I've treated her worse than dirt. Worse than dirt." He shook his head, seeming baffled by himself. "Who knows why a guy like me does the kind of stuff he does. Who knows?"

I shrugged and said, "I don't," exhaling a banner of gray hair over his shoulder.

He grinned. "No, hon, I suppose you don't. But I just want to tell you I have never been sorrier in my life for anything I've done than I am for hitting you. There's just no excuse for hitting a pretty little girl like you. A total stranger. And I just had to have you know that. Especially since, you know, you were being real nice to me, and we were doing something — intimate. You know? The way I behaved was just plain wrong. I am one evil guy. My mama would just roll over in her coffin if she knew what kind of man I have become."

"O.K.," I said, putting the cigarette out in the ashtray near his elbow, "but I need to get back to work." I felt annoyed, familiar, myself again.

He straightened up then, as if I'd caught him in a lie. "I understand. I understand." He cleared his throat. "Listen, I hope this isn't going to make matters even worse. But money is not a problem for me right now, though I suspect it is for you. Here." He handed me a wad of drab green. "I want you to have this as a gift from me."

I took it without looking at it and slipped it into the front pocket of my skirt.

"Thanks," I said, looking at the wall behind Gary W. Jensen's head as he turned to go. His boots squealed over the linoleum and, before he stepped out of the office into the damp curtain of dusk, he turned at the door to its K-Mart Christmas jingling: "Bye."

I tried to smile.

I didn't know why.

The clock said twenty-five past eight, and the river sounded sloppy and fast outside, like someone running away with a bucket of cold black water.

$\mathcal{M}$Y UNCLE ANDY tugs my mother's arm, pulls her up from the couch, gentle but quick, and before he presses her to him she twirls, graceful, and laughs. He scoops one hand up under her breast, arm behind her, takes her hand in his other, and she scratches the back of his neck lightly with her fingernails as they dance barefoot in the living room to no music at all. Her nails are long and frosted, mother-of-pearl, and they make a dry sound as they move lightly across his flesh — a pencil scribbling numbers fast on a page.

She is in a red dress and black stockings, a string of fake pearls like small sea-teeth around her neck. My uncle Andy's nice shirt is starched stiff and unbuttoned to the middle of his chest. He's handsome, and young. He always has new clothes — pressed, pleated pants, skinny belts and ties. Tall and thin, but solid. His dark hair is combed off his forehead but falling, still, into his eyes, over and over. He pushes it back with a fast hand.

In the corner of the living room, the Christmas tree blinks like some stalled car's hazard lights while, outside, the snow gets deeper, deeper, and more deaf. My father is out there somewhere on a two-lane road, trying to get home from another state, some place he's gone to sell something to someone who wants it right away, who doesn't care that it's Christmas

Eve. He calls every few hours to say he's almost home, though still on the way, and it will take a long time in so much weather. I try to look out the window but all I see is their reflection in it:

My mother catches my uncle's earlobe between her teeth. He opens his mouth, and only air comes out — pulling her closer, moving his hand down her spine to pull her hips to his. I press my face up against the black glass, and my breath leaves the shadow of ghost lips on the window, then disappears.

Out there, milk-blue hills of snow have rolled and drifted into smooth slopes, as if they've been butter-knifed across the front lawns along our narrow street, across the driveways, concealing sidewalks, front steps, all the frozen gardens and iced-over birdbaths on our block. All the plain houses, stuck like plastic cake decorations into a deep blizzard of cake, are identical to ours:

Two bedrooms. No dining room. A place in the kitchen to sit and eat dinner or to pay your bills. This rectangle of living room.

Here and there, a garage has been built. Instead of white, someone has painted the shutters red. But other than that, they're exact. Each one with a dry green Christmas tree lit up, making the house a festive firetrap in December. A slow dance behind dark curtains. I hear them breathe behind me, and it's a kind of music — all rhythm, just a drummer's brush.

The lace around the wrists of my pajamas prickles. Pretty trim. Bric-a-brac with little, itchy teeth, nibbling.

I'm too young to be awake so late, even on the eve of Christmas.

When I got home that night, Rick was in blue boxer shorts and a plain T-shirt watching television in our living room. A handsome blond cop dropped to the concrete. Bullets whizzed above him. A mailman put his hand over the mouth of a screaming housewife, hysterical because someone's blood had splattered her yellow dress. But on our television, the blood looked pink as the vacancy sign outside the Swan Motel — neon, phony, cheerful.

Rick turned the TV off.

"Hey," he said, not smiling.

I leaned over the couch and we kissed with the sound of a thin book closing.

Our apartment often smelled like onions cooking in someone else's apartment. Warm, though. Orderly. A few posters on the walls — a man playing guitar, a vase of blue flowers. A row of books on a white shelf.

I went into the bedroom and hung my jean jacket in the closet and then went into the bathroom and brushed my teeth. As I leaned over the sink, mouth full of mint and spit, Rick came up behind me, put his hand on my waist. In the mirror I could see him behind me, his shoulders sharp as wire hangers under his T-shirt. His jaw looked different, too, more clearly a bone than it had been a few months before. My hair fell reddish into the sink, and I flipped it over my shoulder, twisting away, swishing, rinsing while Rick moved back toward the bathroom door.

"How was work?" he asked.

"No big deal," I said.

"Many guests?"

"No. Hardly any. Real slow."

"Want some dinner now?" His skin looked gray against the bright bathroom walls, but his hair and eyes were dark, and behind them I could see his mother as a teenage beauty queen. It was as though, losing weight, Rick had dug up his mother's lost face, exhumed her delicately shaped skull.

"No. I just want to go to bed. Did you eat?"

"Yeah," he said, turning into the bedroom.

I put my hands on my hips and followed him. "What did you eat?" I asked.

Rick shrugged, "I had a salad."

I leaned against the bedroom wall and shook my head. "Why? Why don't you eat something besides salad, Rick? You've lost forty pounds. I hate it."

Rick looked away from me. He smiled, sort of. Again, he shrugged. "I feel really good," he said.

"Jesus," I said, under my breath. "Well, you don't look good. You look *sick*. You look like you're dying. What's the *matter* with you?"

I didn't sound upset, even to myself, though my voice was raised. Instead, I sounded as if I were reading something interesting out of the paper, and Rick just looked at my bald knees, not smiling. He said, "Can't we talk about something else?"

"No," I said. "We have to talk about this. Millie told me today she couldn't *believe* how you looked when she saw you last week. So should I tell her you've lost ten more pounds since then? That you won't eat anything but lettuce, but you *feel really good?*" At the end, I imitated his monotone, folding my arms against my breasts.

"You can tell Millie anything you want, Leila. Surprisingly enough, Millie's opinion isn't all that important to me." He didn't sound angry, either, just blunt.

"What about *my* opinion? Don't you care that looking at my husband makes me sick? Don't you care that this is driving me crazy, watching you evaporate into thin air?"

Rick sat down hard on the edge of the bed, as if he were exhausted, then looked up at me. Even his hair looked different — finer. His teeth were bigger and more white.

"Listen, Leila. I'm tired of talking about my body."

"Well I'm tired of living with it."

He smirked. "Well, that's honest at least. Leila, you're tired of living with *me*, and I'm tired of doing what other people tell me all day to do. I'm tired of my mother nagging and my father foretelling my future in pinball machines, and I'm tired of you telling me what's best to do with my body."

"Well, you're killing your body. Is that O.K. to say?"

My hands had begun to shake when he'd mentioned his father, the future, the pinball machines. It was the one thing I'd never heard Rick complain about before, the one thing I thought didn't fill him with despair and contempt.

"Well, at least it's *my* body," he said. "It's *my* body — " he thumped his rib cage each time he said *my* — "and I can do whatever the hell I want with *my* body. Is that correct?"

When I opened my mouth to answer, it was empty. A wet hole full of wind. In fact, I had to squint: The exactitude of it stunned me, and I closed my lips against breath as he walked past me, back to the living room we shared.

I took my clothes off, put them in a neat pile in the corner of the bedroom, slipped into one of Rick's white T-shirts, and got in bed. I could hear him in the living room. Laughter from the TV and the excited whine of children. I was still awake when he turned it off, came into the dark bedroom, balanced himself into the waterbed and curled against my body before he fell asleep. His breathing was deep, slow, and it made gentle waves on the surface of our bed.

Rick's legs on my legs felt familiar, as if they were my own, as if we were a tree with tangled limbs. I thought about the man with the maroon suitcase, how he'd wanted to see my breasts, and I couldn't remember that man's face, just the pastiness of his body, how it had trembled like soft food when he came. When Rick, in his sleep, put a hand on my waist, I rolled over fast and pressed my breasts against the mattress, warm with water, and his hand ended up on my back. Soon he moved further to his side of the bed, turned away from me in a dream, breathing so steadily I could have counted the long dull minutes with it.

The dark was total, and it pulsed with purple snow and static when I focused my open eyes on the ceiling. Occasionally a bar of light from cars passing by would rise and fall on the wall or smooth its white glove over our dresser as if it were a ghost, dusting. I could hear the woman who lived upstairs run water in her bathroom sink, and I imagined her in red flannel or something slinky and black, ready for bed by herself. I'd only seen her once, climbing the stairs very slowly. She'd had long legs, must have been about forty. She wore sunglasses that day in the dim light of the stairwell, so I couldn't see her eyes. But the woman's hair was darker and longer than mine. She'd smiled and said nothing when I said hi.

Now that woman was getting into a bed above our bed. I could hear the springs squeak and settle, squeak. Then silence. I wondered if the couple under us could hear our bed so well, that swell of water as we got in and out.

They weren't married down there, and they fought every night. Neither Rick nor I had ever seen the girlfriend, but we'd gone to high school with the guy, Bill, and Bill had been popular — a doctor's son — and Rick had seemed to know him pretty well back then. They'd both been witty, athletes, more vivid against the high school's gray cinderblock than I had ever been.

Still, I'd known Bill back then, too, and Rick knew it. Now the two high school football buddies never spoke at all, even when they passed each other in the hallway, at the wall of mailboxes, miniature steel keys popping them open. "Hey," they just said, "hey," under their breaths, dry as the whisk of a broom.

And though we'd never seen her, sometimes at night Rick and I could hear Bill's girlfriend cry, high and wild.

"He's a dog," Rick said once while she was crying, "always was," and he frowned.

Once, we heard her scream Bill's name out the window and heard Bill shout up at her, "Cunt," from the street.

I thought then about Gary W. Jensen. Not until I was nearly home from the Swan Motel, stopped at a four-way stop with no other cars around, did I count the money he'd slipped to me across the counter, and there had been three fifty-dollar bills in that drab green wad soft as a dog's ear, hacked off.

Then I thought about standing up into that slap. How it numbed but hadn't hurt me. I'd been ready for the second one, and I'd moved with it into its own curved momentum. I thought how it hadn't even surprised me — the way the ice-skating instructor had said, years and years before, when our sixth-grade class had been taken on a field trip to the rink in Ottawa City, that the most important thing about skating was learning how to fall: white shavings on the sheen, circling, circling, and falling every few circles into a sting of solid cold, a steam of frost and ice-cindered wind in my lungs. Then, how he'd pushed into me while I was down, looking into my eyes, how he'd pulled out and come on the floor, the dull beige carpet, and my thigh.

Rick began to grind his teeth in sleep. I thought about Gary Jensen coming onto the floor beneath my body, and I rolled further to the edge of the bed, slipped a hand under the elastic band of my panties and touched myself until I was done. Then I fell asleep.

I woke heavy with sleep again when Rick began to toss and mutter in his dream, and I got up quietly then, feeling the groggy weight of my body as if all of it were on my back, and I felt my way in shadows to the couch where we always kept a blanket and a pillow now. I fell asleep again, into and out of a dream in which my mother's grave was a vegetable garden covered over with snow. An inch or two under the snow, there were ten or fifteen beautiful red bell peppers, perfectly round and preserved. At first, while I was clawing them out of the snow with my cold bare hands, they looked like bloody breasts. But they were only waxy supermarket peppers, glossy and big, so many I didn't know what I'd do with them all. But, in my dream, I thought Rick would know. Rick would cook

something for me with them that he'd looked up in a book.
Then I was in a department store, shopping for a coat. Then, I
was wearing the coat, walking across water. And then I woke.

Morning buzzed under me somewhere, and when I opened my
eyes I saw that Rick was already gone. I could smell coffee in
the kitchen getting old. A fat ribbon of dust swelled and sank
slowly in a crack of light between the curtains, and I opened
them. The window was warm. The sun was just a mild yellow
crown in the blurred sky, but high. I went into the bedroom
and saw that Rick had made the bed before he left, had tucked
the ivory eyelet cover into the bulged edges of the waterbed —
a woman's dress over too much flesh. The electronic alarm
clock blinked 11:15. 11:15. 11:16.

Outside, birds bleated softly, sounding digital and sweet.
Orange leaves shuffled on one big tree across the street like a
man shaking his wife's wig in his fist, and someone had set a
pumpkin out on the front steps of the dentist's office next
door: Magic Marker smile. It was a friendly autumn squash
the size of a small and limbless child.

I went to the kitchen — a shiny square. The Formica table-
top and the appliances were naked white. There were no
dishes in the sink, just a checkered dishtowel thrown casually across the faucet's arm and an electric pot of coffee. The
kitchen I thought of as Rick's and spent little time in it. After
I poured coffee and picked my purse off the kitchen chair
where I'd left it the night before, I took the cup and the purse
back to the bedroom and I sat at the edge of the bed, coffee cup
on the floor at my bare feet, purse in my lap. I unzipped it and
counted the money again.

The bills felt limp and damp, but the coins were cold metal.
I weighed them in my hands. A warm sun-bar of gold from the
window moved slowly up my stomach, and I thought about
what I wanted to buy with all that money.

What was it?

Something — a white station wagon? — drove by then, and it lit up the street like an exploding shell.

A refrigerator, I thought.

No.

An ice-cream truck.

A cage of white tigers at the Chicago Zoo on a blinding May day.

But that wasn't it either.

Then I leaned down and opened the bottom drawer of the dresser and felt under the panties and short socks for the jewelry box where I kept this money. I opened it slowly:

The ballerina still danced, but the box played no Vienna waltz. I could see the reflection of my own hand, green with cash from the day before, doubled in the little mirror, and I began to count all the cash in the jewelry box again, though I knew exactly how much was there:

Two thousand three hundred thirty-seven dollars and sixty cents.

And I'd only been doing what I was doing for forty-two days.

Not counting Sundays, my one day off.

*J*T's JULY — a hundred degrees in northern Michigan, and it's like trying to breathe beneath a heap of gray-blue blankets soaked in fever-sweat, yellowed sheets. I've learned to answer the phone.

"Lee-la speaking," I say into its black mouth.

"Leila, sweetie, this is Daddy. Let me talk to Mommy."

My mother's voice is a musical muffle behind the closed bedroom door, and she steps out before I knock. Naked. Her whole body is pale as damp papier-mâché, except her nipples which are glossy, pink, and the thick black patch of hair between her legs. She doesn't close the bedroom door behind her, and I see his dark arms over a pillow. There's the smell of sweat and violets crushed to powder when she passes.

"Hi hon," she says into the phone.

I stay standing in the hallway outside my parents' bedroom. I see him turn over in the bed, sit up, his back against the white-pine headboard. And I stare straight at him, not moving at all.

Maybe my eyes are narrow and dull.

I hear my mother behind me.

She says, "I just can't talk about it right now, Jack. I'm doing two hundred things at once and it's just hotter than hell up here. Call me tonight at dinnertime, will you?

"I love you, too.

"Just come back as soon as you can."

She hangs up as she says, "Bye."

My uncle stares back at me, not seeing me at all, and his chest rises and falls, angry, all that tan nakedness taking up more than half their bed. His whole body sweats.

She moves past me fast when she comes back, and this time I smell something clean as medicine on her skin before she closes the door behind her, and I hear him on the other side of it mutter, "Why the fuck are you talking to him that way?"

"He's my fucking husband," she says, "that's why."

The sun got flatter but warmer in the sky as the day went on. It bounced off the windshields of the other cars and flashed like lightning in my lap as I drove to the Swan Motel. The car windows were unrolled, and the October air tasted pure on my teeth. Indian summer, I thought as I passed the Main Street gift shop and looked up for a moment into the blue eyes of Pocahontas, watching over us like a tacky goddess of tourists and small change, exchanged. In her fixed eyes I was nothing more than a blur of glass and rust on its way to work.

It was warm, but it was October. I could feel the earth tilt, bank further away from the sun with the whole town of Suspicious River on it. Not slipping into infinity and ether, though — stuck. Pasted to its place.

Some of the trees along Main Street were already completely bare, and they clawed at the silver blue of the sky. Bright and quiet, the town had turned away from summer like a stale white cake behind a glass bakery case. As I drove by the pharmacy, I saw my father sitting on a bench outside, sipping a Pepsi, a few ragged leaves scuffling at his feet. But, of course, it wasn't him.

And outside the Red Devil Lounge on the other side of the street, three men in leather jackets stood around a glinting circle of motorcycles. One of the men was staring up at the sky, a long brown braid stretching down his back, his feet apart and his hands on his hips like a man stunned by god. Sun blind. A green bottle of beer shimmered in his fist.

All the buildings along Main Street, except the gift shop with its mural, were red brick and built a hundred years ago when Suspicious River was a boomtown — loggers and trappers with thick mustaches photographed in black and white with their wives in bustles, hair pulled up, grim smiles, posing outside the brand-new buildings they'd raised where there'd been just forest a few months before:

Those photos were pressed like the past into an album at Ed's Photography Shop, and the tourists stopped by sometimes to look at those long-dead faces and think about the town back then. Then, it must have already seemed terrible, and complete, and the future was only a storeroom with nothing except winter in it, and no one had the key.

Who would have imagined tourists then? The Swan Motel? Me?

But those loggers bought tobacco from a German on Main Street, and they ate big meals of bloody beef and boiled potatoes at the restaurant beside the tobacco shop, flirting with their waitresses — the German's daughters, thick-ankled, with Lutheran blue eyes, who scuttled like mice between the kitchen, the garbage, and those meals.

And the money those men spent fed the town just enough to nudge it forward from year to year like a big ship of prisoners and their wives cruising a very short coast for a long, long time. It was no different than the way the tourists slipped a little something into the town's red shoe now as they passed through.

Some of the bricks had crumbled. Many of the buildings were empty. The Star Hotel had once been famous on the western edge of the state for its chandeliers and its Star Lounge piano bar. Peanut shells and sawdust on the wide-planked oak floors, scuffed by heels. But now the Star Hotel was a warehouse for a furniture store owned by a corporation in another town. Even the Palace had been gone so long no one mentioned it anymore. Just a ball of glitter turning above the dance floor like a strange, mechanical planet in the past.

Now, Main Street smelled vaguely, maybe pleasantly, of decay.

Not death, just an attic full of purple evening gowns, crinoline, silk suits shut up in a trunk for a century or so.

Mothballs, and a shoebox of dried carnations.

But no one was sad about that. The elegance of the red brick buildings along Main Street had been replaced easily and overnight by the neon and glass of the new buildings along Eighth Street. McDonald's. Howard Johnson's. A & W. Eighth Street had been nothing but cow pasture until 1972. Now there were dumpsters full of maggoty meat and cow-white styrofoam parked beside our cars while we ate our burgers in a hurry.

Still, those buildings would never be as familiar to us as the ones on Main Street, no matter how long they stood along Eighth Street. Those new buildings were only squares of glass full of air, fluorescent light, and bright plastic spoons. Those buildings had the look of temporary shelters, stuck like afterthoughts into what seemed still to be a pasture. The smell of manure, hen feathers, and horsehair snagged in a breeze that passed between the golden arches every afternoon.

I stepped harder on the gas to make it through the yellow light, and a cool wind knocked at my ear and pushed into my mouth when I sped up. In that wind, I tasted sterling. Like biting down on a coin.

In the parking lot of the Swan Motel, I saw his silver Thunderbird, still there. I pulled in next to it on purpose with the rusty white Duster Rick's father had sold us a few years before for three hundred dollars. It was a reliable car, and it was mine, but it ran nervous and high. Sometimes at a stoplight I felt that if I failed to keep my foot hard and heavy on the brake, the car might fly.

Millie wasn't in the office when I arrived. Instead: RECEP-TIONIST WILL BE RIGHT BACK.

I put my purse under the counter and listened at the bathroom door. Millie wasn't in the bathroom. So I walked back out to the parking lot, squinted and looked around, didn't see her, and then I walked around the office to the back of the Swan Motel where Millie stood in moss-green grass, smoking a cigarette and staring, concerned or bored, into Suspicious River.

The blackness of that water and the way Millie stared into it reminded me of the Magic 8 Ball every child owned when I was a child. *Reply hazy, try again* always rose to the inky surface.

Because Millie's dark hair frizzed in damp weather, it seemed to expand until Millie appeared small and withered, an old petunia, under it. But today her hair was sleek as plastic. A new product, I thought. Gel, mousse, shampoo — something slick in a blue tube — had changed Millie overnight. "Hey," she said, a mouthful of smoke.

I said, "Hi."

The river smelled weedy, green-black, and a swan paddled past. Another stood alone on the riverbank and lifted its wings, then dropped them, shook itself, then lifted its wings, shuddering again. It was like a beautiful woman talking to herself, practicing a speech, mouthing it with nothing coming out. The sun ribboned the water. A thin shiver of light.

Millie said, "God. It's been a really bad day."

The orange eye of her cigarette flared when she inhaled, and I sat down in a lounge chair near her and looked up at Millie's face. It was a pretty face, but the eyes were pale and lost in it. Her long teeth were sharp as an animal's, and severe. She shook her glossy new hair and said, "Mrs. Briggs came in and bitched me out because I forgot to have some guy sign his credit card slip like two months ago."

"Did she just find out?"

"I guess so." Millie shrugged. "She got it back yesterday from the bank."

Millie sighed and smoked and looked toward the other side of the river, which was nothing but bushes, sticks, a steady sway of thin white branches. Now and then a crow flapped out. Occasionally a hawk would circle the air above the nothing, making a slow funnel back to earth in search of something weak or dead.

Millie inhaled and said, "And, Leila, some guy came in asking about you."

She looked away when she said it. Back at the river.

"Who?"

"I don't know. He was driving a white van." Millie cleared her throat. "That's been happening pretty regular, you know."

A warning. I should have known it was coming. Though it didn't matter to me much, coming from Millie, who couldn't do anything well.

There was silence then, except for the river. The muffled sound of a swan's webbed feet pumping just beneath the surface.

"I should probably get to the office," I said.

"Yeah," Millie said, "I'm gonna get the hell out of this place right now."

Saturday October 16. I opened the leather-bound guest register.

Two of the reservations I'd written up myself. Two were in the handwriting of the third front desk girl, Samantha. Big, girly writing. There were circles instead of dots above the i's. Samantha's chubby friendly B in Browski, Mr. & Mrs. John.

Samantha was seventeen, eight months pregnant, and she

worked at the Swan Motel when she wasn't in school. All day she sat on a stool behind the counter and sang Barry Manilow songs to her baby. She'd lean down over her big breasts, hum and mutter to her stomach, and when a guest stepped into the office, jangling the bells, Samantha would look up, open-mouthed, and stop.

Millie's small, loose script, cramped and slack at the same time, was nowhere under the date, so I knew something would be missing that night. Someone would show up with a reservation, and without one. Millie had the busiest shift for taking reservations, and, after all, it was a weekend night. Even in October there were always ten or eleven reservations for a Saturday night.

I looked at the check-in sheet and saw what I already knew, having seen his silver Thunderbird in the parking lot when I pulled in. Jensen, Gary, with Smith in parentheses next to it. How had he explained that to Millie?

I emptied an orange ashtray into the wastebasket under the counter. The ashtray was heavy, for plastic, and shaped like a kidney. It felt strange and dangerous in my hand, heavy enough to explode if it slipped to the floor, or if it was thrown.

I lit a cigarette then and watched the clock on the wall across the counter. There was no second hand, but the minute hand jerked forward hard and mechanical, with only a small clicking sound like someone pulling the trigger of a pistol without any ammunition in it.

I didn't look at him at first when he came in, but he stooped a little, a friendly dance step in his blond cowboy boots, a blue baseball cap shading his face, and he tried to catch my eye. "Howdy," he said, mostly twang.

Gary Jensen was wearing another shirt — also light blue and starched so stiff it would've stayed standing even if he'd suddenly melted to nothing in it. Same stiff jeans. His face looked leaner, maybe a little mean now, with that baseball cap over his high forehead. And he could've been a baseball player, too. I could see the hollows from his cheeks to his jaw like slashed scars or a boy's dimples gouged too deep when he smiled, even under the scruffy stubble of his beard. I could imagine him spitting on a mound.

"You mind if I smoke a cigarette with you?" he asked, reaching into his breast pocket for the package. But his hand froze over his heart like a pledge, and he looked at me with his eyebrows raised for my O.K.

I inhaled and nodded my head slightly, maybe I rolled my eyes, and I mumbled, "I don't mind."

Gary Jensen relaxed then and lit a cigarette without offering one to me, striking two matches to light it. The first match popped and snuffed itself in midair before he got it to the cigarette, and it left a puff of gunpowder in the air between us, hanging. He didn't lean on the counter this time.

"Sure is a beautiful day," he offered, and I nodded, twitching my lips in a kind of automated smile — like the minute hand of the clock, that mechanical snap. That smile could have meant anything at all, I hoped. I hoped it confused him a little — but again he stooped to catch my eye and said, "You seem like a real sad girl, though. I sure wish I hadn't done nothing to make you even sadder."

"You didn't," I said, as if by now I'd grown impatient with apologies and compliments from him, though I'd only met him the day before.

He sucked on a front tooth with his tongue and thought about that before he dragged again on the cigarette and said, "Yeah, I did. Don't lie. It's not O.K. for some asshole to come along and slap you for no reason, is it? Twice!" as if he couldn't believe it himself. "That's got to make you feel pretty awful, sweetheart. That would make anybody feel like shit."

I wished then that the radio in the office still worked or that we had an aquarium stocked with small, panicky, kissing orange fish. Fluorescent aqua rocks. A slimy ceramic castle and a snail sucking up the glass. I remembered seeing one like that in the office of the Blue Moon Inn on the other side of town — four, maybe five years before. But I'd been offered the job here first. I thought at that moment I'd tell Mrs. Briggs about the aquarium at the Blue Moon Inn and offer to pay for the fish myself. Even the fish food, the water purifier, the fake decorations. Money was not a problem.

"Look," he said, "you're probably afraid of me now, and I don't blame you — "

"I'm not," I said, honest. And then, sarcastic, "Sorry, but I'm not."

I shrugged.

And I wasn't. I'd gotten my money, I thought, even the extra, and it hadn't hurt. Not even for a moment had I feared for my life.

Naturally, death scared me as much as the next person — a big, white room with shelves and shelves of books, all with blank pages — and the ambulance screaming down the street bright and blanched while a glitter of steel and needles flashed from the small back window as it passed. I hated that surprise, could never hear the sirens until that thing was right behind me. But I wasn't the least bit afraid of being slapped by a strange man in a motel room. Not in the least. Plus, I'd been paid.

Gary Jensen seemed pleased about that, and he inhaled smoke before he said, "Well, I was going to say I'd like to give our little rendezvous another try" — he held his palms up facing me — "*if* you'd even consider it, after what I done. The money's no problem." His palms were pale and empty. "I'd pay you whatever you want."

I sighed, as if at a child.

He glanced out the glass window to the parking lot, then back at me, and whispered, "You name it. I'd just like to be alone with you again and do it right this time."

"Two hundred dollars," I said fast, looking straight in his

eyes, and I felt a rush of wind when I said the number, as though a speeding car had brushed the right side of my face — wings, or a slap. There was a big white semi pulling into the circular drive, and the wheels and engine rumbled under my feet, in my stomach, up my legs.

"Great," he said, putting a hand over his heart, smiling. "I sure do appreciate this."

$\mathcal{I}$'M IN THE BACK SEAT of a deep blue car. Trees and gray houses, swing sets, and street signs flash by like a slide show, someone clicking the slides on the screen too fast to focus.

But now we're pulling off onto a loose dirt road. My mother turns up the radio — what sounds like the single voice of a hundred young girls singing sadly about love — and glances back at me. Then she leans across the front seat and says something I can't hear into my uncle's neck. He has one hand on the steering wheel while he fingers her knee with the other. It's warm, and I feel sleepy, though I don't want to fall asleep. My eyes open and close, open and close, in slow motion, on their own.

"That's it, baby," my mother says as she turns to look at me, "You go to sleep like a good girl, Leila."

A sliver of wind from the cracked car window shifts my mother's black hair. Her eyes are blue marbles, good ones.

My uncle looks like a boy from the back. Slicked-back hair. His ears are pink around the edges, and maybe he seems a little shy or nervous around my mother. But his skin is darker than hers. His arms are large. Still, when he looks at her there is a kind of stagger in it, astonishment, and he's like a waiter, confused, trying to be casual, carrying a tray that's too heavy with fragile dishes, a silver lid over each one, and he can never remember which meal is under which lid. He pushes the hair over his forehead, casual, again and again, until he's a handsome man with a movie star's profile, surmising, but also with a boy's white and too-eager teeth.

The sunlight is lemon and heavy on my face. "Shh," I hear my mother say in my dream as it begins, shorts out, fades, begins again.

I hear her laugh softly, as if from far away, as the car's wheels buffer us over gravel, dust in the air, sheer slips of it billowing like sheets on a laundry line blown off the shoulder of the road into the woods.

He leans down over her in the front seat, and I can hear them breathe, and it sounds like wind knocking, caught in those sheets hung out on a tight, swaying rope, rising. Somewhere, honeysuckle shudders and dandelions make a high whine — those bittersweet white and yellow flowers singing one shrill note together at the sun.

Suddenly it's night, I'm in my bed, and I think I might still be dreaming, but all the lights in the living room blaze. I get out of bed to see why she is singing, or screaming, and the sound of it is like a knife scraped across a silver platter in the middle of the night. I walk barefoot across the hallway rug.

My mother is wearing a T-shirt, his — he wore it to breakfast the morning before. He has no shirt on, just white underwear, and my mother is on her knees on the living room carpet, her back against the TV.

My uncle leans down, both hands on her left arm, twisting the skin.

It's why she screams.

He pushes her against the empty screen, yanks her to her feet, pushes her into the table lamp, which falls, sparks, sputters out.

My uncle's crying. His face is strung with tears, mucus, pinched up. His lips are apart and ugly — a spasm, a wretched smile.

"Bonnie," he sobs.

He tries to shake her, but he can't open his eyes. She has his hair in her hands, and there is blood. When my uncle opens his mouth, nothing comes out. When my mother sees me, she says, "Go back to your bedroom, goddammit."

I go back.

I close the door behind me.

But the bed has gotten cold.

I curl into just one corner of it and try to sleep, but I hear my uncle shouting, "Why. Why."

It's not a question. It's a note. Or a letter. Y.

My mother isn't crying anymore. She's telling him to shut up, shut up, none of your fucking business you fool.

Then, I seem to fall asleep for seasons. Until time is no longer a straight line. It meanders. My memory has tied it up like a bow, and nothing happens in order anymore. Leaves fall out of the trees, it rains, then leaves fall out of the trees again, and there are flowers at the side of the road. My father comes and goes in his dark car, smelling like cool wind and cigarettes when I press my face into his chest. Someone buys a whole new wardrobe for my Barbie dolls while I am dreaming, and one of the dolls has copper colored hair, like mine. The other has black hair, like my mother's. They're both grown women, though, and wear their sexy strapless evening gowns all night, gowns made of material like metal, stiff and shiny. They dance with one another on the braided rug on my bedroom floor. Their feet, elegantly arched.

Still, those dolls are made of rigid plastic, and their dancing is as stiff as their dresses, and ugly. It looks painful from above. Sometimes they slap each other for no reason — jealousy, or spite — with their outstretched zombie arms. Sometimes they take off all their clothes and dance around and around in circles, their pointed feet pressed together as if their ankles are tightly chained.

When I wake up, it's all pale snow again, and the world is white and vacant as the surface of the moon. An empty book. A concrete pond, drained. A whole era of lost memories, square and barren as a blank movie screen.

I waited a half-hour before I put the sign out on the counter, watching the minutes snap forward on the wall. I wanted him to wait.

When, finally, I stepped through the office door on my way to Gary Jensen's room, the bells jangled and the sound startled a swan who'd wandered onto the parking lot tar, which had gone sticky and soft under the autumn sun, and the swan waddled fast back toward the motel lawn — graceless in its hurry, turning toward the river again, where it had its illusion of safety, of home.

Often the swans wandered away from the water in search of popcorn or old hot dog buns. Sometimes they'd peck at a melted circle of bubble gum in the parking lot with their beaks, thinking it was something they could eat — always famished and always eating, those swans. They were beautiful, of course, but gluttonous, and shameless as greedy, drunken angels at a feast.

I could hear him in 42, whistling behind the door. I didn't knock, just pushed it open.

Gary Jensen was leaning back on his bed, legs off the side of it. Still in his jeans and starched blue shirt. Still in his boots, tapping at the carpet with the sound of an animal scratching at its fur. He looked skinny. A TV cowboy — rangy and weathered with a slow, straight smile. There were a few deep lines at the corners of his eyes, as if a sparrow had stepped there once or twice in wet cement. When he said "Hi," the notched corners of his mouth filled and hollowed. With his baseball cap off, his hair looked messy, thin on top, but it curled a little near his neck. Looking at him, I felt plain, pale, fleshy as a child. I closed the door behind me, and he motioned to the dressing table. Two one hundred dollar bills were on it, worn soft as old felt. He must have had them in his wallet a long, long time, I thought. I picked the bills up, folded them, slipped them into my shoe, under my heel, then went to the window and pulled the curtains closed.

"Come here, sweetheart," he said, patting the empty space beside him on the bed. He put his arms around my shoulders, and the skin of his neck smelled like skin: I couldn't help but sink my teeth gently into the whiskers on his jaw, high up, under his ear.

When I got back to the office, it was full of sun. It smelled like vinyl, softening — the warm seats of an old car on a long drive in the summer. It made me feel slow and tired — like someone who'd been traveling for days. No one was in the office, but there was a brown sack on the counter and a note beside it written in pencil on the back of a grocery store receipt:

> Where are you? I brought you lunch.
> Call me at home. Rick.

I threw the note away, put the lunch under the counter, and slipped the two hundred dollars out of my shoe and into my purse. Then I went into the bathroom and washed my hands and face with hot water and the small pink soap. Afterward, the skin across my cheekbones looked thin, and I took a lipstick out of my purse, put some on my lips, smoothed a little across my cheeks, combed my hair with the black comb. When the phone began to ring, insistent and metallic on the counter, I just let it. I turned the hot water knob off and let cold water run, instead, into the sink. I leaned over to drink it out of the cup of my hand, like sipping from a glacier while the ice age waned, and the cold hurt my teeth, pleasantly, tasting painfully pure.

▼

The first time Rick and I made love, he cried gently and quietly and apologized when we were done. It had been in total darkness on an old couch in the basement of his parents' house. We were both sixteen, and it hadn't mattered to me. It was fine, I told him. Whatever he wanted to do. I stood up from the couch and took off my clothes and dropped them around me on the cold basement floor. My body felt like old stone to me, but Rick ran his hands over it, still in his clothes, as if my body were entirely new.

"Are you O.K.?" he asked me over and over.

"Yes," I said.

Rick stood up to take his shirt and pants off, and I could hear him breathing, a racecar driver trying to change a flat in order to get back on the racetrack, fast. I couldn't see him at all, and I thought then about what it might be like to be blind, or dead. Maybe I held my hand out in front of my face and couldn't even see myself.

"Leila," he said softly afterward, "I'm sorry. I didn't mean to go that far." His head was on my shoulder and I could feel tears squeeze out of his eyes onto my bare skin. "I wanted to wait until we were married," he said.

I wanted to laugh but said, instead, "It's fine."

"Did it hurt?" he asked.

Maybe then I did laugh. I said, "No." I hadn't felt anything at all, and he seemed puzzled, but relieved.

After that, Rick seemed to feel we *were* married, but also that we shouldn't have sex again until we were. He talked to me in whispers when he drove me home from school about how we weren't virgins anymore, and I realized he'd thought I'd been one until then. It made me feel smug, safe. His eyes looked round and dumb when he fixed them on mine. It made me feel loved, the way a bad cat is loved by a lonely old woman. It knows it can scratch up the furniture, piss on the rug, and nothing is ever its fault. I liked the idea of that, liked to let him touch my breasts until he shook all over, and then I'd look into his eyes to see how clouded over with modesty and self-restraint they were. A boy on a diet. A priest. He could've done anything he wanted, and he knew that, but wouldn't. He treated me the way his mother treated him — a fading beauty queen with a crush on something too fabulous to last. There were times I thought I might love him, too, because Rick was tongue-tied, slow, and dull as love itself. I'd search around my chest sometimes at night before I fell asleep, feeling for my heart, but there was never anything there.

▼

The phone kept ringing. I picked up the inside line, which sputtered a red light like an ambulance flasher.

"Office," I said, annoyed.

"Yeah. Hi. I'm in 22. Is this the girl I met yesterday?"

It was the man with the maroon suitcase. He was still there. Millie hadn't bothered to write that in the guest book either.

"It is," I said.

"I'd like to see you again."

I rolled my eyes at the tone of his voice. He sounded like a bad actor playing the part of an ugly, romantic man. I said, "Well, it's going to be eighty dollars this time."

There was a pause. Maybe he was looking in his wallet. "No problem," he said. "When?"

"Give me half an hour," I said.

He said, "See you then."

I put the phone down and picked it right up again, dialed my own familiar phone number. "Rick?" I asked when he answered the phone.

"Leila? Where the hell were you? I looked all over. I was worried."

"I guess I was around back smoking a cigarette," I said.

"I looked there." It wasn't an accusation. He simply sounded confused.

"You couldn't have," I said. "That was the only place I went except the bathroom. How long did you wait?"

"I could only stand around about ten minutes. Dad was waiting for me in the car. We did a repair job this afternoon in Ottawa."

"Hmm," I said, as if I were the one with a reason to be suspicious.

"I didn't want to say anything to my dad about you not being there. I just wanted to give you your lunch and say hi." Silence, then Rick cleared his throat and said, "I'm sorry we argued last night."

"It's O.K.," I said.

"I'm just, you know, tired of being nagged."

I touched my throat. This was the different Rick again. Even his voice was lower, and I stood up a little straighter when he said it. A little surprised. A baby hand of fear and thrill with a few ragged fingernails tickled behind my ribs. The way a big storm announces itself with monotonous blue skies for days.

"Thanks for the lunch," I offered. "Rick, someone just pulled up. I have to go. I'll call you back a little later, O.K.?"

"Sure," he said. "Good-bye."

His room was a mess. The maroon suitcase was still open on the floor. The bed wasn't made, and it looked slept in. A white towel was wadded on the only chair.

"Didn't you get maid service this morning?" I asked.

"I was sleeping," he said. "I told her to go away."

"Oh," I said. I took the bills from his hand, slipped them into my shoe.

Our "maid service" was Mrs. Briggs's daughter-in-law — a fat, damp-white woman who might have been any age over twenty-five, who smoked cigarettes and drank Coke until she coughed up a phlegmy syrup, spitting it over the railing onto the parking lot while she wheeled a stainless steel cart of sheets and plastic garbage bags full of clean or dirty linen slowly from room to room. If someone was asleep when she came by, if the DO NOT DISTURB sign was hanging on the door knob, she never bothered to come back, and almost no one ever complained. Some mornings she'd spend hours in a clean and vacant room watching *Jeopardy!* and *The Dating Game*, emerging later with a pink feather duster raised in one hand like an exotic, captured bird.

I said, "I thought you were only going to stay one night."

He came toward me then, bolder than he had been the day before. Still in the same white T-shirt, though. Same blue slacks. "I stayed for this," he said, pulling my pink knit sweater out of my jeans, yanking it up to my shoulders.

I raised my arms and let him slip the sweater up. He trembled trying to unsnap my bra in the back, so I did it for him. He was breathing hard. I stood with my arms at my sides. His fingers were small and cold. Clammy palms. He made little sucking sounds and groaned when he took the nipples in his mouth. After what seemed like long enough for eighty dollars, I knelt down and unzipped him, and when it was over, he sat down hard on the edge of the bed with his mouth open. His lips, shiny and wet. I didn't say anything while I put my bra and sweater back on, or when I left.

Gary W. Jensen was leaning against the hood of his car when I stepped out of 22. He was smoking a cigarette, looking down at his blond boots. I walked by him without speaking, but he grabbed my elbow in his hands. Lightly, but I stopped.

"Jesus," he said and bit the inside of his lower lip, shaking his head. "Sweetheart," he said, still looking at the boots. Then he looked up at me. "How often're you doin' this anyway?"

I let a moment pass while I tried to decide how to speak to him. He wasn't as easy as the man with the maroon suitcase in 22. I liked his boots and jeans, his easy laugh. He reminded me of a happy con man, the kind you cheer for in the movies — slick, but tenderhearted, with a sense of humor about his own, inevitable death. I'd felt small and clumsy the second time in Gary Jensen's bed. Naked, I thought I looked skinny and uncooked under his solid body, a piece of white fish on a white plate, and nothing to eat with it.

But he'd been shaking, touching me, cooing about *so beautiful, so beautiful.* And it was hard to keep my eyes open. I'd gotten used to being treated like a plaster statue by then, and didn't mind. Just my body, I thought, you can do whatever you want. I'd gotten used to treating the men themselves as if they'd hired me to complete a menial domestic chore, one they'd started themselves and hadn't had time to finish — their couch spot-cleaned, their knickknacks dusted and rearranged.

But this was different. Gary Jensen had been trying to please me — circling, kissing. He wouldn't let me take him in my mouth. He wanted to rub my back instead, which made the inside of my skin feel like static — an electric crackling along my spine beneath his hands, red sparks snapping from my nerves. He said *Relax, relax,* but I couldn't. He wanted to touch my hair, get on his knees between my legs.

His body was thin, but his skin was smooth. A feather-ridge of dark hair at his breastbone, as if there had once been wings, as if they'd been surgically removed. He moved his face down to my stomach, and the whiskers felt like a small fire there. I touched the top of his head, where the hair was thin, and I felt how soft it was, like a child's. He begged me to let him kiss me there, and I imagined he was trying too hard to make up for hitting me the day before, that now he felt he owed me the way I felt I'd owed him for the money I'd slipped into my shoe, and, therefore, didn't fight back when he hit me. So I let him, and he never even came, just tongued and touched me until I couldn't stand it anymore, coming under his warm mouth.

Afterward, he kissed me over and over on the ear while I tried to catch my breath. Smiling, he said he was done, that's all he'd wanted to do, and I put my clothes back on. Maybe it had felt good, that attention, I wasn't entirely sure, but walking back down the concrete steps from his room, I'd felt crushed and numb where he'd tasted my heartbeat between my legs. Foolish and defeated, like a kid. I felt like a child who'd asked for a toy my parents couldn't afford to buy, and they'd bought it for me anyway:

What you want for yourself, and what you dread being given.

"Huh? How often?" He nudged me, squeezing my elbow. Not hard, but I looked up.

"I'd have to say that's none of your business," I said. Then I moved my leg between his legs, my light blue jeans against his dark blue ones, and I pressed my knee into his. "Unless you're saying you'd like to do it again," I said.

He threw his cigarette into the rock garden, and a thin string of smoke rose from the ruined petunias, wadded as they were now, like used tissue, facedown and done. He took his hand off my elbow and slipped his arm around my waist, pulling me into him. Kissing my ear. "Yeah," he said into my hair, "I want to do it again."

22 opened then. Someone looked out from a dark split in the doorway, a man with small bird eyes, and shut the door again.

L ook," my mother says to my father.

They are at the kitchen table, a scattering of empty envelopes between them.

My mother turns her palms up on the envelopes and says, again, "Look. We know Andy will lend us the money. And he's got it. If you won't ask him, I will."

My father is looking into the checkbook ledger as if he's lost something in it. He says nothing, but he swallows.

A drift of snow has leaned against our kitchen window, and in the February twilight, as blank and white as cold bath water, the snow appears to be the sky. Heat rises from the register, scratching — a dry wool sweater over my face, and I stand with bare feet on the black grill of it, burning and frozen at the same time.

I look out the window, over the snowdrift and through the condensation on the other side of the glass, and through it I can see into our neighbors' fenced back yard to where a long brown rabbit is tied by its foot to the low branch of a tree: a cherry tree. In the spring that tree will be bright and fluttered as a hundred doves, and then, in summer, the blossoms will turn to tough red gems of blood.

There's blood under the hung rabbit now — a splash of black in the snow. I watch the rabbit swing back and forth in the wind, closed mouth, its ears still pressed back against its head, defying gravity, or listening intently to the dark. The short gusts of wind nudge the rabbit's form forward like the quick breaths of a woman dying or giving birth in the pause between two blizzards.

"Jeez," my father says. "I hate to take all this money from my brother."

There's silence and, in it, my mother seems to roll her eyes at the white ceiling over our heads. My father doesn't notice. There's an angry rash underneath his chin where he daily shaves the dark whiskers away and washes them down the drain. His hair is too short, cut too close to the scalp, to tell if it's still black or gray.

"But there just isn't any other way," he says and clears his throat, "and anyway, next month." Then he lifts one shoulder in a shrug, as if a bird has landed there and surprised him, as if someone not entirely unexpected has come up behind him and stuck a gun against his ribs.

My mother lights a cigarette. She's wearing a tight tan sweater and a black skirt. Her legs are long and crossed under the table — high heels, black nylons. She'll say she's going to choir practice that night, but practice has already been canceled because of the weather and, hours later, when my father phones the church, worried, the sky will be blood blue, and the janitor there will tell him it was all called off hours and hours ago.

But now my mother goes into the bedroom, stands at her dresser and dabs violet water on her wrists before she puts her camel's hair coat on and leaves. I watch her skate away over the ice, over a crust of snow in those black heels to the car. Behind her, in the hall outside their bedroom, a pillar of violet water rises and diffuses with the furnace dust. Outside, an animal cries, shrill and tinny, at the frozen garbage in the frozen garbage can.

I go to bed early, listen to the wind and to the sound of tires crunching over deep, packed snow.

Kissing my hair, he said again, "Yeah, I want to do it some more."

I leaned in, circled my tongue quickly in his ear, and it tasted sweet, like sweat, a husk, and whispered, "Eighty will be enough. Does that sound good?"

"Better than good," he breathed, lips open against my neck.

"Well," I said, stepping out of his arms, and I laughed. "We can't do it here."

He laughed, too. "No, darlin'. You're right about that."

"Give me an hour to get organized in the office," I said, and he nodded, letting my hand slip out of his hand, slow.

▼

Though it seemed impossible, a horrible, immaculate miracle, within only a few days after that first time with Rick, I knew I was pregnant. My father would be smoking in the kitchen, and the smell of cigarettes made my heart race, made me taste tar and tires on the roof of my mouth, weak enough to faint. I couldn't drink coffee, and my breasts felt suddenly bruised and heavy as old fruit. At night I slept like someone underwater. This was only five, maybe six, days later.

I didn't tell Rick because I knew what he'd say. His own family was so cozy, I was afraid he'd tell his mother and she'd start knitting booties or miniature pink sweaters. His father might light up a fat cigar and invite all the cousins over for a party.

My own father drove across town to the bank every third Thursday to deposit his disability check, dragging his dead leg behind him like a lame, stubborn, but loyal bloodhound. Naturally, it was spring. I'd had him call the school that morning and tell the secretary I had a bad case of the flu. Then, when he'd left for the bank, I went out to what there was of a garden in our back yard — a weak rosebush my mother had planted, which bloomed every June despite itself, red and sudden as a car wreck. It was the only thing my mother had ever planted, and I dug a shallow hole behind it with a teaspoon.

In that hole, I buried a small photo of my mother as a teenage girl. For years I'd kept it pressed like a petal in an old black hymnal with yellow pages, also hers. In the photo, my mother had a strand of pearls dangling in the suggestive V of a black dress, a little cleavage like a stab wound shadowed between her breasts.

That morning, the soil around the rosebush was muddy, sun warming it up. Old grass mixed in, smelling sweetly wet. And there was the smell of something else, something dead, pushing up out of the dirt — a smell that would last all spring, every spring. The rosebush itself didn't look like anything more than the arm of a skeleton that day, its bony hand reaching up from the underworld, up for the sun.

Here and there, a few bald snowdrops glistened against the thawed black. Here and there, the shoot of a crocus reached up, too, struggling from the ground and wheezing as it did, struggling out of bulbs that had been planted by people who'd lived in our house years before we did.

And even a few fat robins already — wandering around, stunned.

When I pressed it into the muck with the tips of my fingers, my mother's photograph curled up wet around the edges in its grave. I used the back of the teaspoon to push the earth back over her, then patted all around it with my palms, letting the darkness seep between my fingers:

It was a superstitious rite, I knew — though I felt natural, even ancient, enacting it — not silly or stiff at all, small-town, hokey, nakedly hopeful, the way I felt when I prayed. I just felt glad and relieved that she was there, buried, while I was here, a week pregnant and alive, the age she'd been when she'd given birth to me. Spring was getting ready to explode all around us like a homemade bomb.

This was the last false image of her I had, the only one I hadn't buried beside the rosebush already.

Later, that afternoon, I called a clinic in Grand Rapids, and they told me I'd have to wait eight weeks for the fetus to grow large enough to scrape. By then, I thought, even the tulips would be blooming, smooth and black, or wagging their red tongues along the sides of houses on our block. By then, April would have come and gone. There would be sparrows darting across the church lawn under the shadow of a cross. Wet wings on Good Friday and a hazy yellow sky. Then another blizzard, though warmer and thick with slush, on Easter Sunday — burying the new color under a rattling cough.

Not surprisingly, nothing ever grew in the spot where I buried the photos of my mother.

What might I have expected?

Some kind of flower, or a dangerous weed? A poppy glaring up at the sun, or something half-human? An orange flower with a child's face in the center of its petals?

That last photo — I even tried to dig it up in August, but it was nowhere to be found, and part of me was relieved that my own black magic always failed, that my bargains with the devil fell through each time.

He didn't seem to want my soul at any price.

▼

I smoked a cigarette in the office, and then I went to his room.

Gary Jensen opened the door before I could knock.

"Heard you coming up the stars," he said, and it took me a moment to realize he'd said "stairs," swimming through his thick accent. He slid his arms around my waist. I put my own around his neck. The kiss he offered was slippery and hot. Our tongues swam over and under each other like river snakes.

▼

The week before my appointment, I said to my father at the kitchen table, "I have to have an abortion."

He stared at me for what seemed a long time, then started to cry. He put his head in his hands and sobbed while his cigarette burned to nothing in an ashtray at his elbow. I watched the top of his head, the short stubble there, and I thought he'd become an old man fast but still had a marine recruit's new hair. After a while his nose was running and he couldn't seem to catch his breath. I reached across the table and squeezed his wrist, which was thin and tangled with blue veins like yarn, something sewn up sloppily. He looked at me.

My father was a big man. Hands like catchers' mitts. A man who might have been a soldier or a football player, who might've been able to beat another man to the ground with his bare hands in an old-fashioned war before weapons or after the big home game, behind the bleachers, over the honor of some girl. Instead, he'd been convinced to sell cleaning products for the rest of his life by a man in a blue suit who'd come to the door the day after his high school graduation: That day, my father had been feeling confused, hung-over, and bored, and his mother was fretting about his future as if it were a case of the flu, a can of tomato sauce in her fist in the kitchen, raised. His younger brother, Andy, already owned a car.

My father's failure as a salesman left him rubbery and nervous in the presence of men. Even at church, he would stand back from the other ushers, who were not as tall as he was but who appeared much taller in their blue suits. Theirs was a kind of height my father never had, and it had nothing to do with height. They'd speak to him kindly, as if he were a much younger or much older man. My father let those other men make all the decisions that mattered — where to park the rich old ladies in their sterling silver wheelchairs, where to set the stack of extra pamphlets about God.

He could never even look the mechanic, with his dirty hands, in the eye. Failure had made my enormous father small and shy, and then his last sales trip had trapped him in the twisted wreckage of his Ford, crushed, finally, and for real — blood and bone meal under the dashboard, crying the whole time for my dead mother while they pried him out — the sound of pots and pans clattering in a restaurant kitchen as they did. The sound of a can opener cutting into dented tin.

"We have to stay over," I said. "I have to be there Tuesday afternoon for tests, and then they do the abortion on Wednesday morning. I'll make a reservation for us somewhere cheap. Somewhere like the Motel 6, O.K.?"

"This is my fault," my father said in a high voice, a statement like a question, wiping his nose and eyes hard with a wadded paper towel. "You're just a little girl. You needed a mama."

He started to cry harder.

"No," I said and shook my head. "It's O.K., Dad. It will be fine. But you have to go with me to Grand Rapids on Tuesday. A guardian has to be with me."

My father nodded his head. "Of course," he said. "Of course, baby. I love you so much."

▼

Gary Jensen caught my tongue between his teeth, gentle, and undressed me without moving his mouth from mine. This time my heart beat hard against the cage of my ribs. I came with him inside me, which had never happened before, not with any man, and the coming fluttered improbably and like a bird dying between my legs. I hadn't imagined it would be like that, and it made me open and close around him like the mouth of something underwater and warm, something not yet born.

Afterward he kissed my nipples again. My neck. My lips and the lids of my eyes, and then he seemed to start to cry.

"God," he said, "Leila — I can't believe, after what I done to you the other day that you're so damn sweet to me. You come up here again like you're not afraid of me at all, and you make the nicest love to me anybody's ever made."

He put his fingers in my hair, and they got tangled and lost in the copper of it.

I noticed a thin scar under the stubble of his beard, stretching thin and red from his neck to his ear. It was white at the edges, as if someone had sewn the skin together neatly with a needle of light. I put my hand, then, on his narrow chest. It was no wider than my own, and, while we'd made love, it had felt soft against me, gently crushing my breasts beneath its bones. I said, "I should get back down to the office. God, what if Mrs. Briggs has been trying to call or there's a bunch of guests down there?"

Gary Jensen propped himself up on his elbow and said, "Don't go yet, Leila, please. I got to look at you some more." His eyes were brown and dry.

I let him look.

"God," he said, touching the side of my face with two fingers, "I can't believe I hit you, baby. I can't believe I did. What the hell is the matter with a man like me?"

I looked hard at his face. His eyelashes were also dark. A scattering of faded freckles on the bridge of his nose was left behind by the agitated boy he used to be. Soft hair. I touched it where it curled behind his neck, and he kissed me again.

"Leila, I got to tell you why. Something about me, so you don't hate me. Because I feel like I could fall in love with you," he said, squeezing my nipple between his thumb and forefinger when he said it. He swallowed. "My daddy used to beat my mama bad." He swallowed again. "And I used to see that all the time. Probably since I was only just born. I bet I never saw him do anything *but* beat her, I guess. And even though I swore I'd never, never treat a woman that way as long as I lived, there's just this thing in me that's him, that's what I seen him do to her, and there I go. I done it again, Leila, before I even knew what I did."

I didn't want to cry, but it seemed like a true story, the way he told it, and I saw myself leaning over the seat of a car, some boy straining into my mouth, his hands in my hair, and I said in a whisper, looking away from him, "I know how that is."

That sentence, as it scrolled out of my mouth, stunned me itself like a slap. I'd never thought of it like that before, and then I closed my eyes, saw myself suddenly in a bright flash against my eyelids at the kitchen table on my sixth birthday. My mother had baked a cake. A plastic Raggedy Ann was stuck in the middle, into the chocolate frosting like a birthday sacrifice. Six candles blazed around Raggedy Ann's orange braids.

My father was on the road, and my uncle had come over with a jewelry box for me, a bottle of red wine for my mother. They'd played some slow jazz on the record player while they drank it and toasted my birthday, knocking their gory glasses together full of red, ringing like old bells. The saxophone sounded scratchy and full of breath, obscene.

I was wearing a petticoat, a velvet dress like a girl in a storybook. It scratched, too, and shuffled, prickling and stiff around my thighs. They both insisted that I laugh — my mother leaning into me with that purple sweetness on her breath like a spleen, clapping, singing, *Leila, Leila, Happy Birthday Leila.*

I wanted to smile to make her happy.

I blew the candles out in one deep gasp, one long forced breath, but I couldn't eat the cake. My stomach hurt. They put me to bed when I started to cry, and my mother and uncle sat at the edge of the bed and smiled.

Make Leila smile, my mother said, and my uncle did a magic trick then, waved his hands in the air, and then he pulled a long silk scarf from my ear. Red. I closed my eyes, and I heard red wind as it passed out of me into his hands. It spun my heart like a plastic top. My mother pretended to gasp, but I knew where he'd gotten it from, and my heart sparked loose and blurred against my ribs:

When Gary Jensen put his face next to mine and kissed my ear, I remembered that. Something deadly yanked out of my body for everyone to see, and now it was in his hands.

Something scarlet, secret, like the wish to die or kill.

His fingers circled my nipple. He moved down to kiss it, then he looked up at me again. "I know you know what I mean," he said, "that you been damaged, too. I could tell that about you from ten miles away."

He sat up in the bed and leaned over the side of it to pick his shirt up off the floor. He slipped his arms in, shrugged it to his shoulders, straightened the collar and started to button. My body felt soft and exhausted, like something left to soak too long in too-warm water. I couldn't move, though I knew I needed to put on my clothes and go back to the office. I knew I should be in a hurry, but I couldn't be anymore.

He stood up and put his pants on. We'd never even pulled the bedspread down. He was looking at the whole bare length of my body on the bed. "Clean yourself up," he said, and left.

He hadn't given me the money, and I knew I'd never ask.

J CAN HEAR them through the wall.

"Bonnie," my father says, "where the hell have you been?"

"Choir practice," she says, and I hear her drop a string of beads on the dresser, unzip the back of her black skirt and step out of it — a breeze of nylon passing polyester, static electricity at her hips, sparking the dark.

"You were not," he says, and it sounds like pleading. "I called the church two hours ago when you were already two hours late, and the janitor said there never even was any choir practice tonight."

"Jeez, Jack," she sighs, "you sure keep track of things real good, don't you?"

"Well, where were you then?"

I hear hangers clanging in her closet, and I can nearly smell the skirts and dresses, limp and empty in that small space, smelling like flesh turned to cedar, bath salts, a lavender sachet, but stale. She must be naked, I think, maybe standing at the edge of the bed, letting him look at her body in the bright overhead light while she slips something silky down her arms, over her pale breasts.

"Where do you think, Jack? We already discussed this."

"What?" my father asks. "What did we discuss?"

"We discussed the money we needed to borrow." She sounds impatient. "I went to your little brother's apartment, Jack, and got the money for you. Sorry if that bothers you, but that's just that." She sighs. "And I couldn't just leave after he'd written us a check for seven hundred and fifty dollars, could I?" Silence, as if she's sipping, or breathing, then she continues, "So I drank a couple beers. His girlfriend, that Amber, was over. I felt like I couldn't be unfriendly right after he gave us that much money, for god's sake, could I? Should I have just gone over for the money and come straight back with the cash in my greedy little hand, Jack?"

"Of course not," he apologizes, "but I was worried, Bonnie. It's a damn blizzard out there. How was I supposed to know where you were, for god's sake?"

There is a weight of silence again, like a fistful of hovering air in an empty glass. She must have kissed his lips.

Her voice is lower, and she says, "I'm glad you worry. I know you love me." More silence; then my father's voice muffled under her lips.

I peer under my window shade to the nothingness outside. Snow lays itself in blankets over snow, and a white truck is stuck in a drift of it, revving and revving its engine. A man shovels, out there, and swears. Through the crack between my shade and the windowsill I can see him, knee-deep in snow and wearing a white snow jacket.

In the kitchen, the refrigerator kicks on and off.

The man disappears and reappears behind a white screen.

For a moment, he is the snow.

Then he is snow shoveling snow in a white crack of refrigerator light.

Finally, he is his own white truck full of feathers driving away.

Then he is sleep, the pillow, sky.

·

When I got back to the office, there was a white-haired couple waiting. They were sitting on the vinyl couch — the light blue couch for guests, though guests rarely sat down in the office, being, as they usually were, in a hurry to get to their rooms or on the road.

"Oh my gosh," I said, pretending to be breathless as I swung the glass door open. "I'm so sorry. There was an emergency," gesturing outside. "Have you been waiting long?"

"Fifteen minutes," the husband said. He was angry, with a small pinched mouth, but his wife smiled her Cover Girl frosted lipstick, Passion Pink, as if she didn't have a care in the world. They both had blue eyes, but one of his was clouded over like a half-poached egg, so their three blue eyes looked up at me as I slipped behind the counter, trying to appear worried, mumbling apologies and lies.

They stood up at the same time and faced me. I said, "Do you have a reservation?"

"Alberts," the woman said. Her hair was piled in soft white curls of seafoam on her head, a feathery tiara. She was petite as a bird, pretty, dressed up for something in a navy blue dress, but old.

I scanned the guest book; Alberts wasn't there.

"Here," I said anyway, making a black X next to Foreseth, Karl, and closing the guest book too fast for the couple to see that it wasn't their name I'd checked, that their name was not in the guest book at all. I looked up then and smiled, "Just one night?"

"No," Mrs. Alberts said, and maybe she did sound worried then. "Three nights actually. We won't be going home until Tuesday morning."

"Oh, of course," I said, nodding seriously, writing 3 NIGHTS in big block letters on the check-in card under AL-BERTS. I assigned them a room as far away from Gary Jensen's as I could. A nice room, view of the river. All day they could watch the swans lean into breeze and pluck their own feathers

out with long, wet beaks, shaking a squall of white fuzz into
the wind like flimsy snow.

▼

After school on Monday, I packed a hairbrush and two print
dresses in a green overnight bag, one that had been my
mother's and which smelled, after all those years, like the
attic itself — formaldehyde and mothballs yawning up from a
yellowed mouth when I opened it.

Four pairs of underwear. Socks. Shampoo. My toothbrush
and a Daisy shaver. In another suitcase, one with a handle that
was broken, which meant my father would have to carry it in
his arms like a large, unwieldy child from our car to the room
at the Motel 6, I packed two white T-shirts for him. Two pairs
of underwear. His electric shaver in its soft black sack. His
denture cream. His deodorant stick. We could hang his pants
and shirt from a hook in the car's back seat, I decided. I had no
idea what else we might need. We'd never gone anywhere
together overnight, ever.

I was sixteen then, a high school junior. My head always
hurt. I had bluish circles under my eyes. In the hallway at
school I'd carry my books tight across my chest and watch the
floor as I walked. The dull shine on it smelled like old turpen-
tine while the janitor in his navy blue jumpsuit, *Ron* embroi-
dered orange over his heart, smoothed a dry mop over it day
after day in slow circles, humming to himself until the floor
was buffed and bright as wax melted over old ice.

It was always too bright in that building, hot and dusty, and
my eyes would water in the morning before I got reaccus-
tomed to so much light. In study hall I would stare at the glare
of my homework under those humming tubes, and the words
would string together like dark pearls, explaining nothing, all
across the glossy paper.

Something sour in the trash cans when I passed. Something
secret in the band room behind a heavy door: the glint of a

black clarinet and scales practiced over and over like a kind of obedient screaming.

I liked music, liked to pass the band room when there was practice, but I didn't play an instrument, and all the ash-blond girls who did — I'd lived in Suspicious River and gone to school with those pretty, smirking girls my whole life, and still I didn't know their names. I might as well have grown to adolescence on another planet. Those girls took their flutes apart, wet with spit, and slipped them into thin black boxes lined with velvet and their own saliva, and I thought about kissing the reed of an instrument until it was ready to play, what that would be like.

Rick would sprint down the hall toward me between classes. He was bigger than I was, and his dark hair was long then, over his ears, falling to his collar. He'd shout, "Leila," behind me, but I'd never hear him until he was already at my side and had put his arm around my shoulder and pulled me in under it as if with a heavy wing. There would be two red triangles at his cheekbones from the school's endless heat, a seal of sweat on his upper lip. He'd seem eager and excited, like a cartoon pet or a TV mother, and he'd kiss me at my locker, then ask, "Do you mind me kissing you in public?"

I didn't.

"Do you feel O.K.?" he'd ask. "Did you eat any breakfast this morning?"

"Yeah." I lifted my eyebrows, though I couldn't remember whether or not I had.

"Oh, Leila," he said, smiling. "I feel so lucky," he whispered into my ear. My back would be pressed up against my locker, which was just a thin sheet of metal, easily dented, painted as gray as everything else and only wide and long enough to hold a body, or a raincoat. The hallway would be empty except for us — everyone else having hurried to class, and we were late again.

Rick's breath smelled like milk in the morning. Mint, or cough medicine, by afternoon.

He said, "All the guys are so jealous," narrowing his eyes and stooping a little to look into mine. "They've all been fantasizing about you for years. And now you're my girlfriend." He took a step back as if to see me better, and he said, "God."

I knew those boys.

It was the girls I didn't know. Their identical ponytails swung like nooses behind them in the halls, confusing. They dressed the same. They even walked the same. It was a house of mirrors, wandering among them down those narrow hallways. Sometimes a girl would stumble into me, on purpose it would seem, and a crowd of similar girls behind her would laugh.

But the boys parted when I passed, making a small corridor for me, alone.

I didn't tell Rick why my father and I were going to Grand Rapids. Rick had a final exam in trigonometry that week and tryouts for baseball: He wanted to make the varsity team and said he'd give me his letter jacket if he did. Already, Rick's class ring felt heavy where it dangled its red glass eye on a silver chain between my breasts. The ring soaked up heat from my skin there, under my blouse, and when I walked, it sometimes felt like a tiny but very solid fist knocking at my ribs to get in, dully humping my heart. I couldn't imagine myself wearing his letter jacket, too, like the friendly girls who dated his friends — tan, rich girls with bright ski jackets and chubby mothers who dropped off Kotex for them at the front desk when they called home, frantic, to say they'd gotten their periods, early, at school.

Those girls gathered in the bathrooms between classes, wearing the letter jackets, giggling and swapping lipsticks, worrying about their hair — ratting it, smoothing it, spraying their hair.

But Rick was a foot taller than I was and weighed eighty pounds more. I thought that if I wore his letter jacket, I'd get lost in it forever, wander around in it like a piece of vacant property, like all that undeveloped land down by the river where they planned to build condominiums but never did. You could wander that scrub for the rest of your life, acres and acres of it, and never be sure where you were. It would be the perfect spot to dump a body or to drop off a dog you didn't want. But then you'd have to find your own way out, afterward, and maybe you never would.

▼

Gary Jensen walked in the office door under a spotlight of sun, and I had to squint to see him. He had a green carnation and a cigarette in the same hand and held them out to me. I took the carnation, and I smiled.

He had the baseball cap on. An orange D glowed over the blue brim. His beard looked shaggier, and when he smiled back at me, only one half of his mouth moved, creasing one cheek above his jaw. A bisected grin. Cowboy, I thought again. Undercover TV cop. I could picture him driving a pickup through a desert, pointing a gun at someone who was running. He'd be squinting, and grinning, in order to aim at the fugitive's heart.

He shook his head, looked at me. "Damn," he said. "You are so damn pretty."

"Thanks," I said, "for the flower."

He leaned across the counter then, smoke rising out of his hand like a charmed snake. "You deserve more than flowers," he said, inhaling and glancing at the ceiling, then back at me, seriously, "and more than money, too. You deserve to be treated like a fucking princess, princess." Inhaling fire, exhaling smoke. "And that's another reason I came in here. I wanted to tell you that I don't just want to make love with you, baby. It's a whole lot deeper than that for me, and you might think I'm some kind of nut or something to say that, when we just met and hardly know each other at all. But I have never" — he flicked ashes into the ashtray at my elbow — "*never* felt like I feel when we're in bed together, sweetheart. You are the cutest, hottest little thing I ever touched." He dragged on the cigarette then and laughed, "Listen to me! I come down here to tell you I don't just want to fuck you, and all I'm talking about is fucking!"

I laughed, too.

He looked down at my hands.

My wedding ring, a thin blond band.

Then he looked up at me and said, "But I want to be *friends* with you too. God, I want to take *care* of you. Isn't that the damndest thing? I just feel like you're my baby already, or something."

He took a step back and smiled, holding his hand out to me, then he gestured to the ceiling as if he were tossing something light and invisible up to it. He said, "Don't laugh at me, O.K.?" and put his hand over his heart, "but that's how I feel. I want to protect you is what I guess I'm trying to say."

He looked behind him.

No one.

Lowering his voice, "I got to confide something else to you, Leila. About my temper. You know how I hit you? God." He inhaled sharply. "Can you believe I did that? Well, I told you, Leila, I just get this bad thing, sometimes, this bad feeling. And I know it has to do with my old man. But once — this is an ugly story, sweetheart" — he straightened himself up at the counter to tell it, bruised his cigarette out — "Once I had this woman. In Boulder." He looked into the distance over my shoulder, remembering. "She was like you. Just so damn pretty and desperate for money. Little baby boy at home I think, but she was just a girl herself, really — and so she was, you know, a prostitute. So, I was staying in a motel there, and I took this girl on up to my room, and, Leila, I done the same damn thing to her that I done to you." He shook his head in disbelief. "I hit that pretty little thing." He clapped his hands together, leaned forward across the counter again. "But you know what, baby? The second — and I mean the *second* — I hit that girl like that, this guy comes bustin' in my room, knocked my fuckin' door down, and he just beat the crap out of me. Just like that. Beat the livin' crap out of me just like I deserved. Man. Baby." He swallowed.

"Leila, that's how I feel like I want to do for you. Like that guy done for her. Beat the crap out of any son of a bitch who tries to hurt you. Because I understand that you got to be doing what you're doing — for whatever reason, sweetheart, and you don't have to tell me why, but I know you got to have the money. And you need somebody to be lookin' out for you." He put his hand over mine, and it felt heavy. "The money is important, baby, but the money is not as important as your life. Money is nothing without that, baby."

The clock on the wall seemed to snap its cold hand forward each time he said *money.*

I thought of that. *The money.*

It's what anyone would think I was doing this for.

But the money was nothing.

The money just bulged out of my jewelry box, green and dry. I only thought about the money when I added more money to it.

Gary Jensen pressed his hand down harder on mine, and sun warmed the plate glass. A bright box, a house of mirrors, a white truck, a palace of ice. What was it? What was I saving the money for?

"Well," he said. "Listen to me, goin' on like a fool. You probably don't have any feelings for me at all, for all I know. I better get back to my room. But, Leila, I wondered if I could see you tonight, when you get done down here, so we don't have to hurry for once. Maybe we could drink a beer. Please?" He laughed at the palms of his hands and said, "God! Listen to me beggin' you like a lovesick kid, Leila. This must make you sick."

I swallowed, smiled. "No. It's O.K.," I said, "I'll come up about eleven."

"Great," he said, still looking at me, backing up to the door, touching the edge of his baseball cap. "That's so damn great." He blew me a kiss.

*T*HE GROUND IS RAGGED with brown leaves. When the wind blows, the leaves sound like women in paper petticoats rustling down the aisle of a hushed and empty church. The trees are naked, the sky is purple. The neighbors' garden is twisted and blond, all the flowers collapsed into one another since summer. The smell of mulch and fusty withered marigolds travels across the chain-link fence in a puff of amber and old bulbs. Damp seeps up from the Michigan dirt, full of Indian bones, tangled tree roots, hard white kernels of corn like teeth buried by squirrels for the winter, worms burrowing into the center of the earth to die or sleep.

The sun is weak, but it shines, and I can feel it flush my face — a cool November sunburn — as I lie on my back on the ground. It's Thanksgiving, and I'm six. From inside the house I can hear the distant tin of TV — a crowd, angry or ecstatic, as my father and Uncle Andy watch the Lions buck and clap against the Chiefs. After dinner, they'd sat down exhausted on the couch, side by side. My mother had her hands in gray, soapy water in the kitchen, feeling the bottom of it carefully for a knife, rinsing it off when she found it. "Leila, why don't you go outside? It's nice outside," she'd said.

I am wearing a plaid jumper with an old, shrunken sweater of my father's. The red sleeves are loose around my wrists, like tongues. I feel how solid and flat the earth is against my back, and I put a forearm over my face. But I can't smell my father in that red wool at all. Just the rusty autumn sun, winter on the way.

I stay out there, on my back, until the sun becomes colorless, threadbare, dipping a cool tin spoon behind the branches, spooning a watery glaze across the sky — and when I go back, slip in through the back door of the house, I see them in the kitchen, but they don't see me. I stand near the hooks where we snag our coats — my father's beige salesman one, flaccid, close to my face — and I watch them around the corner with my eyes nearly closed, holding my cool breath in my mouth and throat.

My uncle unbuttons my mother's blouse, puts his mouth on her breasts. Her skirt is pushed up over her hips with his hips between her legs, moving. His shirttails are down over his thighs, but still I can see the inch of naked flesh there. My mother is pressed up against the sink, her fingers clinging and relaxing at his collar, white as bones in his black hair. I hear the front door open then, and my father hollers, like a question, "I'm back?"

Where has my father been?

My uncle pulls away from her fast. Maybe two minutes pass, slow as heavy church doors with a frantic crowd behind them and maybe someone has shouted, "Fire!" When my father steps into the kitchen, he holds up a sack of, what? Beer? He looks hurried, but he stops dead when he sees them.

What's different?

They already have their clothes pieced together, sloppily, but buttoned. Still, it's there. Electromagnetic. Whether my father notices or not.

The refrigerator kicks in to its automatic humming, square and white, and my uncle picks a dishtowel off the counter and squints at it as if something's written there in a small, cramped hand. My mother is already up to her elbows again in cool kitchen water. "Daddy," I say, and they all turn to see me standing there, and they all look relieved.

"Hey," he says to me. "I got the beer," he says to them, offering the brown grocery bag of it to his brother and his wife.

The expression on my father's face could mean anything, I suppose, but I imagine it means hope. For a moment he's a widower reaching sheepishly into a casket to feel his dead wife's throat for a pulse: a last-ditch effort. Who could blame him for trying?

Hope. My father's expression is blank as the expression of a scarecrow crucified in corn — trampled with crows, their orange wire feet stamping over his face, and a big storm coming, while my father pretends not to notice.

That, or he doesn't notice.

From the back seat of the car I've seen those scarecrows in all the fields around Suspicious River all year long — flapping their plaid farmer flannel in the wind, mouths stuffed with straw.

Even as a child I see that nothing is scared of those.

Pretend men.

Ransacked by the seasons, each season with its own slow torture — rain or snow or burning sun.

Those scarecrows are the ones who are scared to death. Standing out there with their arms outstretched like fathers, stiff and dumb.

By eight o'clock I'd checked four couples and a family from Chicago into the Swan Motel.

The family had been a happy one.

A two-year-old leaned against his father's leg with his face behind the knee, sucking his thumb with loud sloppy sounds, weaving sleepy in a walking trance, looking up with his eyes half open as if from underwater, as if an inch of Vaseline on glass separated that boy from the world. His small forehead was so pale I could see blood under the thin skin, light blue, and looking at his eyes made my own eyes watery and tired, too.

It had grown dark before I noticed, and the air in the office was cold. It tasted like river water when I breathed it, and I wished I'd brought a sweater. I turned the heater on and listened to it hum and shudder. Then, a man began to push into the office through the glass door — until he saw the handle, PULL — but I knew what he was there for before he even managed to get in.

"Hi, honey," he said, taking his wallet out of his back pocket.

The man was tall, wearing a jean jacket and a red baseball cap. He had big white hands, perhaps he was handsome. Thirty-five, I guessed. Blond hair, trimmed blond beard. Six feet tall. "Can I get a room?" he asked, leaning across the counter.

"No problem," I said, "You don't have a reservation?"

"No. Did I need one?" He sounded worried.

"No." I shrugged. "We have plenty of rooms."

I took a check-in card out of the drawer.

He cleared his throat and inched closer across the counter, his chin in his hand, gold watch ticking at his wrist. He said, "How about reserving some personal time with you, sweetheart? Is there plenty of that, too?"

I held the pen in air, hovering over NAME on the check-in card, then I looked at his eyes. Weak blue. I said, "You don't need a reservation for that either." I tilted my head toward him, maybe smirking. "But it'll cost you."

"How much?" He lifted his blond eyebrows, nearly invisible, as if he were amused.

"Well." I had this part memorized, "The room is sixty dollars. I think the company would be worth that, too. Don't you?"

"I sure do," he nodded and grinned.

He told me his name was Barber, Charles. I wrote it on the check-in card and then he paid for the room in cash and said he'd give me my own sixty dollars when I came on over to 31 — a room I'd given him generously, a room with a sliding glass door to a patio only a few feet from the river itself. He hadn't asked to be on the river, and he wouldn't be able to see the swans at night anyway, but I thought maybe he'd like to listen to the river splash past his glass door like a frantic swimmer as he slept. He looked to me like the type of man who might like that — a hunter, maybe, or a helicopter pilot.

"See you in a minute," I said.

I locked the cash drawer and put RECEPTIONIST WILL BE RIGHT BACK on the counter, then took the phone off the hook, turned the heat up another notch, hoping it would be warmer when I got back. I stepped outside, and the air smelled moldy and cool, thick as moss, and I felt it crawl across my back and chest. I crossed my arms over my breasts, holding my shoulders in my hands as I ran around the back of the motel into the damp grass there.

Back there, I could hear river and, beyond it, highway. The sound of tires and wind. There were no stars, just a low frayed blanket of clouds cold in the sky. I rapped on the plate glass of his patio door, and he slid it open for me.

"Here," he said, handing me the sixty dollars, but he seemed angry to be giving the money to me. He seemed different than he'd seemed in the office just minutes before. Not so casual, not friendly, as if a twin had taken his place — this one all business, grudge, spleen.

I slipped the money into my shoe, which was damp from the grass, and I could feel a cold numbness, like river, settle itself into the white flesh of my feet.

It was cold in his room, too. He pulled the curtains, then came up behind me and grabbed my hair, yanked my head backward until he'd pulled me to the floor. He straddled my hips and held my wrists against the carpet. I could hear it out there, churning and wheezing, when he spit in my face.

He held me to the floor with his weight, tore my blouse and came on my bra, then he slapped me so hard I could taste bad coffee on my molars. But it must have been blood. I'd bitten my tongue. When he got off of me, I rolled onto my side and held a hand over my face until I felt I could stand up, wiped him off my breasts with the edge of the bedspread, fixed my blouse the best I could, and left.

Outside again, the river was invisible in the dark, but I could feel it swell and sink beneath the lawn as I ran back to the office, as if the earth were a membrane, a blister, filling up fast with water or blood, as if I were running across the back of a bruise, thinking it was the world.

▼

It was a three-hour drive to Grand Rapids, a two-lane highway through a tunnel of pines. A deer ran across the road outside Ottawa City, white tail flagging and falling in front of our car, then vanished into the woods on the other side of the highway, and I slowed down after that, afraid I'd come that close to hitting another. I'd been so near to that one I could see the sleek muscles tensing on either side of its ribs as it ran.

My father was asleep with his mouth open in the passenger's seat beside me. The weather was cool for May, but bright as milk and shimmering with new leaves. Further, then, outside of Ottawa City, I saw two black puppies sprawled in dirt at the side of the road beneath some dusty wildflowers wagging baby blue above their corpses. The puppies looked peaceful there, like boots, not bloody and ruined like roadkill. They looked as if someone had flung them, dead already, out the window of a slow-moving car.

Here and there a turkey vulture soared and spiraled. A crow landed on a telephone wire, buoying it with black weight, while the milkweed pods just nodded at each other in ditches, dumb as swans.

The cauliflower fields between Suspicious River and Grand Rapids were dank that day, and every few miles there were clusters of small migrant shacks huddled at the edges of those fields. No windows, and their plywood sides had gone gray-green, maybe rotten, through the winter and spring rain.

Soon they would be back — dark-haired children licking popsicles and thin men with straw hats scattered around the shacks. Occasionally in the summer a migrant family might be seen at the grocery store in Suspicious River, looking shy and tired under the bright lights in the narrow aisles crowded with cans, holding tightly to the little ones' hands. But they were seen rarely, and never anywhere but the grocery store — except out there, in those fields, like a human crop.

The migrants had quit coming into Suspicious River and the surrounding towns for anything other than emergencies and bags of bread three summers before when a Mexican boy had been beaten and left to die after a fight at Trini's Bar & Grill. The fight had started at the pool table and ended in the alley between the bar and the branch library — a small room filled with old books that smelled like wet hair and fire-salvaged dresses behind a plate glass window. Just that one Mexican boy — seventeen, the paper said — against a gang of white drunks. He died, slowly, later, in the Ottawa County Hospital of massive head injuries, and the attitude in Suspicious River seemed to be that it was that boy's own fault, being beaten to death — an accident, like falling off a roof — for having come downtown at night. For having asked for a beer in a bar.

It was the biggest bar in town, and that night the owner, Trini, had been there herself. She was an old woman by then, a grandmother who wore her long white hair in a braid pinned at the base of her neck in a tight circle, a blue feather stuck into it on special occasions. She only came into the bar on weekends. Then she'd take a seat, reprimand the bartender once, drink a White Russian, hobble out to her long, pearl-gray Lincoln Town Car, and drive back to the nice retirement village on the river where she rested, in peace.

Trini had even been there when the fight broke out, but when the police came around her retirement village asking questions the next morning, she wouldn't give them a single name of a single man who'd been in the bar when the boy had been hauled out the door — grunting, vomiting blood before they'd even stumbled to the alley. All the men in Trini's were locals that night, except the dead Mexican boy. Well known, regulars, and there was a relief that spread through the town like a minty sigh when their names weren't printed in the paper, never mentioned, never even rumored about at the drug store. Everyone knew one of those old boys at least, or one of their wives, or their mothers — blue-haired and knitting on a porch next to yours. It was said that boxes of flowers and chocolates were sent to Trini for her loyalty, and she told the other old ladies at the retirement village that she'd defend any white man, no matter how bad he was, against any Mexican or Indian or colored with her life.

Time passed. The boy was taken away somewhere and buried, and no one was ever arrested, no trial ever took place, and Trini died, still peaceful, in her bed that winter of pneumonia — suffocating sweetly, bird soul stepping out into the moist fog of her own lungs, blurred, with Morpheus bearing a torch for her through town before they slipped away together, no expression on his face.

But there was a big smiling picture of Trini in the paper the next day above the obituary, the names of fourteen grandchildren were listed, and a large cement angel with concrete wings, too heavy to fly away, was erected above her grave.

When my father and I got to the Grand Rapids city limits, we had to pull over on Division and look at the map to see where we were and where the clinic was.

"Here," my father said, pointing to a thin gray line. "Here we are. We're almost there."

The clinic waiting room was pink and empty, and the woman at the receptionist's desk looked happy to see us. She smiled a lot with long wet teeth and looked me straight in the eyes, called my father Sir, asked if we wanted any coffee, and we did.

My father fidgeted with his watch, winding. He was wearing a thin plaid cotton shirt with a white T-shirt underneath, and he looked old. Maybe even poor, with his short hair over his ears and his heavy black shoes — the one on his right foot scuffed with dust from dragging his dead leg. The chairs we sat in were overstuffed, and my father couldn't seem to get comfortable in his, sitting so low. When the receptionist handed each of us a styrofoam cup of bitter, scalding coffee, she said the nurse would call for me in a minute, still smiling widely. I could smell peroxide. When I looked over at my father, he was wiping something invisible out of his eye with the tip of his finger. When he noticed me watching him, he opened his mouth. Then a woman spoke my name.

"I'm the counselor," she said, and smiled, though the corners of her mouth turned down when she did.

I followed the counselor's black braid into a small purple office without windows. It was cluttered with books and fancy stuffed animals, brand-new and immaculate. A walrus. An exotic-looking polar bear with a smaller bear in its arms. She collected endangered species, it seemed. There was a poster on the wall of an old woman in a long black dress, skipping rope, and I imagined it was supposed to make me feel good — this old woman so full of life, this hopeful future in a long black dress waiting for me with a rope. The office was warm and dark, and the counselor's voice sounded distant, though she was only inches from my face as she spoke.

Leaning forward, the counselor whispered was I sure this was what I wanted, and I felt sleepy. Did I have any problems at home? Had I told my sexual partner? Was I scared? Did I feel sad about this? Did I want to talk about that? Did I have any questions?

I tried to think of a question to offer into the silence. I looked up and asked, "How big is it?"

The counselor raised her eyebrows. "What? How big is what?"

"The baby," I said.

"Oh." The counselor shrugged. She held a hand up and pointed to the tip of her pinkie.

I looked at my fingers, which were longer and thinner than the counselor's, and cool.

The counselor sighed then and said, "Usually on Wednesday mornings the right-to-lifers camp outside. They know that's the day we do the procedures. If they're here — which we expect they will be — there will be some staff outside to walk with you and your father from your car to the back door of the clinic. If you don't see us, just wait in the car, with the car doors locked. We'll get there. We'll be keeping an eye out for you."

"How much will this cost?" I asked, whispering.

The counselor looked at me a little sad then and smiled. "You don't need to worry about that. The secretary looked at the income statement your dad filled out, and you qualify for aid. You don't have to pay."

I didn't want to cry, but I did. I looked at the counselor's poster again, the one of the old woman skipping rope, and I imagined, by now, that old woman had to be dead. The purple walls throbbed around me like kindness, like kidneys, and I felt sick. She handed me a tissue, and it smelled like wet white roses, and it felt damp before I even wiped my eyes.

I COME INTO THE KITCHEN in my nightgown. The red rosebuds on it might look like petals of blood from a distance, and the lace around the wrists still itches. I never get used to that lace.

There's sun coming up through the kitchen window, turning the cold February air to tin. These mornings are tinged with something steel-bright, and silver polish, and it hurts my head to smell it. Waking every February morning into that smell is like breathing frost from the glass coolers at the supermarket. A mouthful of frozen smoke.

My mother is there, sitting in my uncle's lap with her arms around his neck at the kitchen table, and she doesn't move, doesn't even look, when I walk in.

"Morning, sunshine," my uncle says, and I just stare at him.

My uncle's face is my father's face, prettied up. A little feminine, but his eyes are narrow. When he lifts his dark eyebrows, my uncle is an actor. When he bites his lower lip, he's a young soldier in an old movie, a stubble of beard on his chin to let you know he's not a boy — though he still looks sweet and fiendish as a boy.

"Can't you be nice to Uncle Andy?" my mother asks and pulls his face a little closer to her own with her fingers clasped at his collar.

My mouth is empty when I open it. I just keep my gaze on him. My eyes blink like a plastic doll's.

"Look at me, young lady," my mother says, but I don't.

She says, "You look at me. You be nice to your uncle Andy."

My mother stands beside him then, sets the edges of her top teeth against the swordtips of her bottom teeth and smiles as if she could hiss. There's ice melting outside, and it runs down the kitchen windows in sparking threads. My mother is wearing red high heels that match her extraordinary lips, a black skirt and white blouse, and it isn't even nine o'clock on a Saturday morning yet.

"Don't worry about it, Bonnie," my uncle says.

"No." She turns to look at him, her hands on her hips. "I will not forget about it. This little princess needs to learn some manners."

She looks at me. Her voice is stretched tight as a telephone wire, and she says, "You apologize right now to your uncle Andy."

"No." I pout it. I look at him hard and blank, and my mother leans down then and grabs my nightgown, balls it into a fist, and drags me closer to her. Her eyes are wide and blue. She slaps me and slaps me again — a windmill twirling its stiff arms, a sailboat spinning in little manic circles on a small, calm lake. I'm caught in a funnel of feathers and violent air. She slaps me with her small white hands until he pulls her off of me.

"Now apologize," my mother says to me, breathless, glaring over his shoulder.

"Bonnie." He takes her arms in his hands, shakes her once, gently, tries to meet her eyes with his.

"I will not just let this go, Andy. She needs to learn. She's got to have some respect for you if you're going to be her father. She's got to learn to be polite." My mother's voice trails higher and higher, a white kite slipping into a thin white sky.

My uncle drops her arms and his shoulders sag. "Bonnie." He shakes his head, "Don't say that again."

"What?" she asks, her mouth open wide, then her teeth closed together, "What?"

"Don't say I'm going to be her father."

She inhales. "Why?"

My uncle sits back down at the kitchen table and puts his hands on the Formica, shakes his head, looks up at her staring down at him, "Because it's not right."

"What the hell are you talking about?" She grips her own arms in a cage of fingernails, hard.

"Jesus, Bonnie, stop it," he says.

"Stop what?"

"Stop talking about this."

"Why?"

He looks down at his hands then, still shaking his head, biting his lower lip. "Because you're my brother's wife."

My mother takes a step back, inhaling sharply, then breathing hard. She exhales through her nostrils, her eyes widening, and then she smiles with one side of her mouth and spits, "Did you just fucking figure that out?"

"Bonnie," he says.

My mother walks past me fast, the sound of heels and breeze.

My uncle stands up, follows her into the bedroom. There's screaming behind the closed door. Something thrown and broken, someone, muffled, struggling, and I hold my breath so I won't cry until there's silence. Then I climb onto the kitchen counter and take down a yellow plastic bowl, pour Cocoa Puffs and milk into the bowl, and spoon them into my mouth.

The cereal tastes good — something dark and sweet in sour milk.

When I got back to the office I dialed 42, and Gary Jensen answered before I even heard it ring.

"Leila," he said, "Is that you?"

"Yes." I hadn't meant to cry. "I need some help down here."

"What happened?" he asked, loud. "Jesus, Leila, did some creep do something to you?"

"Yeah." The word was a sob. "Gary, my shirt's all torn. Can you please bring me a sweater or something — to wear over my blouse?"

"Oh, baby, yes," he said. "Yes. I'll be right there."

He was breathing fast when he got down to the office, but it took him a long time to get there. By the time he hurried in, I'd stopped crying, but I knew my face was a mess. I crossed my arms over my chest so he couldn't see the ruined blouse, but he came behind the counter and pulled me into his arms, making small noises in his throat like awful grief while he did, petting my hair, making little circles with his fingers on my back.

I leaned forward, weakly, and put my face into the white cotton of his shirt and smelled smoky leaves and deodorant inside his clothes. I looked up and saw the scar just under his beard. The beard had grown even darker in the few days I'd known him. His lips were thin and dry, and when he kissed me I thought I tasted medicine in his mouth. His eyes were nearly closed, a fringe of lashes, a dark stitching of brows.

Then he helped me slip the brown wool sweater he'd brought with him up my arms, buttoning the buttons up the front for me as if I were a child headed out into the cold without a lunch, my arms useless at my sides. The sweater was his, and it nearly fit. Afterward, I clung to him. I couldn't help it. And I began to cry again.

"Look," he took my hand and led me to the vinyl couch, gently pulled me down to sit beside him on it, put both his arms around me and pulled my face toward his own narrow chest. He kissed my hair and cleared his throat. "Look," he said into it, "Leila. It's very important that you tell me who did this to you. I won't do anything crazy, sweetheart. But I got to know."

I was quiet a long time. When I closed my eyes, for an instant I saw an attic full of violent secrets with wet black wings. But I took a deep breath. "31," I said, "Around back." I pointed toward the river with a cold, trembling hand.

Gary Jensen kissed my hair again — a copper shower curtain of hair, tangled as a dragged doll's.

Then he said, quiet, "You go clean yourself up a little, baby. I promise I'll be right back."

Gary kissed my lips. He even slipped his tongue between my teeth and moved his hand over the brown wool sweater, his, and felt my breast, rubbed his jaw against mine, and I felt his beard like dry mown summer grass on my neck.

▼

The nurse eased a needleful of blood out of my arm, shook the vial, and then touched my hand and said, "How old are you?"

"Sixteen," I said, "I'll be seventeen next week."

"Have you ever been pregnant before?"

"No." I shook my head. I thought the nurse would know that from the form I'd filled out in the waiting room.

> How many pregnancies____ live births_____ stillbirths____
> miscarriages____ abortions____?

I'd written zeroes, oval and careful as eggs, in every blank.

"Well," she asked, "You're sure you are?"

"Sure I am?"

"Sure you are pregnant?" Her smile was patient.

The small room we sat in was clean and empty enough to ice skate through in one clean swoop. It was where the smell of peroxide had drifted from, into the waiting room, and it reminded me of frogs. It reminded me of the biology teacher at school pinning one to a board, slicing its gray stomach open in a smooth movement like a grin and, in there, those miniature coils and pouches of frog guts — dry, clean, pink, and perfectly formed.

The light above us buzzed.

"Yes," I said, "I'm sure."

"Well, sometimes girls think they're pregnant, but they're just late. That's why we take the blood."

I said, "Oh."

"Have you decided what kind of birth control you'll be using after this? Did you talk to the counselor about it?"

"Yes." I cleared my throat and looked over the nurse's shoulder to a poster of a skeleton on the wall. There were arrows pointing to each of the bones with the names of the bones in small black letters under the arrows. I said, "She said they could give me an IUD."

The nurse made a check mark then on a piece of paper, and I looked down at the pencil in her hands. The pencil was yellow and stunted, and the nurse's hands were small, too, and chubby, though she was tall, and her body was muscular and lean. Her chin was square, like a man's.

"They can put that in right after the procedure," the nurse said, looking up at me. "The doctor will have a note of it. You shouldn't eat too much before the abortion, O.K.? But you want to have a little something in your stomach at least. Toast, maybe, O.K.?"

I wondered where I'd get toast before seven o'clock at the Motel 6, but I nodded. I hadn't eaten breakfast for eight weeks, since I'd first felt the strange new thing bloat in me, sickened with it, dizzy. I thought about my father then, alone out there in a soft pink chair in the waiting room, waiting.

"Did the counselor tell you about the protesters?"

"Yes," I said.

When my father and I stepped out of the clinic, there was too much air and light. It was four o'clock in the afternoon, and the sky was May-blue, too stone blue to breathe.

▼

Gary Jensen came back to the office one hour later, exactly, and he was smiling. He held his hands up as if to show me they were empty. "I didn't hurt anybody, honest, but that motherfucker won't be back around here, baby. You can rent that room to someone else." He laughed. "I gave him a nice big mouthful of the carpet, too, before he left."

I could smell whiskey between us like old apples. Headlights rose outside and receded. Someone leaving. My whole body sagged, or settled, like an exhausted barn.

Then a dark car pulled into the circular drive. The thump of a bass coming from the stereo in it. Gary aimed a finger at me like a gun and clicked. "Remember," he raised his eyebrows, smiled, "You're comin' up to 42 when you're done."

I nodded, tried to smile in return, while a man in a blue suit eased past Gary.

"Excuse me," the man said.

Gary nodded at the man, aimed at me again with his finger, and said, "Check her out. Ain't she a hot little number?"

"She sure is," the man said, but he sounded bored, or annoyed, looking at the brown sweater I was wearing. His blue suit looked expensive, and he had a black briefcase in his hand. The silver handle on it flashed like a handcuff. The man was tall, with graying hair, *distinguished* you would say. Refined, like processed flour. Next to him Gary looked even more like a con man, an eager mechanic, a minor league baseball player, a little drunk.

Gary said, "She could make you one satisfied customer," and smiled widely at me before he left.

After what had happened in 31, I was afraid, and I felt a hot trickle of acid in the soft red purse of my stomach as I knocked on the door. But when I'd seemed reluctant to come up, the silver-haired man had offered me a hundred dollars, said he'd heard about me from a salesman he worked with, that he'd never stay at a dump like the Swan Motel if he weren't there specifically to see me, or someone like me. I'd stood mute and staring, feeling stiff and ugly in the brown sweater behind the office desk. His face was shaved so close to the skin it looked like chalk, or the underbelly of a woman's wrist. His eyes were plain, indifferent, and he spoke to me with the kind of privilege I'd always understood as money.

There was nothing I could do, I thought, but what I always did.

The lamplight was pale and made a white zero, like a single headlight, on the ceiling above it. I felt stunned by that small light when I stepped into his room, and I noticed the black briefcase, unopened, on the bed.

He was still in his blue suit — a respectable older man with something pricey to sell, something good, American-made, built to last. He didn't touch me or even loosen his tie, but he wanted me to kneel down in front of him while he sat against the sink so he could watch himself slam in and out of my mouth in the full-length bathroom mirror behind me, and I did.

*I*T'S NIGHT, dark as death in my bedroom, but lights blaze through the rest of the house.

It's summer, and the windows are open.

I hear the rustle of leaves like the chattering of a thousand women's teeth, and the sky is far away. It sways with stars — a black hammock sagging under the weight of space. Lights cross it and fall from it. Flash, spiral. A meteor. A firefly. Lightning in another state. Missiles, crescents, asps. Wind gathers itself up in a warm corner and billows my bedroom curtains, sings through the screens.

"How could you do it, Bonnie? How could you fuck someone else?"

My uncle isn't shouting, but there's a swell of energy like an x-ray, an ultrasonic surge that seems to vibrate the wall between us like a tuning fork. A radiant zap.

An angel with a small electric motor buzzing in its guts. A froth of movement and light.

There is fear in my mother's voice when she says, "I didn't."

Smell of metal. A cat growls in the neighbors' garden.

She says, "I lied."

But the blond hair on my arms shivers with static and rises.

My uncle says, "I'll kill you."

He must be touching her because she gasps.

He says, "You know that."

She whimpers behind her teeth.

He says, "I'll cut your pretty throat."

I know the moment he touches her neck with his hands because my own eyes dilate in the dark, and I imagine a hum of light blazes above our house but no one sees.

Samantha came in at eleven o'clock with her thermos of grapefruit juice and her stack of mothers' magazines. She smiled at me and said, "My turn, I guess. Oh well."

The roots of Samantha's hair were brown, a stripe across her skull like a scar where the blond was growing out. Her cheeks were flushed, and she kept one pale hand on her big pregnant belly all the time, making slow, soothing circles with her fingers.

I took the red purse out from under the counter and said good night.

Gary was watching TV when I got to his room. At the foot of his bed, President Reagan looked worried and tired, confused, answering questions with a stammer, shuffling a piece of paper nervously on a podium, but Gary turned the TV off and took me in his arms. He took my hand lightly, and I sat on the edge of the bed beside him. I closed my eyes while he unbuttoned the sweater he'd loaned me and slipped it down my arms. Then he unbuttoned my ruined blouse. He unsnapped my bra, and I stood up so he could unzip my jean skirt, and I stepped out of it after he eased it down my legs and then eased my legs out of my plain white underwear.

There was a chill in the room, and I could feel my skin pull in closer to my bones with it, tight around my nipples, which he tasted with his teeth. But I felt far away from my skin, and, at the same time, only my skin where he kissed it. The rest of the world seemed to shrink and recede like a comet's tail from that room, something dropping vaguely into the shadows out there — a metallic bird slipping out of the sky. I knew Rick would wonder where I was.

Gary Jensen looked at me and said, "Leila, you are a goddess."

Something caught like a fishhook in my throat when he said that. I couldn't swallow. I felt like something feathered and skinned being dragged out of a river, breathing. He ran his hand up my thigh, pushed a finger into me and said, "I want you to show me every place that motherfucker touched you, and I'm going to kiss it away."

▼

That night I thought about Rick while I lay awake in the double bed next to my father's double bed in the humming dark of the Motel 6. I could hear a dog bark in a room somewhere above us — maybe a puppy. It sounded excited and wild. The bedspread was thin and the sheet was tucked so far into the end of the bed that I could barely pull it over my shoulder, so I slid down, shivering.

I wondered what Rick might want to name a baby if he had one. I imagined Rick bouncing a baby on his knee. I watched them together, from a distance, on a plaid couch — the baby laughing, Rick's hands under its fatty arms, a bright look on both their faces. Then I saw myself with the baby, rocking it in my arms, looking at its moist gray eyes. The baby smelled like oranges, or candied aspirin, but I was wearing my mother's black, strapless heels, the patent leather ones she was wearing when she died. I held the baby close to my breasts, wearing those heels, and suddenly I was standing on ice, trying to keep my balance, but I couldn't. I felt the baby slip out of my arms before I woke up that morning to the tiny bells of the travel alarm.

My father woke up with a red crease slashed across his face from the pillow. Even after we got into the car, it was still imprinted there. The road was slick with rain and it glistened like snakeskin. There'd been a storm the night before, and the wrecked splendor of apple blossoms and magnolia petals was scattered like chicken feathers now on the hoods of cars. Spring, skinned, was plastered to the ground.

We were blocks away from the clinic, and I could already see the headlights and hear the commotion. A megaphone. Someone's voice, frenzied, crackled over the quiet damp. When my father and I pulled into the driveway, a surge of bodies pressed up against our car, pink palms slapping at the windows. The sleeves of their jackets were slippery and bright. My father whispered, "Jesus Christ."

We locked the car doors quickly after someone tried to yank the passenger side open, while the windshield wipers gasped back and forth, hypnotic in front of our faces. There were two women standing at the back of the clinic, close together beneath a black umbrella near the glass door. When they saw us they dropped the umbrella on the concrete and ran toward our car with their heads bowed. One of them was the counselor I'd met the day before. My father just stared straight ahead into the inky rain.

The women opened our car doors when my father and I unlocked them, and the counselor, her face close to mine, shouted in at us, "Hurry. Come on." The sound of rain was deafening as static behind them — a rattle, the clatter of small, damp tap shoes.

I stepped out of the car into the soaking dark, and I couldn't see anything, just the counselor's red jacket in front of me and the long braid like a rope ladder down her back. I could smell spilled oil in the parking lot, and then a hand reached through the rain to touch my hand.

When I turned, I saw the face of the man who had taken my hand, holding it gently, at first, like a lover. He was pale, a stubble of black on his thin chin. He held my hand tighter as I tried to pull away. His suit looked new and gray, and he wasn't wearing a raincoat over it: *That suit will get ruined in the rain,* I wanted to say.

The man fell to his knees in front of me. He was crying, or there was rain on his face. "Don't kill your baby," he begged, the fingers of my hand twisting pink and wet now in his, stinging. "Don't kill your baby."

The counselor pushed him out of my way with her hip, blocked a path for me to step around, but I was stunned, looking at that man. His eyes were small and white, but he had them open wide, and they were glassy. He looked drunk, or enraptured. Then someone rushed at me with a poster and pushed it toward my face before I could see what it was. But as the counselor pulled me away in the direction of the door, I looked over my shoulder to see the poster.

It was a blown-up photo of something small and bloody in a rubber glove — a handful of blood with a small human face, like a cupid. It's little mouth was open, only big enough to slip the tip of a pinkie in. If that was human, the hand that held it was big enough to be God's. What would you feel, I wondered suddenly, what leftover breath would you feel if you put a finger in that mouth?

My father was already in the waiting room when I came through the door like something gasped up by a wave, the counselor's hand still clinging to my own. Where had the other hand gone? His had been clammy as a dead man's. I couldn't adjust my eyes to the light, but it was warm and dry in the clinic, and it glowed like pink light filtered through powdered milk, or ashes.

My father looked at the floor, shook his head. The counselor put an arm around me and squeezed. Then she and the woman who'd helped my father through the crowd went back outside. More headlights. Someone wailed over a megaphone, "Abortion is murder," and then a grown man's voice imitating a child's, "Mommy, Mommy. Don't murder me. Don't let them butcher your baby."

"Jesus," the receptionist said, rolling her eyes.

▼

"I should go," I said to Gary.

His head was on my chest.

I'd had my fingers in his hair, and the hair felt soft between them, like a dark web. I felt blunt and numb between my legs, as if I were in love, but my heart was still beating hard in my chest, and it nudged me to get up. It nudged me toward home, though I could barely remember where that was.

Gary looked up at me and said, "I want you to sleep here with me tonight. In my arms."

"I can't," I said, though I wanted to sleep in his arms.

I felt lazy, stupid, my body strung to his with thick wet threads.

There was something about his voice that was as familiar as my own when I heard it. Something about the smell of his beard, the soft stitches of black hair across his chest. His body was no larger than mine. He was thin as a child, and when I clung to him while we made love, I could feel his ribs where they wrapped around his back. His sweat didn't smell like a stranger's.

"I don't want to go either," I said, "but —"

He put a finger over my mouth and said, "I know. You have to go. What time will you be back tomorrow?"

He took his finger from my mouth then and pushed it between my legs. I couldn't answer, gasping. I couldn't even open my eyes. He said, "No, Leila. I'll tell you. You'll be back here by two in the afternoon." I opened my eyes and looked at him. His face had moved closer to mine. He said, "You belong to me tomorrow."

"It's my day off," I said.

"Not anymore," he said.

Rick was asleep when I got home. I took my clothes off and threw them on the floor in a corner of the bathroom, and I put on a T-shirt of his that had been hanging on a hook behind the bathroom door. I pulled the afghan on the couch over my legs, up to my waist, and I woke in what seemed like one flash to the acid smell of coffee.

It was morning, and Rick was drinking a cup of it in the kitchen when I came in. Sun poured over the white appliances, and they pulsed with light.

"Leila." He didn't look up. "Where were you so late last night? I called the motel and Samantha said you left right at eleven."

"I did," I said, pouring the black water into a cup. Weak steam rose in a rippling stripe from the coffee pot. "But I got invited to a party, and I went."

"At the motel?" He looked up then, astonished or confused, and his eyes looked sticky, still, with sleep. His shoulders were bony as a scarecrow's under the cloth of his thin T-shirt.

"Yeah," I said, closing my eyes as I swallowed the hot coffee.

"Well, Jesus, Leila, you could've called." He sounded exhausted as he said it, and I knew he wouldn't argue.

"I know," I said, "I'm sorry."

"You know, it's not a big deal, Leila, but I don't like to go to sleep not knowing if you're coming home or not." He turned his hands up on the table. "I mean, I really think we should look for another job for you. Something with regular hours so we can have a regular life, Leila. This is ridiculous."

"I have to work this afternoon, too," I said, opening my eyes wider when I looked into his.

"What?" He made a V with his eyebrows, but he didn't seem angry. Until that moment I hadn't noticed how much larger his eyes had become as he'd become thinner. He looked like an animal, starving, but not frantic. Calm, or blank. Like a hungry animal crawling out of a hole into the light.

"Yeah," I said, "Millie's sick."

"For god's sake, Leila, doesn't Mrs. Briggs think you have a life?"

"I don't think Mrs. Briggs cares." I shrugged.

"What time are you supposed to go in?"

"I have to be there by two."

"Great," he said, picking his coffee spoon off the kitchen table, putting it back down. "Great." He shook his head.

I looked into my cup. A funnel cloud rose out of it, but I was thinking about Gary Jensen's hands on me. How he'd spread my legs on the bed in his room and said, "Show me, sweetheart. I'm going to kiss it away." When he'd said that, my body had felt used up and brand-new at the same time.

I looked back up at Rick, and his body looked that way, too — something entirely new, remade from the waste of the familiar same.

I HEAR THEM through the bedroom wall. My mother's crying.

"Shut the fuck up." His voice cracks as he says it. "You stupid piece of ass." Each word is a breath: "Shut — the — fuck — up."

"I'm sorry," she gasps it, "I didn't mean for it to happen."

"How the hell could you do this to me? How the hell could you do this to me? Jesus, Bonnie. I thought you loved me." Now he sounds like a child, "But you're a whore is all. You're just a stupid whore." Helpless. He sobs.

"Andy." Her voice is high. "Don't say that. Please."

"God." He's sobbing harder now. "Look at me. Look at me, Bonnie. I've been running around for years with my brother's wife. Sneaking and lying like a goddamn snake, thinking it's bad enough you're still sleeping with him, and I find out you've been fucking some lawyer on the side the whole damn time." He breathes in short, fast stabs, then he continues to sob, "Why? Bonnie? Why?"

Silence.

Silence, then his sobbing.

Maybe she is enjoying his wet gasps. Now she knows he loves her, no matter what she does, that she is the one killing him.

There's a fresh edge to the silence, and my mother slashes it, emotionless, saying, "Andy, I haven't been fucking him the whole time." She even sounds impatient. "A couple times. We need the money, Andy, you know that."

He cries harder, higher, more like a child, "I'd have given you the money. You didn't need the money, Bonnie. Just admit it's all I'm asking you to do. You just wanted to fuck him. That's all. Just admit it." But it sounds as if he's begging. Pure gold fear. A dog about to be kicked.

Her voice is lower when she speaks again, lower, like something rising from a small lake in the middle of the night. Dark ghost voice. Liquid, and someone else's entirely. Afterward, she even starts to laugh:

"O.K.," she says, "Andy, you're right. If that's what you want to hear. I wanted to fuck him, and I fucked him a hundred times and loved it."

She doesn't scream when he slaps her laughter in the face.

I hear him slap her and slap her again; I hear just him, a low groan in his throat each time he slaps her.

I listen to it in the green dark of my bedroom as if it were something on a television in another room, canned.

Or the sound of the radiator kicking off and on.

The washing machine, rocking hard, learning to walk.

Not caring whether or not it will ever stop.

▼

On the way out of the apartment building, I passed the woman from upstairs as she came into the building. She was carrying a plastic bag of green apples. The apples looked small and sour in her hands, and her hair looked gray in the bright light. I hadn't noticed the gray before. I'd thought her hair was the same color as mine. The woman was pregnant now, too, and she walked with her head thrown back, as if her spine ached, leaning into the emptiness behind her like a swan.

It was Indian summer again. After the day of rain, another

dusty afternoon of sun in Suspicious River. A prism of it moved back and forth across my arms as I drove, and it clamped my wrist for a moment with light, then slipped up my elbow like a bangle.

I slowed down at the corner as a long funeral procession of Oldsmobiles and Lincoln Town Cars passed, led by a hearse which crept and bulged like a black snake that had just swallowed a small child, whole. I could see a casket in the back behind a ruffled curtain. Mahogany, and bright. Little orange flags with black crosses flapped from the antennas of the marked cars, and those flags filled the air with the sound of snapping wings. I waited at the side of the road, counting, until they were out of sight.

When I pulled into the parking lot of the Swan Motel, it was 2:30, and I parked as far from the office as I could, hoping Samantha or Millie wouldn't see the car, or that Mrs. Briggs wouldn't notice it if she happened to come in that afternoon to reprimand Millie.

An older woman from Fennville took our day-off shifts, and she had my hours that evening. But if the woman from Fennville saw my car, she'd think nothing of it, I knew. She didn't notice much. When she wasn't working part-time at the Swan Motel, she ran a beauty shop out of her basement, styled hair — though her own hair was long and unkempt, hanging down tangled over her shoulders the way I imagined my mother's Spanish moss had hung sticky and clotted in the Louisiana trees.

The woman from Fennville complained a lot about the Swan Motel and its guests, with a sneer like someone terribly depressed, someone who'd barely managed to get out of bed that day, who didn't wash her coffee cup, who wouldn't pull up the shades in the living room because she hated the weather, no matter what it was — someone who couldn't help but blame her bitterness on all the smiling people on vacation in their coordinated outfits in Suspicious River at the Swan Motel.

When I thought about that woman, I didn't want to live to be forty.

Gary Jensen was sitting on the hood of his Thunderbird with the heel of one boot up on the fender, smoking a cigarette. He looked up when he saw me pull in, and then he walked around his car, got in the driver's side; his face disappeared behind the glass as he slammed the car door shut, vanishing, then, into the belly of all that silver, steel, and smooth chrome flooded with sun.

I ran across the parking lot toward his Thunderbird, so much light bouncing off the car that I had to squint, even with my hand like a visor at my forehead, clutching the red vinyl purse against my stomach with the other hand while I ran. I pulled open the door like a big steel wing, and I slipped into the passenger's side beneath it, next to him.

He'd already started the car. "You're late," he said.

He looked perfect, a little slouched at the wheel like a man with supple bones and no worries. Blue work shirt and jeans. The brass buckle of his belt was dull, but glinting. He smiled with half his mouth, and it was sexy and lean.

Until that moment I'd never felt the need to stare at a man the way men seemed to need to stare at women — women on the glossy covers of magazines, their hips thrust forward and their slick mouths open, or on billboards — women peering suggestively out of television sets while husbands in their armchairs tried not to stare in front of their wives, but did. At the drug store, those men would be lined up around the magazine rack all day, thumbing through slippery pages of women they'd never meet, never touch, whose voices and names they'd never hear: flattened, one-dimensional women who fingered their own nipples and stared back at the nothing. The oblivion ahead of them. Splayed, those women were just angles and lines and light against shadow, and, looking at them myself, I'd remember reading in a social studies book in high school about some lost and primitive tribe who wouldn't let the white man photograph them, who believed their souls were snatched by cameras.

These women were proof of that, I thought: The world was nothing but a fake backdrop, as if nothing before or behind them had ever existed, or ever would.

But when I looked at the side of Gary Jensen's face that afternoon, I suddenly knew why they stared. Gary gazed into the windshield as if I weren't beside him, and I understood in a flash how it was to want someone whether he wants you or not — just imagining, under clothes, skin, and how it would feel to press your own skin into it, and under that skin, blood — a human heart bobbing warm and soft, a carnal apple. I knew, then, that I'd want him no matter what. Even if I had to pay.

Finally, he said, "Hi," looking over his shoulder, backing up.

There was an inhalation of breeze through the car windows as we pulled out into the road, and then he touched the bare skin above my knee with the tips of his fingers and looked at my face. He smiled. "Well don't you just look like a fine little slut this afternoon," he said.

I breathed.

I looked out the window.

I could feel blood climb my neck, and something hot and liquid seemed to laminate my lungs, like phlegm, or shame. I'd worn a short black skirt and high heels, checked myself twice in the mirror before I left. Tight white blouse with black buttons. I'd felt sexy. Looking at myself in that mirror, I'd thought fleetingly, but with pleasure, of a dry, abandoned field set on fire by a homely little girl.

"Hey," he said, looking at me as I turned my face away, "I was just kidding, baby. You look fine." He squeezed my knee, higher this time. "Mighty fine."

Still, I couldn't look at him. The sky was perfectly blue through the windshield. A shock of red against it in the trees. As we passed the gas station, I caught a glimpse of a girl I'd gone to high school with — a woman now, I thought. She must've been twenty-four, by then, or twenty-three. Once, she'd been a pom-pom girl. All breasts and bleach-blond. Now, she was filling up her black Pinto with gas, frowning, her face turned against the fumes. Rainbows of old oil at her feet. I thought I saw a baby strapped into a baby seat in the back of that Pinto. Its mouth was open and pink — yawning, or surprised.

"*Mighty* fine," he said, lifting my hand out of my own lap and putting it on his pants, under the brass buckle, pressing it down on his erection. "Feel that?" he asked. "You must look hot, huh?" He leaned toward me as the red light changed to green and said, "Look at me, Leila," his hand still pressing against mine. The car roared when he stepped on the gas, and I looked up at him, and then he smiled. "That's my girl," he said. "That's my precious."

Gary Jensen drove straight down Main Street until we were out of Suspicious River. He kept his hand on my hand against him all the time, and I said nothing. It was just my hand. I looked down at my bare knees. Just knees. And I felt tired. When I closed my eyes I saw Rick against my lids. He was naked, a skeleton, with arms crossed over his ribs. *It's my body*, he'd said, with an authority that staggered me. The sun felt warm on my legs and in my hair.

"Leila," Gary said, "you know, you would give any man a hard-on. You know that don't you?" He pressed my hand against it more lightly, then harder, and then he shifted a bit in his seat and moaned. "God, baby. I want your body for my own." He was breathing hard. "Baby, is it mine?"

I couldn't look at him again, but I tried to smile ahead of myself, at the sky, the tree, the speed limit sign.

"God, Leila. What man could resist your body, baby?" He

glanced at my legs and then at my face. "I bet many don't even try to, do they?

"Do they, Leila?" Pressing my hand.

Still, I just smiled at my own blank smile in the windshield, but he was waiting.

"Do they, Leila?

"Do they?

"Do they?"

I bit my lip hard between my teeth because I couldn't smile anymore. I had no idea what my answer should be. I didn't know if he wanted my body to be everyone's body or only his. I didn't know if I should be modest or bold about my body. I wanted to please him, but I was just guessing at what would please him. A stab in the dark. I shrugged. I said, "I guess not."

It was the right answer, and I was relieved when he grinned then and said, "You got the most incredible body, Leila. There's some men might say you just look like a cheap whore, but that turns me on, Leila. Thinking of you going down on all them guys makes me hard."

I pleased him.

I looked out the window again, feeling better. We were nearly as far as Fennville, and the pine trees shivered in the breeze like poisoned arrows. Poisoned arrows, I thought. Poisoned sparrows. A huge bird circled over the highway in a funnel of air, tunneling further and further down to earth, slow as a bad idea or a sharp, black kite. He said, "You going to go down on some guys for me today, Leila?"

We pulled off the exit to Fennville, and Gary turned left, tires spewing up gravel and crunching it like jaws. I'd never been down that road before. I had no idea where we were.

Still, his hand on mine.

"Huh?" he nudged. "You know you'd like that.

"You'd like that, Leila. I know you'd like that. There's nothing wrong with liking that, baby.

"Leila? You gonna turn some tricks for me today?"

I swallowed and squinted — just dust in my left eye, or an eyelash swimming loose across the pupil, turning the world in that one eye to water.

"Answer me, Leila." He squeezed my hand so hard against him that it hurt, little bird bones. "Are you gonna, or do you want to go back?"

I shrugged again, again not sure what I should say, feeling naked and ashamed, but I tried to smile.

He pulled over then and unzipped his pants, pushed my face hard into his lap, holding onto my hair. I thought I'd cough, but I couldn't. I couldn't even taste him. I didn't even need to breathe. I was that far away, barely tethered to myself by a thin, white thread — though Gary was pushing, alive, in total control, taking over for me. I recognized my body as I hovered above it, but it wasn't my body. It was just a glimpse of someone I'd known once, changed — like the pom-pom girl at the gas station. I closed my eyes. Afterward, I wanted to be slapped, but he just kissed my numb lips softly.

It wasn't enough. I wanted to hurt, the way that blond man in 31 had slapped and dragged me back into this world. A newborn. The way Gary had, that first time, knocked me into my skin from the oblivion where I'd been — seeing stars, bloated, colorful planets, comets dematerializing as I passed back into the atmosphere, bruised, landing on his carpet in my red shoes. I wanted something to suck me into my body, knock me back to earth, make me feel. I was high, like a white moth caught in a gust of wind — helpless and thrilled at the same time, farther above my small hometown than I'd ever dreamed of being. I was too precious, too delicate and bright-winged now, too much sweetness in me, like a wedding dress on a laundry line, that moth landing in a swaying ocean of lace — or a clear plastic bag of sleep, opened, sparkling in the breeze. Like Rick, all crisp bones, ready to be blown away. I wanted to plunge down into the dirt. I dug my nails into his neck, and he snapped me back by the shoulders with his hands. He didn't slap me, though I was gasping for it, bending closer. Instead, he murmured against my neck, into the curve where it met my chest, "God Leila, god, I'm falling in love with you."

My eyes stung, my heart was a poisoned sparrow. I wanted to throw myself against the windshield glass, then, like a bee, stinging and droning myself to death against the impenetrable sky. But he'd turned soft while my heart fluttered in its bloody nest. Something passed the car, and the hood of it flashed with light: It was a trailer with a white horse lashing its tail at a cloud of dust behind it.

▼

I was cold, naked to the waist on a table. A nurse, the one with the jaw like a man's, was squeezing my hand. The whir of kitchen machinery between my legs, and I heard my mother scream, perfectly, above me. From the round ceiling light, or from the huge glass jar of cotton balls on the counter next to the tissue box and rubber gloves, I heard my mother scream, "You're *killing* me."

A last electric hum, and it was done.

Quiet, shining, empty weight, and that round light in my eyes.

"Are you all right, sweetheart?"

The nurse leaned down to me to say it, and the light behind her head blacked out her face. I didn't say anything, but I held tight to the nurse's hand. She said, then, "It'll just take the doctor a few more minutes to put the IUD in, then we'll take you to another room to rest."

Rest, I thought.

Water was running in another room. From one room to another room. From a distant source, fast, maybe miles and miles away, and the rush of it passed through pipes in the wall near me, sounding pressurized. A river. A warm flush. The doctor cleared his throat between my legs and prodded me open with his rubber gloves and with something metal like the barrel of a gun. A door, half closed — he was propping it open, saying nothing. I couldn't see him, and I thought of the dentist, his face close to mine while he ran his fingers over my teeth. Our breath on each other, mingling — his, always warm and yellow — and I'd close my eyes so the dentist wouldn't have to look into them while he leaned seriously across my body, into my face.

But the IUD felt like a fishhook going in, and I caught my breath. Snagged, I thought. The ceiling light seemed to reel me up out of darkness, blinding me with air, as if I'd suddenly been born — wet with sweat, not screaming, spilling bloody onto a stainless steel table into a stranger's sterile gloves. And I never did see the doctor's face — just his back as he left the room, the loose blue surgical scrubs hanging off his bony shoulders, angular as a mannequin.

The nurse left, afterward, too, so I could put my clothes back on. I stood up and dropped the white hospital drape on the table where I'd been lying. The table was wrapped in white paper, like a mummy, a gift, or a steak. I slipped a spring dress with pink flowers over my arms, and then I held tightly to the edge of that table so I wouldn't fall, and I touched myself between the legs before I slipped my underwear on. Blood. On my fingers. On the linoleum under me. I took a tissue out of the box on the counter near the glass globe of cotton, and I leaned down to clean up the floor. Glare, a rush of liquid in my ears and then the rush of an empty cup. The blood was nearly black on the tissue, and my chest ached.

In the room where the nurse led me to rest, a girl was crying softly to herself while an older woman, the girl's mother, I thought, squeezed her knee as they watched a beautiful blonde mouth words about bleach on the TV. A white sheet flapped across the screen. The blonde's teeth flashed. Pristine, or sterile. The sound was turned all the way down. I looked at the mother with her daughter for a while, and when I looked away from them, they looked at me.

The counselor came in, smiling shyly, like the hostess of a disappointing party. She was wearing a thick purple sweater that looked homemade. She handed me a Dixie cup of purple Kool-Aid with a napkinful of Wheat Thins, and I could feel blood coming out of me faster — my own blood passing out of me, spreading warm through the Kotex between my legs, then turning cold into the world.

Two

. . . .

*S*HE SCREAMS, "You're killing me."
I sit up in bed when the damp smell of leaves presses down into my sleep like a slinky piece of sky.

It's October, and I'm seven.

Black wings, black fur, mulch outside in the midnight blue-black as grass. The clammy hair of a pumpkin, all guts in the carver's hands. A slash of moon in the crack of curtains, and the musky smell of an animal's stomach.

I've smelled those guts before: once, when my mother cut open a yellow melon, and it was rotten — and once while the neighbors cleaned a doe in their back yard the second day of hunting season.

That tearing sound of a small-toothed comb through long blond hair when they opened the doe. Dogs sniffing around with their hot, hollow breath while it swung from a rope and ran with rusty water — though the dirt soaked it up like an old blanket, old leaves turned to rags, wet for a while, then stiff with it.

I follow the scent to my parents' room. I see my uncle, first, sitting at the edge of my parents' bed. Blood on his white T-shirt. It's steak pink, and it smells like mud and meat, tang of iron in tap water, a dark layer of decay just beneath the ground.

My mother is in a red silk slip on the bed.

A red silk slip yanked up over her belly, just covering her breasts, naked legs. Black patent leather heels on her white feet. Naked arms. Black V of hair between her legs. Mouth open. A pink froth.

But it's blood, not a slip, sleeving down over her breasts like silk.

Three
. . . .

$\mathcal{S}$HE WAS BEAUTIFUL — like a mannequin in her casket, which was quilted in satin and flashed its glamorous hinges at the church ceiling. She was wearing her favorite black dress, a sweep of chiffon, light as crepe or charred lace over her long legs. Nails painted dusty rose. A string of pearls around her swan-white throat. When flashbulbs snapped in my face, they left black stars behind my eyes, and each star had a thin filament of light in the middle, like the bright spine of a moth.

I stood with my hand in the minister's in front of the church, and I cried gently while they carried my mother down the stairs into a purple late-October afternoon — two men on either side of the casket. I could hear my mother shift inside, and someone rushed in to photograph my tears:

There I'd be the next day in black and white on the front page of half the newspapers in the state — my face screwed up and ugly with sobs. They'd quote Reverend Roberts saying, "Bonnie Murray was a member of our church since she was seventeen. I don't care what else she did, she had the voice of an angel, and the person who did this to her will be punished for all eternity in a lake of fire."

I imagined my mother with Uncle Andy there, in eternity, the lake on fire.

She'd walk across the water with her arms outstretched.

She'd be wearing a white choir robe, and it would be in flames, like awful wings.

I don't know why, but I start to cry.

Gary pulls over on the road into a dirt circle beneath some trees. Suspicious River runs back there — the very water that rolls past the Swan Motel all day. Through Fennville, through Ottawa City and Black Springs, to the huge cold blue of Lake Michigan, and then?

I can smell water, and I want to know where it goes.

He puts his arm around me, and I'm happy to have an arm around my shoulders, which feel cold and bare. I can smell him, too. Smoke and soap. I feel my stomach throb like a heart full of want and blood, or a lung of smoke. I want him with my stomach. Hunger, and emptiness. I like the way he smells, as if he is a meal.

"Leila," he says gently, "Look at me."

I can't.

"Look at me," he says and takes my chin into my hand as if I am his child.

But I'm ashamed for him to see me cry, to see my face puffed up, slick with tears. My makeup must be running, my skin gone gray as something old and melted. When I try to turn my face toward the car window to hide it, he holds my chin harder. He says, "I haven't been very nice to you so far today, have I?"

I just shrug. There's wind around my ears like a cool, churning bath. It's an apology I don't need to hear. Instead, I want to be touched. That tug of the stomach. My uterus, maybe, I think. Maybe it's the cool breeze in my guts, but I feel opened, my insides gently exploded and exposed.

"Well, I'll tell you why," Gary sighs. He moves his hand from my chin, drops it to his lap, and looks out the windshield ahead of him. He takes a deep breath and says, "I was mad at you, Leila, that you went home last night to your husband, dammit. I wanted you to stay at the Swan Motel with me."

When I inhale, I'm still drowning in my body's water — tears and snot, and I'm trying to bury my face in my own hands now, thinking *he wanted me.*

He wanted me.

He wanted me all to himself.

It's why he's been so cruel.

Gary reaches into his breast pocket for a cigarette and offers one to me, lights them both with a single match between us, and the little flame moves from my face to his like a tiny, blazing ladybug before he snaps it out quick with a movement of his wrist. The car windows are rolled up now, and the air around us fills with smoke, which dries my eyes.

Gary inhales and turns to look at me. "Isn't that stupid, Leila?" He swallows, looks away, "I guess I felt like you didn't trust me or something, you know? I felt like you should trust me, 'cause I kicked that guy's ass for you in 31. You know? But now I realize how dumb that was. Why the hell should you trust me? You don't know me from Adam."

He looks at my face again, more closely. He says, "But, Leila, I feel like I know you. I feel like I know your heart."

When he says that, he puts his right hand over his own heart and blows a gray stripe of smoke into my hair. "Leila, do you forgive me? Do you forgive me for being — I don't know — *distant* with you this afternoon?"

I nod my head, which feels weighted with the smoke. I remember how he came back to the office flushed, how he buttoned his own sweater up over my ruined blouse. Like a father, he'd proven his love. I whisper, "Yes."

He seems relieved, then, and says, "Let's get out of the car a minute before we get goin' again, O.K.? I just want to talk to you and hold you where I can look at your pretty face. It's so

damn beautiful out. But not long, O.K.? I got to take you to
Ottawa City this afternoon and show you off to my friends.
O.K., beautiful? O.K.?"

I smile and wipe my eyes with my wrist. There are tangled veins like thin blue yarn just beneath the skin, also thin,
the color of skim milk. The veins are so close to the surface,
so nearly exposed, that I can barely stand to look at them.
Sometimes I can't bear to feel my own pulse under that skin,
at the crook of my neck, that blood throbbing under gauze,
sickened by the thought of my own fragile membranes, my
blue sap bubbling. Seeing that fork of veins, I know someday I'll die, as everyone does, but next to Gary I feel warmer,
and alive. I step outside, and Gary takes my cool wrist in
his hand.

It's a canopy of red in the branches over our heads, gold. The
light is hennaed. The color of my hair. I feel pretty when he
looks through a cool burnish of leaves at me. Two squirrels
chase each other through high branches, chattering, and the
sun pours lavish onto their copper fur. Like my hair, which he
touches with the tips of his fingers. I feel beautiful because he
wants me, and the river shivers and ripples like a black sheet,
a wet velvet dress.

Gary lies on his back, and I crawl on top of his body, put my
arms around his neck, lay myself out flat on him, pushing my
hips into his. His brass belt buckle sticks soft and dull into my
stomach. A rush of blood, a runnel of wetness, warm fluid and
desire between my thighs. He closes his eyes, hands at my
waist, and I put my head under his chin. He's warm and solid
as earth beneath me, and the sun is warm on my back. The
slow rise and fall of his breathing lulls me, as though I'm on
the deck of a ship in still, calm water. The blue work shirt
smells like him. His heart under there, inside a cage of bone.
His thin ribs. His hands on my back, no larger than my own.
His arms around me, no wider or longer. Even his hips fit

against me. He's my height, my length, and my body feels safe with his, as if I am desiring myself, as if there's only one of us to please. I say, "I'll stay with you tonight if you want me to," and I lift my head to look into his eyes.

Gary pats my hair, easing my head back down to his chest. "We'll see what happens," he says. "Tonight's a long way away."

Now, I feel naked, ashamed. I feel he's seen the muscular redness under my skin, the yellow fat, draped with that chaos of veins. I whisper, "I just thought it's what you wanted." There's shame in my stomach, too — shame expanding my bladder. Shame in the surging river. I say, "It's what I want, too," apologizing for my shame.

He clears his throat and says, "Tell me something about you, baby. I don't know nothin'."

I close my eyes and the light behind them is white as a slide-projector screen, a white slide projected. I can't think of anything to say about myself. It seems to me he knows it all, whatever there is worth knowing. He's licked my breasts. He's held my hair in both his fists. Although I'm lying down, I shrug. I say, "I don't know what to tell." He waits. I offer, "I was born in Suspicious River."

"What do your parents do?" he asks.

Again, the white slide, the white slide, another white slide. I don't want to talk about this today, there's so little to say, but he slips his hand under the waist of my skirt and pulls out my shirt. His palms smooth the flesh there, hard. At first it's cold, the flesh, exposed — the air coming cool off the river. But then his skin warms mine, and I say, "They're dead." The naked skin feels almost hot beneath his hands.

"How'd they die?"

I shrug again. I say, "My dad had a heart attack five years ago January. He was shoveling snow."

"Shit," Gary says, shaking his head back and forth against

the ground. "That sure happens a lot. I had two uncles who went that way. Damndest thing."

The way he says this makes it simple. A bald fact: a routine. I gain courage from this. I say, "And my mother died when I was seven."

"Oh baby, that's sad," he says and puts one hand in my hair, kisses it.

I close my eyes tight. For these kisses, I'll tell him whatever he wants to know. I'll remember details, specifics, names, places, dates, if he'll just slip his hand into my shirt. If he'll tell me he's in love with me, I'll show him the bed where my mother died. What difference would it make? She's dead, and I'm alive. "How old was she?" he asks.

"Twenty-four," I say, "same age I am now."

When I say that, my mother's face flashes on the screen. Her mouth is open, as if she might say something, or sing, but I open my eyes, and Gary's beard is what I see. Getting darker every day. Spreading down his neck. It hides the long white scar that divides his face like a seam — the dark side from the other, brighter side.

He says, "So she was real young when she had you. Seventeen?"

"Yeah," I say. He makes tiny circles with his fingers on my shoulder. I go on. My voice is a little louder. "I don't have any brothers or sisters. Just me and my dad after that."

"Oh, Leila." His voice is muted in my hair. He slides my body off his body into the grass at his side, eases me onto my back. I feel the earth come up cool and damp through my clothes. He says, "I want to take care of you, precious. I want to take care of you for the rest of your life. I don't want you to ever be alone again."

I close my eyes.

With each of his words there's the click of the slide projector. I think I've never been in love; am I in love? With Rick, there was never this physical undertow, this dredging of the bottom of my stomach like a lake. With Rick there was only a kind of lull like sleep when I was in his arms. And with the others, just the body — and the body like teeth set on edge, a hiss and a sigh and a scream at the exact same time.

But with Gary Jensen on my body, there is flash after flash of empty brightness. White air. A square ceiling light. Sun/nothing/sun. Photo after photo snapped of no one.

I know I am in love.

He rolls on top of me, and even his thin body is heavy. His weight pushes my weight into the ground. Pure gravity. His tongue pushes into my mouth. His hands are cool, and he pulls my shirt up, my skirt down, without lifting his body from mine, until I'm nearly naked against the earth, shivering, just his body keeping my body warm. He doesn't even unzip his pants, just pushes up against me for what seems like a long time. He spreads my legs under him, presses against me hard. I can see the muscle working in his jaw like a piece of the machine, but he is blank-eyed as someone in a trance, until I think I can't keep breathing. The bone of my pelvis bruising under the brass belt buckle. He thrusts against me as if I were not there — violent, but quiet, and then he's done.

Saying nothing, he stands up over my body, which is shaking, splayed beneath him on the ground like something shot out of the sky and fallen naked at his feet. My face is full of tears, and my thighs are numb. I am a meal, I think, a picnic. I feel pretty and close my eyes, and when Gary goes back to the car, I open them. I hurry, scramble to put my clothes back on, fingers trembling at the snaps and buttons, afraid he'll leave without me, and then what would I do? I'd have to follow the river home, and maybe I'd never see him again.

But when I get back to it, he's just waiting in the car with the radio on. A guitar screams steel against steel — music like a car wreck or a riot. He has his pants unzipped and he's cleaning himself off with a red bandanna. "Look at the mess you made, Leila," he says. He shakes his head. "Man." He smiles. "You could make a million bucks with that ass of yours, baby."

I cannot breathe quietly enough. I am afraid the sound of my breathing will make him angry, will make him sick of the sound of my breathing, so I try to hold it for him.

Then he snaps the sun visor on the passenger's side down so I can see myself in the narrow mirror — brown scraps of leaves in my hair. I look scratched, ragged as some animal a hunter has chased out of the woods and into the street. Gary says, "Clean yourself, woman, would you? You're a fucking mess." He laughs.

I feel lucky that he laughs, looking at the mess I am. Lucky to be here, to be alive, to hear him laugh.

▼

In the middle of the third night after the abortion I woke up burning and soaked, stripped off my nightgown, which was ruined with blood, and lay down on the floor of the bathroom, holding my knees against my chest. I woke up again to my father pounding on the door, and by then I was cold, drenched in sweat. "I'm O.K.," I mumbled to him over and over, but my teeth chattered. I put my hands over my face when he turned on the bathroom light, and I could see that my fingers were blue.

At the Ottawa County Hospital, my father sat at the edge of my bed.

The doctor cleared his throat, and his voice was watery. He wouldn't look at me. He spoke to my father as if I weren't in the room, as if I weren't worth speaking to — so vague to him, a cup of melted sherbet — and his back was wide and white. His hair was wet and white. Speaking to my father, it was as if he were reciting something he knew already by heart: "Your daughter has a perforated uterus, Mr. Murray. It's not the fault of the abortion as you were thinking. It was the IUD. It was inserted incorrectly, and instead of rejecting it, as it should have, her body pulled it up, into the abdominal cavity."

"Is she going to be all right?" my father asked weakly, like a TV with its sound being slowly turned down.

"She'll be fine, now that it's out. But of course there's a lot of scar tissue. Which might be just as well. She won't be getting pregnant again at least."

My father looked up as if he'd been punched. He put his head in his hands and gasped for breath.

But I exhaled my life, lying back utterly into the starched white hospital pillows.

I imagined that IUD like a fishhook — I'd never seen it — caught in my belly, bloodying me like my mother, snagging me out of the cold river water and reeling me up. But someone had decided to toss me back after all.

$\mathcal{F}$OR A MONTH after my mother died, I woke up every morning on the floor. Cold, a cotton sack of bones.

I must have fallen out of bed, but I never woke. Just dreamt I was slipping through dark space, naked, a hundred hands touching me as I fell.

I wasn't afraid. The noises I heard at night were still familiar: my mother crying, my Uncle Andy humming. Only now it was just the furnace humming, or my father's radio in the basement weeping with my mother's voice.

"This is just a small town," the *Detroit Free Press* quoted our neighbor, an old lady I'd never seen before. On the front page of the paper, she waved her hands in gray, photographed air. She said, "What a way to get on the map."

Our house looked ordinary behind her, empty, though it wasn't. And next to our house, a map of Michigan — bloated hand, an arrow pointing north, pointing out the black circle of Suspicious River in it, on the fat pinkie of that mitten.

No one told me where Uncle Andy had gone.

Lake of Fire?

Halloween came and went with the smell of burning leaves in human-sized piles. Though no one came to trick-or-treat at our door, I could hear them shuffling through the neighborhood in costumes. The voices of other children, muffled under masks and sheets, passing our haunted house by:

The smell of fermented apples, soft and rotten, and the air was like a black orchard, trampled under boots as big as God's.

When I looked at my father, he seemed like a ghost now, too. It seemed someone had slipped him off in the middle of the night — like my Uncle Andy — but zipped something entirely else into his skin.

Expression painted on, head stuffed full of straw. Winter was already blowing in and out of my father's empty mouth when he opened it to speak. Like a white silk scarf that had belonged to my mother.

Gary says, "Here we are." He slips his Thunderbird between two faded yellow lines, then looks at me.

The parking lot glints with nice cars and pickups, a rusty van with an airbrushed painting of snowcapped mountains on the side. Gary says, "Let's have a drink and see who's here." THE BIG CITY BAR blinks green from a small dark window with a limp curtain in it.

Inside, the bar is dim and warm. The smell of old beer and sawdust, like every bar up North. There is a couple standing near the entrance, outside the restrooms, arguing. The woman, tiny and pale, with long black hair, leans against the gray wall wearing only tight cutoffs, topless. Her naked breasts are a little shriveled, nipples huge and burgundy black. *My mother*, I think, without looking at the woman's face: that casual nakedness, standing in front of a man as if she were a statue, a Venus, a marble madonna, but topless. Without thinking about it, I know, in the very center of my stomach, that when you look at a woman with her breasts exposed, in a public place, on a bright day, nothing good will happen. She is as accessible as something dead, and so are you. Your own body is exposed through your own eyes. The way someone's soul is always snatched by a photograph — the photographed or the photographer, depending who is weaker. Depending on who pays.

The man has his hands on either side of her face, and he leans into her, barking, "What? What did you say?" He's also thin and small, maybe younger than she is, and not as strong. The woman seems annoyed but not afraid, and she glances at us, a rectangle of sun between her face and the man's cutting sharp lines of light across her stomach and breasts as the door opens before us, closes behind us. After it's closed, for a moment I'm blind. The woman says, "Shut up, Doug. Hi, Gary."

"Hey baby." Gary gives her a little wave, and I feel as though I'm following someone important. The man with the key to the place. I feel the way the girlfriends of rock stars look. A little curious, but calm. Look at me, don't look at me; I matter, and I don't matter at all.

*T*HEN IT WAS WINTER. The girl said, "Your mother was a whore."

I'd won the second-grade essay contest that day. Something I'd written about the last passenger pigeon, how there weren't any more in the world once that one died. I'd gotten the idea for it from my *Weekly Reader,* and I'd stayed up half the night to write it in big block script. I'd wanted to win, and when I did, when my name was announced, there was the grudging applause of my classmates, looks passed to one another fast while I walked to the front of the class to receive the certificate: FIRST PRIZE, with *Leila Murray* written carefully in black felt pen underneath.

Then, if I'd noticed, it might have been like laughing gas seeping through the cinderblocks, the cracks between the windows. A green cloud rising from the floor.

But Miss Lovette asked me to read my essay to the class, and my fingers trembled as I did — paper fluttering in my hands like weak white wings. I was trying to read it loud. I felt my voice shoot to the back wall, a flat echo like the snap of a rubber band against it — while, outside, the snow rose higher and higher and a yellow plow whirred under the classroom window, tossing snow into the gray school-afternoon air. Miss Lovette had a frozen smile on her face when I finished reading.

I could tell by that smile that I'd won nothing but the pity of Miss Lovette. She hugged me hard to her soft and empty breasts.

This girl was the prettiest and smartest girl in the second grade. The girl whose name should have been written carefully under FIRST PRIZE. Daughter of a dentist. Ponytail slick and nearly white as a fall of water. She stood facing me, snow to our knees, and I could feel that snow seep into my socks. The straps of my red boots were broken, and they flapped loose, like the long red tongues of cats as I walked. The girl hissed, "It was in the paper."

My mother had been dead two months, and no one had said a word to me about it — not since the police in their dark suits. They'd looked at me carefully, coaxing, slowly, seeming to think I was much younger than I was, a baby, or that I was a fragile glass animal with diamond eyes, something expensive that could be shattered by their voices if they talked too loud, too fast. They'd made me feel precious and tired, and I didn't mind answering their questions. I could have done that for them for the rest of my life.

Those policemen circled and touched me when I cried, and they smelled like men. One of them let me crawl into his lap, put my face into the starched white of his chest for a long, long time. Something musky and fresh. Maybe it was just his sweat.

We sit down at a round table near the back and Gary asks, "What'll you have?" "No," he interrupts himself, "let me answer that." He smiles, squeezes my knee under the table and says, "I'll be right back."

The music isn't loud, but it is mostly bass, and I feel it in my stomach, under my lungs. The bar isn't packed, but there's a small group of men close to the front. A curtain of smoke lifts and closes around them. Mostly young — twenties, thirties —

mostly wearing jean jackets and old jeans. There might be a
chain looped through with a belt, and keys on that. A few of
them look at me when Gary turns his back at the bar, ordering
our drinks.

The men are gathered around the small stage up front like
gawkers at an altar — five splintered sections of plywood with
a bathroom rug draped over it. I imagine it's where a woman
has been dancing, maybe the woman who was arguing at the
entrance. A greenish-blue light bulb hangs over the stage, and
dust dances under it now. Maybe there's a strobe.

I know what this is all about. I've been to a topless bar
before. In Suspicious River, there's a block of them. All with
windowed mirrors. When you glance at those bars from the
street, you see yourself. Maybe you look disheveled, fat, or
embarrassed. I remember sitting near the back with a man's
wide hand on my knee while the stripper stooped and twirled,
too far up front for me to see. The man I'd gone there with was
divorcing a librarian at the high school, and he'd picked me up
in the parking lot there after he'd been escorted from the library by the school's principal for having shouted at his wife in
the library as she scurried away, deeply flushed, pushing a
metal cart of books. He'd craned his neck to see the stripper
and pressed my thigh at the same time. I felt sorry for that
man, but the cocktail waitress, topless, seemed to feel sorry
for me. In the restroom she asked me if I was O.K., if I wanted
her to call someone to give me a ride home. "He's pretty old
for you, isn't he?" she asked, and I just lifted my eyebrows as if
I were surprised and shook my head no.

Gary comes back to our table with two drinks. "Jim Beam
on the rocks," he says proudly. "You ever drank that before?"

I sip it. Warm as cough syrup slipping down. "I think so," I
say, and he looks disappointed.

"Well. You ever been to a strip joint before?"

"Once," I say, and he stops smiling.

"Jeez," he says, sipping his drink. Maybe he looks annoyed,

but he eases his hand up my thigh. "You done it all, haven't you?" Someone turns the music up, and Gary has to shout above it. "Who's been bringin' you to strip shows, sweetie, your husband?"

"No." I lean toward him, nearly shouting to be heard, "Just once. I was in high school. An older guy."

Gary shakes his head, mouth full of whiskey, which he swallows, and says, "I knew you was naughty the first time I saw you. Knew you'd do whatever I wanted, baby. I like that." He puts his arm around me, up under my arm, and he feels my breast. I move away at first, as if to dodge his hand — as if I wanted to or could — but then he reaches up to put it on my breast again, and I let him keep it there. I'm happy, because he's smiling. Because he's touching me. He says, "Nothin' much surprises you, does it?" And I think he sounds pleased as he says this.

I sip from the drink and shrug.

The woman we'd passed near the restrooms comes out then, and there's a weak swell of applause under the booming music. She has her black hair hanging over her breasts now, and she passes close to the men at their tables as she walks to the stage, taking long, loose steps to the music in her high red heels. A few of the men reach out to touch her thighs or her cutoffs, and she lets them, but she doesn't smile. Neither do they. Some of the men lean forward in their chairs, looking carefully at her, as if they're memorizing something, or trying to read small print. Some lean back, unimpressed, while the man she'd been arguing with stands in the back drinking from a bottle of beer with long, deep swallows.

The woman dances for a while in a small circle, lifts her long hair off one breast and shows it to the men, offers it up with one hand. Then she lifts the long hair off the other breast. Finally, she flips the hair over her shoulders and stands close to the edge of the stage, shaking her breasts, leaning forward, and the men don't applaud — just drink, stare. The music pounds. The woman unzips her cutoffs fast and then steps out of them. Black lace panties under that, naturally. She plays with her nipples while she dances, licking the tips of her fingers first, then dancing her fingers around the nipples in circles while she dances, also in circles. The nipples get hard, briefly, but they go soft and slack again when she stops touching them.

The woman pulls the panties down to her knees, and her pubic hair is thick. She dances for a while with the underwear at her knees. She stumbles a little when she steps out of the panties, then picks them up and throws them to a guy at a table in front of her. She puts her hands on her hips, legs spread, still dancing, but not well. She's lost the rhythm. Maybe she isn't listening to the music anymore. Then she pulls the lips apart with both hands, showing them the pale, shell-pink, and Gary squeezes my breast hard when she does that.

Faded now, I can barely hear the music either, and I feel surprised when he touches me too hard. Surprised to be alive. I am reminded briefly of my own body, receding in the smoke, the blue-gray haze.

When the music stops, the woman picks up her cutoffs, and the guy with her panties hands them back to her politely. She walks naked through the bar, but no one tries to touch her as she leaves. When she's gone, the restroom door closing with a whoosh of air behind her, there is quiet applause.

"I'll be right back," Gary says. "I'll get you another drink."

Now that there's nothing on the stage to look at, I stare into my glass. Ice melts oily into the whiskey. Maybe I'm already drunk. I feel a little like I've been shaken up, myself, in a glass. Gary's left his pack of cigarettes on the table. I light one, and smoke curls out of my fist as if my fingers are on fire. When I've finished the drink, I want another, but Gary hasn't come back.

Behind me, there's only the wall. Cinderblock and beige,

and the man who argued with the stripper leans against that wall, his arms crossed over his chest, staring straight ahead, working a muscle high on his throat. I'm the only woman now in the room, and a few of the men up front have turned all the way around in their chairs to look at me. I don't look back. Once, I saw a show cat on TV. Pure white fur and a rhinestone collar around its neck. Now, I feel like that show cat. Stretching casually. Letting the judges look. I keep my eyes on my empty glass, turn my nails over in my fist to appraise them myself. That cat, licking its paw.

I look up when a man with long, red-brown hair comes over to the table, smiling. The others watch him move toward me. He asks, "Can I buy you a drink? Or is Gary going to be right back?"

I'm surprised that everyone in this bar knows Gary's name, and it sounds familiar on their lips. I shrug. I say, "I don't know," leaning back a little in my chair.

"Well, he won't mind me buying you a drink, I bet." The man winks. "Let's go sit up at the bar."

I follow that man to the bar. A horse to water, I think. He's tall, overweight, but solid as far as I can tell. So large and thick I feel like a child behind him. I put my purse on the bar and fold my hands together on top of it, and when I glance over the man's big shoulder toward the entrance, I see Gary. He's laughing. A blond man with a trimmed blond beard smokes a cigarette next to him, also laughing. And before I realize who he is, I've already thought *old friends*.

Then I see the friend more clearly, back framed in a square of smoke when someone opens the door behind them. I'm not sure at first, but then I am: the man from 31. I see myself for a moment curled on carpet, tasting blood on my tongue, but I swallow. I say "Thanks" when the bartender pushes the whiskey and ice in front of me. I look over at the man who's paid for it, slipping his wallet back into his pocket. "Thanks," I say again, to him this time, and what I feel is gratitude, simple as that. I don't look over my shoulder at Gary with the blond man again. There are explanations, I think as I sip, for everything. I think of my husband crossing his thin arms — *It's my body*, he said. That, I could understand. The span of obligation and forgiveness reaches no wider than the span of your arms. I always knew it, but now I *know* it.

The man who paid for my drink puts his huge hand lightly on my thigh — on the thin cloth of the skirt, first, then pushing underneath the skirt. "Sure," he says, though I no longer know why he says it.

The bartender's old. His teeth look soft. He peers down over the bar at this man's hand on my thigh and smiles with those old dog teeth. I sip the whiskey, ice knocking cold against my own teeth.

▼

"I know you didn't want me to," my father said. He was putting the phone back into its black crib when I walked into the kitchen, his face as foggy as old ice. "But I called Mr. Schmidt, and I told him what his son did."

I could smell cut grass in the neighbors' yard, turning dry and blond in the sun since they'd mowed, and their honeysuckle, also getting old, stinking sweetly in the May heat, like something moldy, bloated. I looked out the kitchen window into a hedge of white lilac, a shock of forsythia beyond that, yellow and fancy as a new dress against a wide blue sky. I hadn't bled for a week.

"Why?" I asked. I could tell my father was cool and sweating by the smell of his T-shirt. Cotton, salt, cut grass.

His mouth trembled, lips pursed, as if he had something half-alive slipping over his dentures, a garden snake. As if he were trying not to cry. He said, "This boy got you pregnant, and now you can never get pregnant again. He ruined your *life*, Leila. You're just a baby. You're just seventeen, and you don't understand about this yet, but that boy *ruined* your life. It's something his father has got to know, Leila. That boy owes you."

The river had only just melted — that's how long it took spring to creep up North. And every year, when it finally did, the season exploded in Suspicious River — half crazed with wildflowers and sun, ecstatic daisies sucking up to it like junkies with their fuzzy yellow tongues. I didn't feel like my life was ruined at all.

In fact, I felt as though my life had just begun.

But I saw my father look into that life, then, like an empty room. No point in buying furniture for it now, he seemed to be thinking. No sense painting something that will always be so plain and gray. I'd thought *no baby, ever* in the hospital room that night, and I'd felt the whole quiet, shining weight of that pure emptiness for a moment in my arms like a white paper bag swept up by a breeze. But then I saw myself as a woman on film — myself, but someone else. Maybe I was thirty years old, wearing a beige trench coat, waving to a cab. There was something in my arms after all — a briefcase, a book, a yellow legal pad. I hadn't felt sad when I saw that.

When Rick called a few hours later, I answered. My father had taken a painkiller for his leg — not the leg itself, which felt nothing anymore, but the ache that hovered like a halo around his leg, the pain that came and went for no reason, the bloodless angel of old pain — and he'd fallen asleep on the couch. Whispering hello into the phone, I looked over at my father to see if he'd been jarred awake by the ringing, but he just slept. I wondered, in the scene of me in the trench coat, where had this heavy, hurting presence of my father been? Who would be here with this man, taking care of him, if I were thirty years old with a briefcase, waving a cab in Chicago, or even in Kalamazoo? He shifted in his sleep.

Rick sounded as though he'd been crying. "Leila, why didn't you tell me?"

I shrugged, but he couldn't see that gesture through the

phone lines, stretched tight between our houses, crisscrossing the town of Suspicious River, taut across the country, hooking our small house up to the White House if we wanted, or a skyrise in New York, where a little old lady in a green silk dress smoked a cigarette, looking out her window to the west.

Here and there a few crows settled on those lines, then flew up into the blue — a ring of black and, in the air behind them, a trail of smaller, more intense birds, snapping their little wings furiously, looking tossed as a handful of feathers into a breeze which blew them backward as they flew. The windows were open, and the curtains in the kitchen billowed. I could smell violet water, a bright pillar of it, moving through the kitchen, shimmering, then leaving through the open back door, passing silently through the screen.

"My parents think we should get married, even though you're not having the baby." Rick sounded grave, old. He swallowed. "And I think they're right."

*M*Y LEGS were bare, turning pure white in the February wind — stung at first, then numb. It was a marble-heavy morning of old snow, a low sky pressing down dully, like duty, the color of a spent flashcube. I was wearing a purple dress, a spring dress, in this dead of winter, and the broken boots. I hadn't zipped up the jacket, and I was a half-hour early for school, waiting outside. No one else was there yet, and when I blew on my fingers, they softened and began to burn.

"You're early, Leila," Miss Lovette said. She was coming up behind me from her car, wearing a huge black coat that made her look like a mother bear. She said, "It's cold. Come in."

The lights weren't on in the school yet, and I felt peculiar, out of place, being there. I'd never seen the school quiet and dim. "You're legs look cold, Leila. You need to wear warmer clothes."

I nodded. I hung my coat on a hook in the hallway, and it looked deflated there. I hadn't meant to be early or to be invited in.

Miss Lovette put her own coat in the closet. She flipped the light switch on, and those long white tubes stuttered above us, then buzzed, then hummed. In that glare, my bare knees looked shiny and simple with shame, so I pulled the hem of my skirt down over their faces. The numbness had worn away in the warmth, and I was shivering again, but when Miss Lovette came over to hug me, suddenly I felt I was spinning away from my body, a naked puppet trembling at the end of a string, and, I didn't mean to, but I was sobbing before I could stop — water ruining my dress, too, a puddle of urine hot under me. It stung the cold skin of my thighs.

Miss Lovette pulled back fast, a pinched look on her face. She squinted at me as if I were a little dangerous, the way you might look at a dog you hadn't noticed was injured until you'd already put it in your lap: Then, you see blood under the matted fur. You want to offer whatever comfort you can, but it repulses you, too, makes you think you might gag — so your hand just hovers in the air above the dog.

I was holding on to the edges of my desk but it was rocking under me. Something inside my body was shaking its way out.

Even after the bell rang, Miss Lovette made the other second graders wait in the hall until she'd gotten me as clean and dry as she could. A few of them had their faces pressed to the glass in the door. They must have seen Miss Lovette, then, lift up my wet dress and wipe my bare bottom with a brown paper towel.

"Hey," Gary says, slipping onto the barstool next to mine. He glances at the hand on my thigh and then at the man on my other side, the one who is touching me, the one who bought my last drink. My legs feel cold and bare, but Gary ignores the man's hand and puts his own arm around me. "You see who's here?" he asks. "Our buddy?" He nods his head in the direction of the blond man from 31.

"Do you know him?" I try to keep my voice steady as I ask it. I picture my voice as a flat line above my head on a monitoring machine, but there is still life in my breath when I ask it. Emotion. I look down at my hands.

Gary laughs, "Well, just from the other night. Hey, Ralph."

The man on my other side swallows smoke from his own cigarette and says, "How ya doin', Gary?"

"Good." Gary nods, sounding happy. "These mine?" He points to his pack of cigarettes.

"You left them on the table," I say.

His shoulder feels familiar, nudging mine, and my own shoulder feels a little like a muzzled animal bumping, toothless, back into his. I know his body now, and he knows mine. I don't even care about the blond man from 31. When I blink, I see a barn owl circling out of the sky — a wide-eyed child with prehistoric wings. Brown and slow as a bad decision. I step aside from my body between these two men at the bar, and what I've stepped into is pure air. Like that owl. Like waking from a dream when the phone rings, but it's too late. You're hovering, already, above your body, your bed, ready to answer and crash wide awake onto the surface of the world.

"Jim Beam," Gary says to the bartender as he taps a cigarette out of the pack, and the bartender starts to pour.

Gary looks across me to the man with red hair beside me. "Am I interrupting anything?"

"I don't know." The man shrugs, looks at me. "Is he?"

I just look into my glass. I say, "I don't know."

"Well, hell," Gary says, "then I must be. No problem, baby. I'll be over here if you need me." He picks his drink and the pack of cigarettes off the bar in the same hand, and he tosses three dollars from his front pocket on the bar with the other. The red-haired man's hand moves farther up my thigh.

"Want to go to the back room?" the man asks.

I don't know exactly what he means, but I know what he's talking about. I say, "Whatever you think. I don't know."

"Should I pay you, or Gary?" looking in his direction.

I shrug. I say, "Him, I guess."

And the man says, "O.K., baby, I'll be right back."

I take a last sip from the drink, and the man is already back. "O.K.," he says and takes my hand.

The back room is by the entrance — a small door opens into it across from the Ladies' Room. I hadn't suspected there were rooms on the other side of this wall. When he opens the door to let me in, I think of Alice stepping into a mirror as if it were water, surprised.

But what girl would ever think to try a trick like that? Walking into glass?

Some part of her already knew there was something there beyond her own reflection.

Someone had told her, or she'd seen it in a dream. I couldn't remember the story at all.

In this back room there's a brown couch. Not old, but worn. A coffee table, a table lamp. It looks like someone's den, but there's no carpet, nothing covering the linoleum floor. The light is gold and warm. An ashtray. An empty bottle of beer. He locks the door behind us and takes his jacket off.

Now I can see that his arms are even larger than I'd imagined. He isn't fat, as I'd thought. He's been lifting weights. Solid muscle and a drab olive dragon tattooed above his elbow. "O.K.," he says. It's all he says.

I start to unzip him, but he pulls me off my knees and pushes my skirt up, pulls my underpants down, and then he moves me back, toward the couch, as if we're doing a gravity dance, and I sit down. He eases me backward onto the couch, kissing my neck, saying, "O.K., O.K.," and then he unzips himself and eases himself in.

It lasts a long time.

Twice, someone tries to open the door, barred by the lock.

Finally, someone knocks and says, "Hey. Hurry up."

I think maybe it's Gary, but I don't recognize his voice behind that door:

Gravity dance. A dance of gravity. I keep my hands on the

man's chest to keep his weight from crushing me, but I feel small and exhausted, worn out under him. He never looks at me, just stares straight ahead, groaning loud when he comes. Then he zips himself up and puts his jean jacket back on, leaving the door half open when he leaves.

When another man pushes the door all the way open and steps in, I'm dressed again. He looks around as if maybe he's in the wrong place. I recognize him as one of the men who's been in front, near the stage, who's been wearing a slippery baseball jacket and a cap. He'd grabbed the dancer's leg when she walked by, but after that he'd just sat slouched through the rest of her dance, as if she'd disappointed him, as if the whole thing bored or insulted him, or made him mad.

"I already paid Gary," he says.

I nod.

It's as if the room is suddenly coming into focus, as if it's *my* room now. Details. The plaid pattern on the couch is tan threaded through with black, the beige behind it stained, and the paint on the wall behind the couch has wept a suture loose. In that crack, plaster crumbles gray and dry as mouse dust. The ceiling seems to settle a little, easing down on me like a darkening sky. There's comfort now in the plaid of these couch cushions scratching at my thighs. *Down-to-earth,* I think, and I know now what it means. Exactly. Gravity; nothing flies. No birds, no moths. No shock, loss, disappointment. No personality, maybe. That focus on physical detail. It's all I notice now. That plaid, that crack.

I lean back, and he kneels in front of me. "Oh, man," he says, hands shaking as he pulls the shirt up over my breasts. "You're the most beautiful thing I've ever seen around here. Oh, God." He pulls hard at my nipples with his teeth, then rubs his face back and forth across my bare chest. The stubble on his chin scratches at the skin there, but I'm glad he doesn't want me to do it for him. He comes in his own hand, touching himself while he presses his mouth to my chest, sucking, then biting the flesh as if it isn't real. I barely breathe.

Gary comes in afterward, looking worried — I've pulled my shirt back down, tucked my hair carefully behind my ears. Gary says, "He didn't put it in you, did he?"

The sound of his voice — a wavelength of pale light through the dim room — I hear concern behind the accent, behind the anger. A kind of love, I think. I say "No," and feel that we are partners in this now. I feel relieved to have someone share the burden of what I've been doing alone for what seems like a lifetime now, like finally showing the raw throat to a doctor, opening your mouth when he tells you to, saying, "Ah" — a revelation, or a lover's sigh.

"Good," Gary says. "He didn't pay for that."

▼

Rick and I got married kneeling at the altar where, ten years earlier, my mother had been laid out like an arrangement of black flowers in her coffin. My father was wearing the same bright blue suit he'd worn to her funeral — the only suit he'd saved from his salesman days, out of fashion and brand-new.

Reverend Roberts asked us a string of questions, though he'd already told us how to answer, and Rick squeezed my hand hard when he said, "I do." His shoulders shook. I felt naked in a white sundress in the church, all shadows and the cold sweat of marble settling on my own shoulders like a fever. *Infertile,* I thought, realizing I was, walking in front of my father and Rick's parents back up the aisle we'd just walked down — a cold white ruined bride leading a silent procession.

The word hadn't occurred to me until then, and then it seemed to hover over me. And other words — barren, sterile. Husk. I'd never wanted a baby, but now the world would be full of nothing but the babies I hadn't wanted. Fresh and squirming flesh under the hospital nursery's too-bright light. My father's limp was an empty echo behind me as we passed the vacant pews and stepped out into a shock of bright green sky.

It was June, and the whole town seemed doused with light. I looked at it differently that day, stepping out of the church into the town where I'd spend the rest of my life. The sky was just a backdrop, flimsy — the illusion of depth and space — while a faceless scarecrow stared out of a vegetable garden bordering the church, sun burning dust off the scarecrow's blank face. In the distance, a shotgun blast punctured the flimsy membrane of sky with a furious hush of gray wings everywhere at once. When I looked up I saw there was a thunderhead swimming toward the church, fast, like a sphinx. It seemed to paddle the air, grazing the trees, with its webbed feet.

Afterward we went back to the Schmidts' house and ate white cake. Layer after light, white layer on plain paper plates. Two tiers of nothing but cake with a stiff plastic bride and groom up to their knees in frosting at the top. Rick's mother poured black coffee for us into brittle cups, which clamored against their see-through saucers when we lifted them to our lips and set them back down again. She smiled at her only son over and over again across the table — a nudge of comfort, encouragement, consolation.

Rick smiled back, but he wouldn't meet her eyes. He ate no cake. Already, he was exchanging his body for a thinner one, slipping quietly out of the fleshy boy he'd been into a gradually descending suit of new bodies while we slept. As if no one would notice. Like the Russian dolls that have smaller, identical dolls tucked away in their hollow stomachs. Rick was working his way down to the smallest doll.

That night we slept in Rick's childhood bed. It was narrow and the springs, when we shifted, squeaked like a small dog being beaten with a stick.

We had to be quiet because his parents were sleeping together on the other side of the wall, so I put my face in Rick's pillow to cry. I thought about my father alone now in our house, sleeping alone in the bed where my mother had bled to death. I didn't know if there was blood on that mattress. I'd never looked. But the smell of blood had never gone away. We'd grown used to it. Like the taste of well water. A red fox sneaking through the snow and a coop of ruined chickens: I missed the smell of that house.

Rick rubbed his hand up and down my spine. "It's O.K.," he said over and over, sounding far away or shrinking. "O.K.," he kept saying, "O.K."

When we woke up, it was still just June, and the lawns on the Schmidts' block were scattered with shredded petals, smelling like newly cut hay — scratchy and sweet in the breeze that carried it in from the miles of farmland that circled the town. Daisies swayed under an impenetrable sky.

▼

"Oh shit," Gary says when we pull back into the parking lot of the Swan Motel.

I recognize her pickup.

He says, "My wife is here."

"It's O.K.," I say. I want to make things easy for him. It's been a long day. I say, "I'll go home." My head hurts from the whiskey anyway, and it's past two in the morning. I'd planned to spend the night with him; I'd wanted to, but maybe this is just as well. I have no clothes with me to wear to work tomorrow afternoon. And Rick. Our apartment, with its white shelves.

"Look," Gary says, putting his arm around me. "You did great tonight. I'm so proud of you. You made a lot of money for us, baby. Tomorrow we'll split it up. Whatever you think is fair." He leans over to kiss my hair. "You and me are gonna be so happy when we straighten everything out." He nuzzles into my neck, groaning a little. "Leila, you were so hot. God, you don't know how much that turns me on — all those men wanting you, and you're all mine."

He kisses me long and hard on the mouth. It's warm. I hold on to his shirt loosely with my fist. I think, is there anything that belongs to me under my skin that couldn't just as easily belong to him? Or am I empty? A gift box of tissue. I've even stopped thinking, dreaming. Just snow, now, smoke. When I close my eyes, I am alone.

Earlier, I'd even gone to the Ladies' Room at the Big City Bar and *tried* to think. I'd looked at my hands, but they didn't look like hands, and the bathroom tile was cold beneath my bare feet. I hadn't bothered to put my shoes back on or button my blouse because it didn't matter who saw. I was a white wall. I tried to think, but the thoughts were only bits of branches tugged along with river water as it rushed through a narrow tunnel. I couldn't see anything separately or long enough to understand what it was, so I'd gone back to the room, pushed through a crowd of men who touched me as I passed. I left the door open behind me, took off my clothes again, and lay back naked on the couch in that room's dull light, waiting. I imagined silver coins in my stomach, melting into mercury, pure liquid sterling, and I felt cold. I even spread my legs.

Let them see it all, I thought. Let them have it.

I don't want to let go of Gary's shirt, but I do when he says, "I got to take care of this now, Leila. I'll see you tomorrow. O.K.?"

As I walk from his car back to my own, I see that she's just sitting in her pickup alone, in the dark. Not even the light of the radio is on.

$\mathcal{M}$ ISS LOVETTE paced in the principal's office, taking small hard steps in her wide black pumps between his desk and the chair I sat in across from the principal's desk.

Miss Lovette was large, and her skin smelled sweet, doughy. Maybe she was only thirty years old, but she could have been any age — all smooth skin, earth mother, like a mown hill. Her hair was neither blond nor brown. She wore it short, and her ears were small as a baby's, pink and smooth as shells.

There was a cold wind coming into the principal's office through a crack under his window, even a little snow, a few flakes of it blowing across the room before disappearing into the air above the radiator's thumping. He sat square behind his desk, chin rested on his fist, his hair oily and black. There was a photograph near his elbow of a thin blond woman and two dark-haired children sitting together on a sunny day at the edge of a pool. One of the children, a boy, was splashing the aqua water with his feet. In the photo, light and water frothed beneath the boy. The blond woman looked annoyed. I could tell that woman and the children belonged to the principal. They all resembled him.

Miss Lovette said, "It's not a problem. Leila can stay with me until everything's all settled. O.K., Leila?" She smiled, but she still looked worried. She knelt down at the side of my chair, squeezed my wrist with her hand. I looked down at that hand, noting the skin over the bones, how it was clammy and thick, how those bones seemed fragile and lost in flesh, though her fingernails were full of little rising moons.

She spoke quietly to me, "You understand that everything's fine, don't you? But your daddy had some trouble on his way home from Benton Harbor, and the doctors have to make sure he's going to be fine before he leaves the hospital. He'll just be gone for a little while. But he'll be fine. Tonight we'll call him from my house."

Fine, I thought, and Miss Lovette said, "Won't it be fun for you and me to spend some time together?"

I nodded and tried to smile, but the air coming up under the principal's windows was like raw iron. It hurt my teeth, my shoulder bones. The windows seemed to bend with it, but eventually February would shatter those windows altogether. In a few weeks, an ice-heavy branch would be blown by wind into the plate glass, and then it would be as if the sky had fallen onto the principal's desk and exploded into a million jagged pieces of blue light.

One minute the principal would be looking at the nice photo of his children splashing in a motel pool, and the next he would be sitting in the sky.

Snow in his hair, in his eyes.

A dust of frost on the dark sleeves of his suit.

Rick gets up and comes into the bathroom while I'm taking off my clothes in the dark. In the first flash after he flips on the light, I feel like something captured. And his image in my blindness is an x-ray. A negative. I see his bones blaze in the glare, his skeleton standing in the door. I'm naked in front of him — my own body doubled, but brighter, behind me in the mirror.

"Leila," he says. His face is a blank. As he loses weight, his eyes seem to creep back in his face like animals retreating to their caves. "You're having an affair again, aren't you?" he asks.

I pick a limp T-shirt of his off the bathroom floor and slip it on over my arms, then look at him. I bite my lip, swallow, and say, "Yes" — feeling merciful, thinking it's better than the truth.

"Is it Bill again?" He doesn't look angry or afraid, just tired. He looks the way my father used to look when he had the first pains around his leg. As if a drink, a pill, a few hours sleep were all he wanted or needed on this earth.

"No," I say fast.

"Someone else?"

"Yeah." A whisper.

Rick exhales and steps back, shaking his head as if to shake something annoying out of his hair. A little bird. An insect building a web. "Jesus," he says, "Leila."

He goes back into the bedroom and sits at the edge of the bed. When I step into the room, he looks up at me. I must be featureless, framed in light from the bathroom behind me. A silhouette. The kind of tracing the TV policemen make around a body on the sidewalk where it's found.

"I'm sorry," I say.

"You're sorry," he says.

I catch my breath. His voice has changed. It comes from a deeper part of him in this moment, as if it has echoed in his ribs awhile before rising from his throat.

I lace my fingers in front of my stomach and look down at my feet. They're shiny, white, cool as two skinned doves.

Rick looks at my feet, too. "Leila," he says, "I can't keep on living this ridiculous life."

I exhale, then, from my nose. Perhaps it's a laugh. Rick looks at me, quick and angry.

"You think that's funny." He doesn't raise his voice. "Well, it's not funny, Leila. Not anymore. I've been taking care of you for years while you just drag your body around this town and screw every man who crosses your path. And everyone around here knows exactly what you are and what a dumb fuck your husband is for sticking around."

Under the silence there's an electric hum. For a moment I think it's coming from Rick's bones.

"Look," he says, apologetic now. "I just want out. That's all I want. I'm not jealous. I'm not angry. I'm just nothing. Maybe it's not even your fault, but I'm done with it, Leila. I'm done feeding you and waiting for you. I'm done doing what other people tell me I should do."

*M*Y FATHER had been driving too fast for the conditions, they said. He'd been trying to get back to the house before I got home from school. It was February. The roads were slick, and there was too much on his mind. The car spun across both lanes before it hit the median, and then February crumpled up his Ford like something childish in a huge, white glove.

He would be fine, though. Just a few days in a hospital. Just a simple procedure on his leg, and he'd be home again. Until then I could stay with Miss Lovette.

After school, she drove me to my house, and we got in the back door with a key we kept hidden beneath a brick of concrete outside. I showed Miss Lovette where we kept that key. Then, when we were in the house, I showed her where I kept my clothes, and she grabbed underwear and socks by the handfuls out of the dresser drawer and put them in a paper grocery sack.

The house was dark without my father there. Without the TV on. And Miss Lovette seemed nervous. In a hurry. She seemed like a different woman than the one who taught my second-grade class — quicker, less polite than she was when she was at the school. There, she smiled and spoke in a high, singsong voice. Here, she looked harder, out of place. Her voice was low when she spoke.

We hadn't taken our coats or boots off, and scraps of gray slush melted onto the floor beneath us. Miss Lovette seemed to shiver in her bear coat. When she had two paper sacks of clothes and my toothbrush, she asked if I could think of anything else I might need that week, and I couldn't think of anything at all.

Maybe, then, Miss Lovette smelled old blood.

I was standing in the hallway when she turned to look at me. The house was quiet and gray-cold. Outside it was getting darker, and the sky looked thick with fog, Brillo blue.

At first she hesitated. But then she seemed to sniff the air and said, her voice still low and unfamiliar — as if she didn't want anyone to hear, although no one was there to hear — "Show me where you found your mother."

For a moment it was as if the wind had been knocked out of me by wind. As if someone had pushed my face into the freezer, fast. But I moved through the hallway of the house, blind, through a blizzard of quiet, and I opened the door to my parents' bedroom to show Miss Lovette what she wanted to see.

It was deep blue in there. The shades were pulled. The bed wasn't made. The imprint of my father's head was still pressed heavy into a pillow. Miss Lovette walked into the room with her mouth open.

Still, she seemed to be smelling.

I looked up at her face.

Miss Lovette's lips were wet, and she looked hungry. But her eyes were narrow. Like someone who imagined being kissed.

She went over to the bed and smoothed her hand across the rumpled sheet, then turned to me with her eyebrows raised and asked, "Here?"

I nodded, crossing my arms over my stomach, feeling empty. I remembered my bare bottom in the classroom when

Miss Lovette had pulled my underwear down and wiped it with a paper towel.

The other children had seen that, hadn't they?

They'd pushed their faces up against the glass to see it better.

I thought of my face, screwed up and puffy in the newspaper, the fuzzy photos making me look younger than I was and fading quickly away.

It was as if I were inside out. Nothing private, not even in my guts. Was I naked, I suddenly wondered, or wearing clothes? Maybe my dreams could be seen hovering above me in my sleep. Maybe my thoughts were all out loud. What difference would it make? Miss Lovette looked excited, sexual, and I remembered how most of the people at my mother's funeral I'd never even seen until that day. They weren't crying, either. Instead, they'd peered carefully over the edge of my mother's coffin. Curious, full of desire. They'd watched me, too, hadn't they? — though they'd looked away fast when I looked back.

And only a few days before, an older boy had cornered me on the playground and whispered, leaning into my face until I could smell waffles on his breath, "Your mother was naked with high heels on when he stabbed her and stabbed her."

How could he have known?

That boy made a stabbing motion toward my stomach with his fist while he said it, and I was exposed in my own clothes. Even with my coat zipped up.

"Is this the same bed?" Miss Lovette asked, looking down at it.

"Yes," I said.

She was breathing hard, touching it, and sniffing.

"I'm out of here tomorrow morning, Leila. You understand?"

"That's right," I look up, feeling a stab of anger, but it's dull. I say, "It's your life. It's your body." Then the anger's gone.

Rick nods. "That's right," he says, "and it's the same with you."

There's a barn owl outside somewhere. Or an old lady laughing. We get in bed as we always have, but Rick sleeps on his side all night, quiet and still for the first night in years. I keep my arms around him, my body curled like warping wood into his back.

I can feel his ribs.

I can feel his spine.

I can feel how cold the shoulder bones are under the thin skin, how simple what we're made of is.

I can feel where the bones are fused to one another.

Primitive.

Elementary as a kit.

He is a skeleton, after all. We all are.

I sit up in the dark to look at Rick's face, and it's all skull. A candle flickering behind his eyes, flickering out. I hold him in my arms all night, and he gets thinner and thinner in his sleep. Until, by morning, he's completely gone. Just some dust, a few dark hairs left on his pillow. T-shirt and boxer shorts lying without his body in them where his body had been the night before. Nothing in my arms.

I go to sleep again while the sun is coming up cold-steamy, pink against the tooth-rim of the sky, and when I wake it's two o'clock in the afternoon, and I'm going to be late for work. I hurry to take a shower in water so hot my skin itches afterward, red as meat, and I put a blue dress on over no underwear — a cotton dress with small pearl buttons and a full skirt. No hose. Flat black shoes. I can feel the dress against my nipples. Material slippery and close.

I open the bottom drawer of my dresser and take the money out of the jewelry box. I look at it, smell it — old green pages — and I wad it into my purse. Today, I think, I'll buy that flat white thing:

The thing that's flashed and receded like a horizon at the

back of my mind every day for months. A smoke signal. A flare. Something projected into the air. A missile. Or a weather balloon, moving slowly over the sky:

Vinyl. Chrome. A piece of bent sheet metal reflecting water, or snow.

Something carved out of soap, enlarged.

A sandblasted statue.

A slab of marble.

A huge bowl hollowed out of bone.

When I put the jewelry box back into the drawer, it feels light and empty in my hand. Then I hurry down the stairs and out into an afternoon as bright and vacant as my hope. Hopeless. Hopelessness.

There's even a hook of day-moon hanging coatless over me in the sky.

*H*E WAS THE BOY who'd known my mother was wearing high heels when she died.

He'd known that at first it had looked to me as if she were wearing a red slip pushed up above her breasts, but it was blood.

I must have told someone. Maybe the police. Maybe the detective who'd rocked me in his lap while I cried — though I didn't remember telling anyone that.

I was walking home from school when that boy caught up with me. It was a bright, cool March day. By then I was eight years old, and the boy must have been nine or ten. The snow had begun to melt, but the boy had a gray handful of what was left of the snow — bits of sticks and mud in it. He was wearing mittens and I wasn't. The boy grabbed the back of my coat and yanked me to him, pushing the handful of snow to my mouth.

At first I tried to spit it out, but I couldn't breathe, so I just let him keep the gloved handful of snow, finally, against my face. I opened my lips and let him shove it in, and I could taste it — dirty water melting against my teeth.

Later, in April, that boy would ask me to pull my shirt up in an empty garage, and I would do that, too. Passive, just the taste of old snow on my tongue. What difference did it make?

No part of me was private, I could tell. I'd heard someone say "sacred cow" on TV, and I imagined cows on thrones. Cows with gold shawls over their heaving sides, all animal breath and the dank smell of mashed grass in their mouths.

But the cows in the fields around Suspicious River weren't sacred at all, standing stiff as junked stoves and freezers at the dump under a plain white sun.

The garage where I took off my shirt for that boy smelled like garbage. An animal had gotten into it and clawed open a styrofoam container of old chicken. The thin bones of it littered the middle of a dried puddle of oil, and I stood for a long time with my shirt pulled over my small pink nipples — the place where I didn't have breasts yet, where I didn't even suspect I ever would.

The boy's mouth hung open. "Take off all your clothes," he said.

Behind him I could see two other boys watching us through the garage window. I took off all my clothes and let them fall around me like chicken feathers onto the greasy floor of that garage.

When I got home, my father said, "Hi, Leila sweetie," from the couch. He'd come home from the hospital after his accident dazed with pain, and now he was always home. Dull-eyed and groggy. No longer a salesman. One hundred percent disabled, the paperwork said.

"You're an hour late," Millie says, "I tried to call your apartment, but no one answered. I was just getting ready to call Mrs. Briggs."

"I'm really sorry," I lie, "I had car trouble. I ran out of gas."

"Well," Millie says. "Can you come in an hour early tomorrow to pay me back?"

"Of course," I say, "Sure. Of course." But I know full well that tomorrow is a blank — a wide, white, drive-in movie screen shut down in an abandoned field: some empty place you glimpse from the highway as you speed by. Tomorrow, I won't be in at all.

"I'm going home then," Millie says, still sounding angry. "Pretty dress." She nods at my dress, and I notice that Millie's hair is combed carefully and smooth today. She looks prettier, younger, than she's looked in a long time — as if her heart were pumping a bit more blood. Or like someone just coming out of a damp cellar after spending a week or two down there. "But aren't you going to get cold in that thin dress?" she asks, looking like a mother. Like my mother, I think, though Millie is younger than I am: My mother would be, too, I realize then with surprise, and I'm transfixed for a moment by Millie's skin, which glows. She purses her lips and says to me, "It's not summer anymore, you know. Did you even bring a sweater with you?"

"I don't care." I shrug, wanting to be honest.

She stops in front of me and looks sharp into my face. "Are you O.K., Leila? I don't want to get involved in your personal business, but people are talking about you, you know. It's only a matter of time before Mrs. Briggs hears about it."

I look more carefully at Millie, into her eyes, to see if she wants the truth or the lie. I want to tell the truth, but her eyes flicker away from mine and back, so I give her the lie. "I don't know what you mean," I say, and she looks relieved. She straightens her spine until she's taller than I am. I cross my arms over my breasts as if they're bare — loose and cool under the light cotton of the dress. I feel protective of them.

"Yeah you do," Millie says, bolder now that she knows I won't tell her what she doesn't want to hear. She slips her jean jacket over her plaid shirt, and I know she's glad I lied. It gives her sole ownership of the truth between us like a veil of white lace. Her veil, but I can see her through it. Her voice is thin and tight as an electric wire, though she isn't angry anymore. She says, "You're making some extra money around here with a lot of different men, and it's perfectly obvious to everyone why you're coming in here half dressed and you hardly ever answer the phone and your car is parked in the lot all day on your day off. But it's none of my business, Leila, and I don't give a damn about Mrs. Briggs and the Swan Motel. I just hope you'll be O.K. I hope you don't get hurt."

I shrug for her. I look at the clock. When she grabs my arm, I stare at her hard: I don't want to hear it, and I won't. I can tell by the turn of her mouth, the hesitant teeth, that she wants to say something about my mother. Something like *Do you want to end up like your mother?* Millie was a girl here when that happened, too, and no one ever forgets a thing like that.

But Millie can't say it.

Again, too true.

Then, a breeze over Suspicious River throws a handful of pebbles and branches on the roof of the Swan Motel. I imagine Millie's hesitant teeth are a handful of those small stones. She can't say anything with those.

She squeezes my arms. Under her breath, like a secret, she says, "I hope you don't get killed." And then she leaves.

After I put my purse under the counter, I dial 42.

"Yeah?" Gary answers.

"It's Leila."

"Hey precious. How's my baby?"

My pulse starts to beat like a tiny bird heart in my left wrist when he says that. I say, "I'm O.K. I'm here. I'm down here in the office."

"Great," Gary says. "I got somebody who wants to meet you. Why don't you get your pretty little butt up here?"

"I better wait," I say, opening the guest book. But there are only two reservations in it. "Oh," I say, "it's O.K. I'll be right there."

"That's my girl," he says, hanging up.

▼

It was after school. June. The trees had exploded like a can of green confetti, leaves shaking their streamers at the blue sky and air. There was a crescent moon rising up the horizon in the middle of the day like a dangerous kite.

I was seventeen, tired, a mediocre student in a small-town high school, headed, really, nowhere at all. I dressed simply, in pastels and short white socks, like a child, and looked even younger than I was. The kind of girl you might never have noticed if you didn't know that her mother had been stabbed to death by a lover, naked and bloody, in high heels, on a Tuesday night.

But it was a small town, and you'd have known it whether you wanted to know it or not. You might even have heard she'd been tied to the bed that night, that she'd liked it that way, that there were other men there when it happened.

Maybe the sheriff.

Maybe a high-stakes gambler from out of the state.

If you weren't at the funeral yourself, you'd have heard from someone who was there that Leila Murray never cried — even when they lowered her mother into the dirt.

Eerie. It had been eerie. As if that girl were in a trance.

If you'd been a teenager when it happened you'd have heard, and maybe even have believed, that a green light hovered over the cemetery every night. That a man from Chicago paid the local florist to leave a dozen fresh red roses on her grave every other day.

Someone might have told you that Bonnie Murray was a Playboy centerfold once.

Or that she'd been born in a whorehouse in New Orleans.

You'd have heard, maybe, that Leila had watched her being stabbed. That they'd made her lick her own mother's blood off the knife.

Sometimes, seeing that girl, awkward and small in her secondhand sweaters, seeming average as real life, you could barely believe all these stories about her mother. But there

was something else you'd know — from living in Suspicious
River so long:

That it's the ordinary-looking houses that aren't.

It's the good dogs that go mad on a Sunday afternoon in
April and tear an infant apart.

Only fences help. And keeping to yourself.

They said Jack Murray had cut off all his wife's black hair
before they buried her. He kept it in a Ziploc bag, and he slept
with that package of hair at night.

That day, I was walking in the direction of home after school
when a car pulled up beside me.

"Hey."

It was Greg Adams. His parents owned a laundromat, and he
had to work at it on weekends. Making change. Hitting the
coin slot hard with the heel of his hand when it was jammed.
Sometimes I saw him there on Friday nights when I went to
wash our towels and sheets, my father's socks and shirts, my
pastel sweaters gently. But Greg Adams had never spoken to
me before — just watched me, sometimes, or so it seemed,
while I folded, sorted, read a magazine. "Hey, Leila," he said
that day, "want a ride?"

"O.K.," I said, and I got into the blue Ford that belonged to
Greg Adams's father. I could smell an old cigar like a small
snuffed fire in there, and I could see clouds through the tinted
windshield, getting whiter and fatter as summer got closer.

Greg drove slowly, looking at me occasionally from the corner of his eye. He took the back roads, and there were purple
weeds back there in the swampy ditches, cattails lolling under
the blue sky, seeming to gag. He unrolled his window and I
could smell June like a fresh white bed — soapy, starched. A
film of lint, ash, stardust coated everything in sight, and when
we were halfway to my house, he stopped at the side of the
road, under some trees, and he swallowed.

Greg Adams was stocky, with a pale shaved beard. He

looked dumb, and his teachers believed he was, so he had a history of getting in trouble at school for doing nothing. He just seemed to bother the teachers, the way he'd look straight ahead at the chalkboard, taking no notes, his lips parted, clenching and unclenching the stubby pencil in his hands. His forehead was wide and always a little damp with sweat.

"Look," he said, "I — " He cleared his throat. "Some of the guys at school said you would do it." Then he looked at me, scared, pulling back a bit as if he thought I might hit him. I felt sad about that.

I leaned over and kissed Greg Adams with my eyes open. His mouth was small and sour, but he kissed back hard. He seemed timid when I started to take off my clothes, so I just leaned back and closed my eyes, as if I weren't there at all, so he wouldn't have to be shy. Above us, there was the sound of something hovering around the trees. The sound of scissors cutting cloth. Maybe the whacking blades of a helicopter.

He did what he wanted, and it didn't last long.

▼

"This is Leila," Gary says to a man who's drinking whiskey out of a plastic glass, sitting on the edge of the bed.

Gary is wearing the same blue work shirt, the same jeans. Blond boots. But his beard is fuller now. It makes his face look round, and less hard.

"Hi, Leila," the man says, standing up.

Gary kisses my neck, dry and quick, and says, "I'll go hang out in the office for you and make sure everything's cool, O.K.?" Then he looks at the man, who's running his fingers through his gray and spiky hair, "Take your time, but don't take too long. Right?"

"Right," the man says, winking at Gary.

Gary closes the door behind him in a short gasp of cooler wind.

The man's left eye wanders a little when he looks at me, I

think, but I'm not sure. He must be sixty. Thin and worried-looking. He might've been a shoe salesman, a minister, retired early, I think. He says nothing, but he feels all around my dress as if he's lost something in it, and there's something frantic about it, even when he pushes me back on the bed and pushes the dress up to put himself in. Then he bites at my lips like someone who's never kissed, and I think of Gary, in the office, looking after things for me, like a mother.

*T*HAT SPRING I'd often wander to the river. I was eleven, dreamy, and always cold — thin white-blue fingers. I'd be humming an improvised tune against my small white teeth, as if against a plastic comb. The tune was a bit like London Bridge, but slower, falling down. I held the sound of it on my tongue like a small music box buzzing in my mouth.

To see me walking down the sidewalk, scuffing my unlaced tennis shoes in the dirt, looking up at the sky, my long hair copper-colored and tangled by then, you might have mistaken me for a blind girl. Something missing. But you'd have known me, known I wasn't blind. You'd have remembered when my mother sang in the church choir, when they'd carried my mother out of the house like a feast laid out on a table under a long, white sheet. I'd walked by your house twice a day for months, even Saturdays and Sundays — as if no one had told me the school was closed. Leisure. Nowhere to go. Nothing in my hands — no books, no gloves — maybe making a loop around your half-dead pear tree, a sapling you planted years ago that got smaller and sicker every summer — just a fistful of blossoms now in the front yard and one tough, stunted pear per year. I'd lean back, holding on to the thin trunk, and sway around it like a Maypole. You'd have known who I was and exactly what was wrong. "That's Bonnie Murray's daughter," you'd say when you passed me in your car, windows rolled up tight on a brisk, silver, scalpel-sharp Saturday morning in early spring. "Poor little crazy thing, no coat in weather like this."

Sometimes I'd wander past the Shell station, and a man in an orange jumpsuit would come out of the glassed-in office and say, "Hi, Leila." Once, he gave me a quarter, and he winked as I turned it over and over on the tips of my fingers. That coin caught the lukewarm, northern spring sun like the flat wing of a jet.

"Going to the river?" he asked.

"Yep," I said.

"Down by the trestle?"

I nodded.

"It's nice down there," he said. "You have fun. Buy yourself some candy with that quarter. I know your daddy. I'll tell him I seen you if he comes by."

The man's orange jumpsuit was clean and stiff. He looked like a spaceman in it, smiling his gold tooth down at me like a little planet.

Late April, there were tulips pushing out of mud, shocking the ruined hair of the grass and the still bare branches with their scarlet lips, like plastic, or screaming, but beautiful, and new. The town seemed empty — a bright package with nothing in it — and the sun sailed over the neighborhoods like a hollow ball of pale fire, tossed. I walked.

Here, all the houses for blocks and blocks were the same. I'd know where to find the bathroom in any one of them. I'd know where the broom closet was. Here and there, an old bike had been left out through the winter, leaned up against a shed as if it had fallen out of the sky. A rusty drum of water. A hubcap. A shiny, white van with no one in it. A scrawny dog leashed to a tree growled suspiciously as I walked by.

I followed a muddy footpath to the river, which was high

and dark with melted snow by April, and I slid a little, inching down to the edge of it. A circle of gray birds flew over me. I heard train brakes far away. Steel on steel. A rat paddling. I stood and watched the river ripple by like a black stripe on a huge flag. A handful of brown leaves. A plastic sandwich bag. A ribbon of oil.

At first I thought it was a tree branch bobbing with the current — rising and falling, gray at first, then sinking, then emerging, sharp and white — tumbling past. Its face rose for a moment over the surface of the water, as if it were sniffing at the air — then it turned again, smooth, slow. Its hoof. Its bent leg. Then the blond fur on its back. Antlers again. Then the curious face, black nose nudging the surface until the surface broke. Looking out of the water's fissure with its dead eyes. The river rolled it past and away from me for a long time, and then I wanted to go home.

"The phone's been ringing," Gary says when I get back down to the office.

"Oh," I say, and smile. He's sitting on the vinyl couch, smoking. His teeth flash at me, cold-white in the white light.

It's warm in the office, and the sun outside is dry and brittle on the red leaves as they circle and fall in slow motion. A little dreamy, or hopeless. Gary's got one leg crossed over the other, an ankle on his knee, shaking his blond boot. I slide down next to him and put my arms around his neck, kiss his ear. It's dark and clean in that narrow tunnel. He holds the cigarette above my head and smells my hair.

"Look at me, baby." He nudges me back so I can see his face. "Look, you know you don't need this job. This job is just getting in our way."

I look around the office, and I can barely see it, having seen so much of it. I can smell the pink soaps in the bathroom, though — medical and sweet — and that man's flesh where it sweated into mine like a body of fog beneath my dress. I hear a swan honk by in the river. And the river, just sloshing, foamy, getting colder. On the wall, the clock hums and twitches its silver minute hand, and I think, *He's right. He's right.* I've barely glanced at the checks Mrs. Briggs has written to me in the last six weeks. They amount to nothing when I put them in the bank, which gives me only yellow squares of paper and numbers in return. I imagine a vault in the basement of that place, locked, with nothing in it — symbolic. Just the idea of money, of future, of invisible food and a weekend in a ghost town for vacation.

But the jewelry box in my bottom dresser drawer — that box had begun to bulge like a rat-fed snake, smelling moldy with old dollars, a tangible fact.

"I can't stay here much longer anyway," Gary says. "I can't afford no sixty dollars a night for the rest of my life."

I haven't even thought of that. "Gary," I say, happy to have something to give to him for free, "you don't have to pay for it. I'll just rip up the slip with your credit card number. No one will know but me." I smile. I kiss the top button of his shirt, and it tastes like plastic, smoke, and salt.

Gary nudges me back again to look at my face, or so I can see his. "You'd do that for me, baby?" he asks with his eyebrows raised, his brown eyes wide as a child's.

I laugh. "Of course." I kiss his lips smiling, my hands in his hair. I push my tongue between his teeth, to taste him deeper, and in my throat there is a small animal sound that surprises me when I do — a dove, or a cat nursing kittens. I hear the sound in my own throat as if it's come from someone else, but my heart is like that dove now, fluttering loose in my dress — pursued. Is that love? I want to take the dress off and wrap my naked body around him. I can barely stand to take my mouth from his; that's how in love I am.

"You'd do that?" he asks again.

And, again, I say, "Of course." I laugh, stand up, walk behind the counter. I open the cash drawer with the key Mrs.

Briggs keeps hidden naively on a magnet underneath the drawer. I sort through the credit card slips and receipts until I see his: Gary W. Jensen. I hold it up so he can see, then I rip it to shreds while he smiles.

Afterward, I lock the cash drawer and hide the key again, and Gary stands up and walks over to the counter. He puts his cigarette out in the ashtray, then reaches to take my hands. He squeezes them hard, and I lean as far toward him as I can with the counter between us, the sharp edge of it in my hips. He reaches out and takes my arms, and I cradle his elbows in my palms. Gary kisses me and moves one hand into the scooped neck of my dress, rubs the back of his fingers against my breast, and I breathe faster, pressing my kiss deeper into his, my nipples tightening until they're small and hard as the pearl buttons on my dress.

He leans back again, still with his hand against my breast, and says, "I love you, Leila."

A hundred frantic doves. Or pigeons. White wings flagging a white roof, rising. I say, "God, I love you, too."

He turns his hand on my bare flesh, squeezes the nipple between his fingers, and says, "You don't need this job no more, baby." My body buoys toward his as if my hips are strung to his with cobwebs and damp weather. There's snow somewhere on its way, I think. I open my mouth, and only a little gasp comes out.

He says, "You've got me."

"Can I just leave?" I ask him, widening my eyes until they water in the glare. "What about Mrs. Briggs?"

"Who gives a damn about Mrs. Briggs? She's gonna fire you if you quit?"

I laugh. He's smarter than I am, and older. A father. A sexy god. He pulls me closer to him, and I kiss his new, dark beard. Then he looks serious again. "We need cash, though, Leila. I'm runnin' low."

I shake my head and say, "No. I've got twenty-three hundred

dollars in my purse, Gary." I point to the purse. A splash of red under the cash drawer.

Gary stands up straighter then and smiles, surprised. "Whoa. Leila. You're a rich woman. What the hell we hangin' around here for, baby?" We both laugh.

He looks behind him. No one there. He lowers his voice anyway. "What about in there?" he asks, nodding at the cash drawer. I look at it over my shoulder while Gary's fingers circle my wrist — my wrist, which is laid out on the counter like a piece of white fish now, a little light blue where the blood rushes under the thin skin. "How much is in it?" he whispers.

"I don't know," I say, reaching underneath the drawer for the key.

When it's open, Gary says, "Looks like a lot."

"A few hundred, anyway," I say, touching the bills. They're soft. Then I glance at the tips of my fingers, as if the green dye might have come off.

"Let's take it, Leila," he says. "We're starting a new life, baby, and we need it. I'll pack my shit and meet you in the parking lot in ten minutes."

I breathe, nod. I say, "What about my car?"

"Leave it," Gary says. "You don't need it."

Without counting it, I gather the bills and hand the money to him. Gary unbuttons his shirt and slips them inside, next to his heart. He winks at me, pushing backwards out the glass door, looking heavier with cash.

When he's gone, I open the guest book again. For the last time, I think. *Monday October 17: Blackwell, L. Farr, C.*

I stare at that date.

October 17. My new life.

Like a carpet of stars. Pure time.

Monday.

It startles my eye in the guest book, like a white moth on a white flower. Cool and empty in my lungs and fifty million light years long. A galaxy. A sheet. The smell of bleach in a cool breeze.

When I hear high heels click by on the cement outside, I look up. But it's only just begun to rain — hard, fat drops on the sidewalk and on the windshields and on the bald garden rocks.

W HAT are you doing here, Leila?

The footpath was scattered with old leaves.

He stood in front of me.

Looking at the river, I said. A dead deer. A dead deer just swam by, did you see it tumbling in the black like a slow, blond dance?

I pointed, but it was gone. A branch again. A ripple. Nothing.

He laughed. His orange jumpsuit swelled with light in the sun.

Where's your daddy, Leila?

He's waiting for me. At home. I've been gone too long.

Does he know where you are?

No. He doesn't know. I have to hurry.

Not so fast. He doesn't know where you are?

No. He'll be worried. My father's waiting.

Wait.

The river didn't notice.

The shiver of a sapling.

Over there, the willows milled around like restless men.

I ran to them. My arms open. I ran and ran in the wrong direction, mud sucking at my shoes. A child trying to fly —

stupid, wingless bird. Mud on my hands, oily as blood. The earth kiss of mulch in my copper hair. I fell down there.

Randy McCarthy buttoned up his shirt in the back of his mother's station wagon.

"I don't get Rick," he said, shaking his head in the dark. His hair was white-blond, cut close to the scalp, and it glowed like a smudged halo on his head. "He doesn't have a clue, and nobody tells him shit. It's pathetic. And he *married* you. Man. He thinks you're the fucking Virgin Mary or something, doesn't he?"

I pulled my sweater down over my face. "No, he doesn't," I say — quick but flat, like a lie. "Rick knows me."

Randy McCarthy laughed. "A fucking nympho Virgin Mary is more like it."

When he said that, I swallowed. Someone had written it on the wall of the girl's bathroom in black Magic Marker that never washed off — two years before, and on my last day of high school, it was still there between the mirror and the dirty roller towel:

Leila Murray is a Nimphomaniac.

For two years the girls I went to high school with, crowded around with their hairbrushes and lip glosses, adjusting the cups of their bras, tugging up their beige pantyhose like a second skin on their legs, would go silent when I came in and washed my hands right under that black sentence.

Randy McCarthy was always angry afterward. All hands when we were in the back seat, like a raccoon ravishing the frozen garbage with its little human claws, looking skillful and sweet, then slinking off, body close to the ground, bandit mask making its long face look mean.

Most of the high school boys were like that. Winter lasted a long time in Suspicious River — child-sized chunks of ice dragging along the banks, knocking at the docks and the aluminum rowboats tied to them rusting and unused. Most of the girls in town were afraid of their fathers, who shot deer in the woods and strung them up in back yards before the first snow, or they were afraid to get pregnant, or they wanted to marry someone who owned a store. They couldn't relax — always complaining, fidgeting with their clothes, straightening their skirts down over their thighs, yanking their bra straps back over their shoulders.

But I was quiet, hovering ten feet above my body all the time. Maybe being with me was no different than being alone. You could be as mannerless afterward as you wanted. Maybe that was my appeal. Or was it what made them angry?

Randy dropped me off a few blocks from the house and didn't say anything when I got out. It was mid-June, a pulse of stars in the dark overhead. I looked up at those and thought I saw a few fall fast through the sky. But it might have just been my eyes.

The light in the Schmidts' house was yellow when I got to the back door, and Mrs. Schmidt was gluing something together on the kitchen table. A ceramic ballerina. "Look." She held it up for me to see when I stepped in. "Look what the cat did."

The delicate head, hair tied back with a pink painted ribbon, had snapped right off, and I could see into the ballerina's body through the splintered crack at her throat. Inside, she was hollow and pure white. Mrs. Schmidt laughed and put the bottle of glue back down on the table. "It's hopeless," she said. "Oh well. Who cares? Sweetheart, did you eat?"

"Yes," I said, "I ate."

"Well, Rick and his dad are probably having McDonald's as we speak. They rented a trailer and went into Ottawa City to haul an old pinball machine to the dump. I guess they might not be back until midnight, so I ate a salad myself."

Rick's mother picked at salads for lunch and for dinner, even when she'd roasted beef for her husband and son. It would seem the green leaves had only been rearranged by a finicky rabbit when she was done. But at night, in the quiet dark, while we were all in bed, I could hear her rummage through the kitchen, illuminated only by the refrigerator's private light. I imagined, from Rick's bedroom where I pretended to be asleep, that Mrs. Schmidt was in her bare feet, a white nightgown, her graying beehive looking as if it were wound with frost in that light, eating vanilla ice cream from the carton with a cold spoon. Then she'd slip back into bed beside Mr. Schmidt, who slept like death beside her. She'd be cold as snow between those white sheets, and in the morning, she'd be innocent at the kitchen table again, sipping at her black tea while Rick and his father ate the greasy bacon and eggs she made for them.

This trick was similar to the silent art, the sleight of hand, by which she could tell them what to do — those two big men — without ever opening her pink mouth. The way Rick would change his shirt if his mother looked at it a certain way. He'd emerge from the bedroom with another one on, buttoning, asking, "Does this one look O.K.?"

"You're not hungry, then?" she asked me.

"No," I said, "I'm fine. But thank you for asking."

It was warm in the house. The windows were closed, and the rain that was on the way would not blow in under the cracks, as it always had in my father's house. The windows were secure, sealed as if by a law of physics my father hadn't understood. Mr. Schmidt fiddled around with the doors and the storms every weekend, it seemed. Patching the screens. Making sure nothing squeaked.

"Are you sure you're fine? You look tired, Leila."

"No," I said, "I'm fine."

"Sit with me a minute, dear. I want to tell you something."

I liked Mrs. Schmidt, but I didn't want to sit with her in that small, clean kitchen, sharp as a cube. My legs ached. I could still feel Randy McCarthy around my shoulders, like a bracelet of bruises cuffing my upper arms. I could smell him — a

little boozy, a little like his car — exhaust fumes. Old Milwaukee. Still, I sat down. Mrs. Schmidt's eyes were dark like
Rick's, but her eyelashes were pale. She'd retained her prom
queen's smile. Despite the graying hair, you could picture her
in a pink satin dress. Or twirling a baton. The prettiest and
friendliest girl in the school. Someone you wouldn't swear
or smoke around, but who wouldn't condemn you out loud if
you did.

The ceramic ballerina lay broken on the kitchen table between us, utterly submissive now, and on her side. Her pretty
face wasn't ruined, but it was useless. Little pinprick eyes.
Rosebud mouth, pouting. Separated from her body by a few
inches of pure and invisible air. Beneath us, the guilty cat,
white, purred and snaked around our ankles.

Mrs. Schmidt reached across the table and squeezed my
hand. She inhaled and said, "I know how hard it must be for
you right now, being married, and so young. But things will
get better." She opened her eyes wide — exclamation points
— "And Rick loves you *so much*. He's a good boy, like his
father, and he'll always take care of you. And so will I." Mrs.
Schmidt smiled that high school smile then, which reminded
me of women on the covers of *Ladies' Home Journal*, the faces
of those models on the racks at the grocery store checkout line
— models chosen for their ordinary beauty, meant to imply
you could be me. Under her smile, in bold letters, HOW TO
TELL IF YOUR HUSBAND LOVES YOU and *One hundred
new cookie recipes!* Mrs. Schmidt's teeth looked like white
thumbtacks, blunt and rounded, or dulled, stuck carefully into
her gums, and she smiled wider. "You're my daughter now."

"Thank you," I said, but I was breathing too hard. "Thank
you, Mrs. Schmidt. I feel so happy." I touched my heart when I
said it, as if I had something to prove. My ears were ringing,
but the only real sound in that kitchen was the refrigerator's
drone, its bad imitation of a busy hive of bees. "I need to go to
bed," I said, my voice getting higher, and I stood up. My hands

had gotten cold, and I couldn't feel them anymore, as if they'd broken clear of my body.

Mrs. Schmidt stopped smiling, and the ballerina rolled onto her back without being touched. She said, "Sweetheart, you're sure you're all right?"

"I'm fine," I said, "I'm just so tired."

"Well, Leila, I was going to say that I'd be honored now if you would call me Mom." She took my hand again, and I was embarrassed that it was like ice. I nodded. I tried to smile, and Mrs. Schmidt let it go.

When I got back to Rick's room I pulled the shades, took off my clothes all at once, and threw them on the bed. My period had started. Dark red clots like ruined fruit. I went to the bathroom and ran cold water in the sink for a long time, cleaned myself up, rinsed out my panties, and then I went back to bed, waiting for sleep or for Rick in the silence, just as his mother on the other side of the wall waited for her husband, her son, her own dreams, her secret feast waiting for her in the kitchen when she thought we were asleep.

But I could smell my own blood in the dark. Old blood coming back to me once a month. My mother's long white legs. A cup of blood. Communion. I could smell the red silk slip of it between my legs, and I knew I wouldn't sleep all night.

▼

As we pull out of the parking lot of the Swan Motel in a blue, muggy rain, I look back at my rusty car, the white Duster that belonged to Rick's father, its muffler dragging the road behind it for years, sparking the dark like an old tail. I say good-bye under my breath, and Gary squeezes my thigh. He says, "I like it that you don't have any underwear on, Leila."

I smile with my lips over my teeth because they feel cold. Or maybe I feel shy, staring straight ahead.

He chuckles and says, "You're a wild one — especially for

such a quiet little thing." He touches me between the legs, and I don't move. It feels like nothing there. He glances at his hand and says, "Jesus. We're gonna be happy as hell, sweetheart."

I close my eyes and feel his hand on me, feel the road float under us like a river, the rainy sky float lower over us like a river, too, and my body floating in slow motion between those rivers of road and sky with Gary, fast, sweeping toward my new life, which waits like a mother at the end of a long, white tunnel of light.

L EILA, does your father know where you are?"

The taller one blocked out the sun behind him, scraping the sky, before he knocked me to the ground, and the human trees moved in, breathing.

The younger one might only have been sixteen. Maybe he was scared.

He also knew my father.

He fixed our car.

He was wearing a cowboy hat, a stiff black one, and it made him pale. He didn't take it off. His upper lip was prickly and blond, and he had a small scar in the middle of it, skinny and white as a worm.

The older one knew what he was doing, maybe even why. But the younger one seemed embarrassed about his penis, hands cupped over it after he pulled down his pants. He fumbled for a long time. I cried out for my father again, but neither one of them would look at my face. The older one looked out across the river like a man surveying what he deserved to own, angry that he didn't.

Those men know.

Those men smell all the girls around them as they pass with their pink fingernails and ankle socks, schoolbooks pressed to their chests. Those men put their noses to the breeze and they know which girls will always run in the wrong direction, every time. Which ones will never tell a soul, shame snaking a thin blue thread through their veins; they're just surprised to be left alive. Not grateful, certainly, not willing, but familiar with the customs in that bad part of the country, that fat wasteland. The currency, the dull thud of a fist, or a penis, or a mouthful of mud.

The older one was teaching it to the younger one. The way they do. Next time he'd be able to smell it out for himself.

A pheasant with birdshot in her belly, but still alive.

A nest of rabbits.

A girl watching the river unravel.

Next time he'd know, too.

"Leila. Are you asleep?"

I open my eyes.

"We're here, baby." Gary smokes a cigarette beside me in the Thunderbird — coffin of silver and glass. Pure light. He says, "This is where I live."

It's a small white house with aluminum siding. There's a long, cab-yellow car in the driveway, and a line of trees in the front yard, blind with red leaves — luxurious skirts rustling in an adamant wind. The rain has stopped, and the sun cracks behind the clouds, snuffed, and the clouds make a tunnel between the earth and sky — low and purple. The house is at the end of that tunnel, at the end of a gravel road with no other houses around it, just the chaos of a vegetable garden that's done for the summer, all blond stalks now, a collapsed sunflower, and a slow-rising hill behind it. A row of pines, and what must be the river in back of that, slipping through the mud and bushes like a wet knife. The ground is littered with leaves, scarlet and wild.

Someone parts a curtain inside the house and looks out, but the window is too dark to see the face. From a white birch, peeling its bark like bandages near the front stoop, a thin black hound strains at its chain, snapping at the air in silence toward us. The birch shudders a little each time the dog lunges; yellow leaves drift onto the windshield and a few stick to the dog's sleek back.

Gary says, "Let's go in."

My legs feel cold and weak when I step out of the car, and I realize I'm wearing nothing but a summer dress with pearl buttons, and winter's on its way. The telephone line stretches loose and swaybacked from the house, and a crow lifts off of it, beating its big wings hard against the weather, which will be raw and magenta from now on — until winter finally smothers it over with nothing and snow.

The dog sniffs in our direction. As we walk across the yard, I keep my arms crossed over my chest to protect it, but the wind just cuts right through my dress and handles what it wants. I'm numb and scorched, like freezer burn, before we even get to the door.

But, inside, the house is warm and dark. The man who'd looked out the window is wearing a down jacket, jeans, and boots like Gary's, only newer. His hair must've been black once, but it's thin now. A gold tooth glints when he smiles.

"Hey Rob. This is Leila." Gary puts his arm around me and squeezes. "She's my sweetheart."

Sweetheart, I think. I like the word. I like it better than the words *wife, daughter, mother.* I imagine my heart as a sticky, red dessert.

"Nice to meet you, Leila," Rob says, holding his palm in my direction. His hand is dry and cold, and he passes over mine lightly with it.

The living room smells like old wool, or a dog. A plaid couch. A TV with a wide black screen. A La-Z-Boy, a newspaper folded on that. Someone has done half the crossword puzzle in pencil. A coffee table with a coffee cup, a glass ashtray, a stack of *TV Guides*. In the hallway that must lead to the bedroom, I see a child's red-sparkle tricycle. Shiny, with white plastic streamers on the handlebars. When the dog in the front yard starts to howl, I look out the window at it.

"Don't mind him," Rob says. "He smells something. Probably a rabbit, or a cat."

But the dog is throwing itself into the distance beyond its chain, snapping and staring at it — the chain jerking him back, strangling him back. The dog circles under the chain to escape it, howling and frantic, chewing at the air, before it lunges and chokes, and chokes again.

$\mathcal{T}$HE WIND RAGED THAT DAY, lifting a blizzard off the lake, scissoring it across the sky over Suspicious River, then shredding it to scraps of white. Only a few skiers were staying at the Swan Motel, and they looked windburned in their colorful jackets, seeming healthy and rich. I liked the job. I'd only just started, and I was serious, careful. I added the credit card totals twice on squares of scrap paper before I wrote them permanently on the carboned slips. When guests opened the glass door and stepped into the office, a gust of December trailing them like frozen smoke, I said, "Welcome to the Swan Motel."

Inside, the office air tasted sleepy and warm, like a mouthful of blanket or toast. Somewhere deep in the coils of the electric heater, an old bed seemed to be smoldering nicely, its fibers settling in my lungs.

The door opened then, jangling its bells, and Rick and his mother stepped in — shyly, it seemed, smiling weakly at me. Mrs. Schmidt's hair was covered with a white wool scarf, and she wore an old, loose coat, colorless against the glass behind her. Her lips were pale pink as the bathroom tiles, and Rick, beside her in his father's hunting jacket, washed her in an exhaustion of electric orange. Seeing them in the office of the Swan Motel, I realized how ordinary and unathletic they looked in comparison to the guests who usually stood in front of that desk — my teenage husband and his mother, where there'd been those skiers in their slick purple jackets, sunglasses reflecting the drywall, blizzards, and my own pale, melting face in plastic as they scanned their bills.

"Hi," I said.

"Hi, Leila," Rick said, lifting his hand into the air. It looked enormous in a black glove. His mother's eyes were wide, as if she might cry, but she smiled. They walked together toward the counter, their faces disturbingly similar and familiar, and I saw them as they were. Humble, useful people. Foreign to me, but mine. I knew I didn't love them, didn't even really know them, but somehow, now, we all belonged to each other. Discovering their faces suddenly at the center of my life was like finding a box of someone else's snapshots in your attic: None of these aunts and uncles smiling intimately into the camera is yours, none of these happy holidays, these puffy infants. But if you don't keep them now, you'll have less than you had before you found them. Something will always be missing. Something that claimed you, as if it could enter your memory, your life, and then it did. I realized at that moment, *This is what family is.*

"Leila," Mrs. Schmidt spoke to my throat. "We need to call Mrs. Briggs and tell her you have to leave."

"Why?" I could hear snow being plowed outside, thrown heavy, human, and wet to the side of the road.

"There's an emergency," she said.

Rick grabbed my hand then, and when I tried to pull it back, his glove slipped off between us on the counter, empty. He opened and closed his small white fist beside it like something immodest, exposed.

"What?" I put my hand under my breasts, over the place where my ribs met each other in a bony seam. "What?" I could feel my heart beat soft and bloody behind that seam.

But the tin bells shook on the door then, and two skiers

stepped in — a woman with long blond hair and an orange tan and a man with a red hat who looked much older. Her father, I thought, though his hand was making small circles on her hipbone as she leaned into him, looking drunk, or stunned, or stoned. Or, maybe she was in love. The blizzard melted fast on their shoulders, and the slippery sound of their jackets became louder as they walked toward the counter. They laughed while, outside, the snow buried the sky.

Gary opens a door from the hallway, and I follow him into a yellow bedroom. The double bed isn't made, but the sheets are bright. They look as if they've only been slept in once, by someone very tired. The curtains are open and through them I can see a small storm of wet, gold leaves spin in a violet wind. When he flips the light switch on, the room throbs and the windows go dark.

"Here," he says. "Just relax in here. I've got to go to town, and when I come back we can get some dinner." He kisses me quickly, his fingers on my jaw. In the bathroom on the other side of the wall, I can here someone — Rob? — whistling. There's the insistent knock of hot water in old pipes.

As he leaves, Gary's boots thud on the floor. I watch his back. His dark hair over his blue collar. His narrow shoulders. From the back, in those jeans, in that work shirt, I imagine he could be any thin man from Texas, though I've never been to Texas and still don't know if it's where he's from. Florida license plates, I remember. But the accent. Beneath his boots the floor sounds solid and dead. No basement, I think. He closes the door hard, and my mouth goes dry. I close my eyes tight, knowing I'd wait in this yellow room all night, or forever, for another taste of his sweat.

I swallow with love as he disappears, and I turn the light in the bedroom out, crawl into the bed, pull the sheets and a scratchy white blanket over my ears, and roll onto my side. From there I can see out the window. I can see him get into his silver Thunderbird, face lowered against the wind — the wind, which sounds like an old train rushing by before he closes himself into the driver's side. I watch his headlights, then his taillights, a trail winking away — night around his car like a silky cave. I imagine a red scarf unraveling from my heart, pinned to his, and then he's gone.

I don't look around this room. I close my eyes. But already, by accident, I've seen a photograph of a woman and a child, both blond and smiling, on the nightstand. The photo is framed in black. A string of green plastic beads has been stretched out carefully on the dresser, and the lampshade has a chain of rosebuds hand-painted around the edges. I can smell a woman, all water and flesh, beneath the sheets, and the white feathers in the pillows smell like perfume, sage, a plucked, feminine bird. I hear the wind outside pick up, die, then lift itself again, higher this time.

I open my eyes and close them, and then I'm dreaming. Then, I'm walking up the front walk to my childhood house through a shaft of snow. A dog howls. The sound of breathing in a tunnel. Something has been tossed or has fallen at the end of the walk, near the front step of our house with its blank face. A white sleeve flaps like a tongue of light.

I bend down to see it, but all I see is my own face reflected in an icy pool, looking younger than I am, and suddenly I realize I must be someone's child. A dog howls again, and when I wake up, the light is on, and Rob is standing at the foot of the bed, smiling kindly, his gold tooth gleaming.

"I'm sorry I woke you up. Is it O.K.?" he asks, touching the top button of his shirt apologetically. "Gary said it would be okay. But if it's not, don't worry, I won't bother you."

"It's O.K.," I say and close my eyes again.

▼

"Leila," Mrs. Schmidt said, pressing my hand when we were finally out of the Swan Motel and into the car, driving, heater humming, the night parting around us as we traveled deeper into it, "Your father had a heart attack. He was shoveling snow."

"Oh," I said.

I was between them in the front seat of Mr. Schmidt's long Ford. Rick put an arm around my shoulder. I leaned forward, pressing my mittens against the lids of my eyes. Stars and blood. I could see my father against that sparking, red velvet backdrop — snow falling fast, rising around him, and he was moving too slow through it with his dead leg to escape. I saw his mouth frozen open, icing over like a small, safe lake. Two little blizzards in his blue eyes.

▼

I taste mint on Rob's gold tooth. Though the skin on his arms is lax as an old man's, his chest is hairless as a boy's and he seems cold, or ashamed, slipping his clothes off onto the floor fast, hurrying into the bed with his arms crossed over his bald stomach. He wants me to move on top of him, and I do, slipping my arms around his neck, my mouth pressed into the pillow near his head. He pulls the blanket up over us, and it's warm with him under it. While he rubs one hand up and down my spine, the other searches softly across my breast. I kiss his neck and imagine it's Gary's neck, but shaved soft as candle wax or plastic.

"That's right," he says, pushing my hip against him with his hand. I feel my heart beat harder between us. "Oh you're so sweet," he says, holding onto me.

Rob whimpers when he comes, and I don't let go until I'm done, too. He stays quiet under me, hands slow over my body as I press my pelvic bone against his. Two skeletons under our skin. And I remember Gary pressing into me with his clothes on at the edge of the river. How I'd been trapped, burning, beneath him, as if he were an avalanche. My eyes, full of white.

Afterward, I curl into Rob's bony chest and fall asleep again, but dreamless this time, with wind and clouds parting their curtains around the bed in this strange dark, in the twenty-fourth October of my life. The one with the weather my mother never rose from, dank and velvet with death.

*T*HE FUNERAL DIRECTOR wore plaid pants and a green golf shirt in the middle of December, and, in the basement where they displayed the coffins, he looked wildly alive. A parrot in a leafless tree.

"This is our least expensive," he said, lifting his soft palm toward a gray one with a dark blue pillow built right in. Comfortable looking. Something you could sleep in one long night for the rest of your life.

But I said "No," and pointed at a glamorous white one like the one my mother had been buried in. It was quilted in white satin. Silver hinges. It looked like an elaborate ice chest, and I could imagine my father in it under the ground as if he were a trunk of gems. My mother the Snow Queen beside him in her pearls:

In the winter they'd be frozen into opalescent statues. In the summer they'd explode together with white petals on black branches, pushing out of the dirt.

"That's typically a woman's coffin," the funeral director said, "and it's twenty-three hundred dollars more than our standard model" — but he was writing a number onto a piece of paper. He looked up and smiled. "Though I can certainly see why you might prefer that particular box for your father. It's really lovely."

"Fine," I said.

"Can you drop your father's suit off later tonight?"

"I think so," I said. "I'm not sure where it is."

The funeral director looked worried about that. He said, "If it needs dry cleaning, there will be an extra charge I'm afraid," and he made an extra note on the paper with his yellow pencil. The fluorescent tubes of light droned and burned above us.

It was cool and dry down there. Not like an ordinary basement. Not like being under the earth. The coffins smelled like plastic, or brand-new cars. There were ten of them in different colors, sizes, styles. One was no larger than an infant, and it was also white. Upstairs, Rick waited with his parents, and I could hear someone pace above our heads, muffled by the ceiling tile and a furnace duct wrapped up like a mummy in gray, asbestos bandages.

"To whom will I be billing this?" the funeral director asked.

"To Leila Murray," I said. "Leila Schmidt, I mean." And my old name drifted past him, something erased, before settling like chalkdust in my father's bright, new coffin.

I wake up in Rob's arms when Gary says, "Well look at the little lovebirds."

Rob wakes then, too, and sits up. Gary's brow is pale in the dark of the doorway, and a cold oval of air blows over his shoulder, passes us, rises into the yellow ceiling above the bed — an invisible balloon with winter in it.

▼

We went to get my father's suit. The house was dark and cold, not like the Schmidts', where I'd lived since June. There, I'd gotten used to the claustrophobic smell of dinner cooking day and night, or having just been cooked. Boiled down to something soft. And the gold light that comes from a dim lamp in a living room on a winter night.

Here, it had never been like that, even before my mother

died. I remembered my uncle in a sleeveless T-shirt and underwear standing in the doorway of my parents' bedroom, shivering. "Damn," he'd said, "it's always freezing in here."

It was my uncle I saw standing there, frozen, when Rick and I went back to that house to get the suit to bury my father in. "Bonnie," he was saying, "Turn up the goddamn heat."

I saw her walk naked toward him with her arms open, nipples tight and pink. "Here it is, Andy. Here it is." The heat, she meant.

My father's suit looked out of fashion in his closet, and never worn.

"Here it is," I said, holding it out to Rick.

He wouldn't enter the bedroom. Maybe he could feel them in there, too. My mother under the sheets in black panties and a black bra. My uncle's fingers hurrying over the lace and hooks. A river of blood swelling under them like Indian mounds, then drying. Just a bed of red clay now, the color of a barn. And now, my father, too, was finally and completely gone.

*H*E LOOKED ANGRY in his coffin for the first time in his life. It was the way his eyebrows had fallen together, relaxed in death. In life, he'd kept them raised in an expression of humble confusion, always, as if he might be saying "I'm sorry," even as he watched his wife sail into the distance with his younger brother, waving her bikini top in blanched air — a mirage, disappearing, then reappearing, smaller, gleaming, until she was just a spool of glitter on electric water. The whole time, those eyebrows raised in apology.

But in his blue suit in that white casket, hands waxy over his stomach, eyes closed, with that new expression at his brow, my father no longer looked as if he forgave us all. He looked like a man you might be a bit afraid of if he were alive. Someone who'd died shoveling snow after shoveling snow his whole, long life, and who was finally bitter about it. After Reverend Roberts said what he had to say about dust to dust, Rick's mother squeezed my shoulder as she peered over the flashy rim of the coffin, a treasure chest full of my father's death. "He loved you," she said.

The church was decorated with holly and red ribbons for Christmas, and it smelled like pine needles and melted wax. Only two pews in the front row were filled, and they were filled with Rick's uncles and aunts, cousins, second cousins, his grandmother — a skeleton herself, bent over a silver cane, resembling a mummified bat: brittle, black wings pulled in around themselves. She smiled ecstatically whenever she caught my eye, waving all her bony fingers at once in the air, as if, with them, she were imitating the way snow falls — fast and scattered.

None of them had known my father, but they didn't look at their watches during Reverend Roberts's sermon. They stared straight ahead, politely, into the dim light that skimmed and glinted off his too-bright coffin. They were there for Rick, who belonged to them.

Afterward, Mrs. Schmidt had everyone over for ham sandwiches with Miracle Whip on small brown buns that tasted grainy, dark as a harvest, as if they'd been buried a long time, dug up, warmed in a toaster oven. And each of Rick's relatives touched my hand and said, "I'm sorry."

The women in Rick's family had shiny, sprayed hair and wore navy blue dresses with crocheted collars, or manufactured lace, and white hose. Their husbands looked winded and uncomfortable in ties, and each one looked at least a bit like Rick. Thick, black hair. Brown eyes. But among them, Rick looked large, like someone trying too hard to blend into a crowd. There was something exaggerated about the way he shook their hands when they said they were sorry and congratulations at the same time. Sorry that his father-in-law had died. Congratulations on his recent marriage. Each time someone said it, Rick looked surprised, as if he'd been the last to hear about these changes in his life. As if they'd been arranged for him while he was out of town.

And Rick was the only one who didn't kiss his grandmother on her spotted lips, pretending she wasn't insane. He couldn't even seem to look at her, but his cousins would say, "Yes, Grandma," when she asked them if Rupert, her husband, dead for decades, had carved the turkey yet. "Of course," when she asked them if the mortgage papers had been thrown onto the fire, then "No, no," when she looked alarmed. But when the old woman fixed her eyes on Rick, when she said "Rick" and touched the air in his direction with her pale hand, he pretended he didn't hear — though there was a film of sweat on his upper lip, like mist.

Gary leaves the light on but shuts the bedroom door behind him when he leaves. I hear his boots back down the hall, and Rob sits up at the edge of the bed, slipping his black socks on over his bald feet.

It has grown darker while we've been asleep — pewter blue now — and it smells like winter on the way. Wet feathers, rags, old apples fermenting, turning to soft brown bruises on the ground as it gets harder. The light makes the yellow walls of the bedroom shine slick as lemon skin or sherbet, and I hear a voice drifting in from the living room. At first I think it's the television, but then I hear Gary ask a question and someone else answers. A woman. Then I hear her scream, "What the hell are you bringing your whores around my house for?"

Rob leans over me then with his elbows on either side of my face, kissing me with his dry lips. "Don't worry about her," he says, sitting up again. But he doesn't explain. He finishes putting on his clothes, tucks his white shirttail into his jeans, pulls his boots on and tugs the pant legs down over them. Then he blows me a kiss and shuts the bedroom door behind him. Still, I hear her voice rise and fall on the other side. A wind instrument. Someone practicing a clarinet. Sounding frantic, but no words to go with it.

▼

A few days after my father's funeral, Mrs. Schmidt said, after breakfast, after Rick and his father had left for the day, stum-

bling together across the back yard to Mr. Schmidt's car, taking long steps through the deep snow in their big boots, "You
need to think about your father's house now, Leila. You need
to think about selling it. Or renting it out. It shouldn't sit
empty very long."

A silver sun had risen that morning in a clear sky, surprising
and blinding us all. I'd thought of my father in a drawer at the
morgue: It was too late, or too early, in the winter to bury
him, they'd said, and I imagined him in his blue suit on a
slab in the dark. Perhaps he would be startled back to life
when they pulled him out again into the glare of those lights.
A thin, hibernating bear without fur. His white coffin, in stor-
age, would be unbearably bright. The way my own eyes could
barely open in the glare of that new day, after so many weeks
of gray.

"Maybe we should go over there today, Leila, and at least
bring in the mail. Do you want to do that, honey?"

I nodded. "I'll do that," I said.

"I'll go with you," Mrs. Schmidt offered as she brushed toast
crumbs into her palm. She kept a clean kitchen, decorated
with flowers and swans. Thick, pink sashes held the curtains
apart like braids, or arms, tacked to the window frames. Mrs.
Schmidt had never seen my father's house, and I could already
imagine the look on her face when she saw that kitchen.
Naked.

"No," I said, "I'd rather go by myself."

Mrs. Schmidt asked over and over if I was sure, and I was.

▼

When Gary comes back into the bedroom, I have my blue
dress on again, my knees pulled into my chest, my back
against the pillow, my feet under the sheet. He has a beer for
himself and one for me, just like the first time, when he'd
made the joke about my job, that I couldn't drink on duty but I
could have sex with strangers — the time he'd slapped me,

twice, across the face, and I'd heard something with silver wings fly over the Swan Motel.

"Thank you," I say when he hands it to me. The bottle's smooth and green. The glass numbs my hand as I hold it.

Gary sits at the edge of the bed with me, and he fingers my knee, pushes the dress over it to touch the bare, blank face of the knee itself.

"Look," he says, "I have to tell you something." He stares straight ahead at the yellow wall as he says it, and I watch the side of his face. Under his thicker beard, I can no longer see the bones of his jaw. No trace of the scar, like an earthworm buried back in the earth. He draws a breath. "Look," he says, "my wife is here, and she wants me to go back to her place with her tonight. To see our boy. You understand?"

He looks into my eyes, and I nod.

"I'll be back as soon as I can." He smiles. He says, "I love you," and he closes his eyes when he kisses me.

My own are open. There is a bright flash from his wrist-watch. 8:12.

He turns the light off when he leaves, and I sit up in the bed, in the yellow dark.

My new life, I think. Right now, I should be behind a counter at the Swan Motel. Instead, I'm here — headlights rising and falling against a stranger's bedroom window and the ink-wet sky, wavering and radiant as UFOs or saints. I hear the woman's voice once more, a syllable, in the front yard. She says, "Wait." Boots through leaves. The dog is running free, now, with his chain dragging against the ground. The sound of damp air in and out of its lungs. Then nothing. Rob must have gone, then, too.

I finish the beer, every drop. There is something comforting in the last sip of something bitter. My own apartment seems far away. The car, the rusty Duster. The Swan Motel. This is like being born again. At the very bottom of the bottle, the beer tastes sweetest — sugar and amber on the back of my throat. Some harvest long ago, melted. A whole bronze season in it. A farmer with a pitchfork smiling beside his sour wife.

I wait a little longer before I stand up from the bed, open the door, look down the dark hall into the dark emptiness beyond it, and step out.

*T*HERE WERE ANIMAL TRACKS in the driveway where my father had collapsed — his heart squeezing shut, I imagined, with the sound of rusty hinges on a cellar door.

Cat feet. Hundreds and hundreds of them in the snow. The glare of the bright sun on those paw prints made them shimmer like new coins — coins and diamond chips scattered all over the snow in the spot he'd died. Someone had propped his shovel up against the fender of his car.

Coming into the house out of so much light, my eyes could barely adjust, but when they did, I saw nothing I didn't already know was there. I could have kept them closed.

I got on my knees and touched one of my father's bedroom slippers. It was under the kitchen table. Old and plaid. Still warm, I thought, before I realized it couldn't possibly be. I smelled it, but there was nothing other than rubber sole in there. I'd forgotten why I was in my father's house. The slipper felt foolish against my heart, where I held it, so I put it back on the floor. Then I remembered the mail.

The box was stuffed with it, all junk. MR. JACK MURRAY, YOU MAY ALREADY BE A MILLIONAIRE. Mr. Jack Murray, subscribe to *TV Guide* now and get seven issues FREE!

But, slipping between the slick pizza coupons, there was an

envelope that felt small and plain in my hand. I turned it over. It was addressed to Miss Leila Murray in black felt pen.

"Hi," he says when I step into the living room, and it startles me. It's been so quiet, and I hadn't heard anyone pull into the driveway. He's sitting in the La-Z-Boy with his feet up.

"Hi. I'm Leila," I say, holding my hand up in the air and waving it in a little circle.

"I'm Gary's friend. Andy."

He looks uncomfortable, but I sit down on the couch across from him with my legs pressed together, and I smooth my thin dress down over my knees. Maybe he's thirty, but he looks younger. Brown hair with sloppy sideburns. A weightlifter. He's wearing a light blue T-shirt with TAWAS BAY printed in white letters across the front, a line drawing of a boat's sail, and his big arms and chest are pressed across the T-shirt from inside, bulging, making it look like a second skin. Outside, night rustles around the house like something creeping secretly closer.

My purse is still on the couch where I'd tossed it when I followed Gary into the bedroom, and it looks strangely familiar there, like something I'd owned in another, longer life. Or something I'd thrown away years ago, mysteriously returned. I pick it up and put it in my lap like a pet, a red vinyl pet, while Gary's friend looks at his wristwatch, watching it. I can hear the watch tick, fast, a tiny machine gun. Or a small white rat scratching rhythmically at an empty tin can. Or rain. And when I unzip the purse I'm not surprised to find the money's gone. The whole green fist of it. The whole green paper heart of it, gone.

I think of the ballerina, paused forever in my jewelry box.

The tinny waltz, smothered.

Now, the emptiness of the purse makes a sound of its own. A cool yawn. A broom sweeping baby powder off the floor. White wings and air.

Twenty-three hundred dollars.

The car keys, too.

Now, it just smells like old cigarettes in the stomach of that purse, but there aren't any cigarettes either. No matches. No ashes.

Suddenly, the diamond-shaped window in the front door fills brilliantly with light. Headlights. The sound of motors, killed, car doors slamming. But as I walk toward the beaming diamond in that front door, it goes black, and I think maybe I've finally bought what I'd been saving that money to buy.

▼

When I turned sixteen, I went to the Ottawa County Library to look for my mother. It hadn't occurred to me before. Then, suddenly, the clear idea of it was right in front of me, obvious as a dead rock dangling in the sky — the thing I'd always dreaded and longed for filling my empty palm with mercury and moon.

The librarian was a red-lipped man with soft white hair down to his shoulders. Even when he smiled, he appeared to be a sad clown. Delicate, with long fingers, his skin was soft, as if the outer layer had been peeled off, as if he'd been buried in mud or wrapped in wet bandages for years in the library's basement, then dug up, unwound. He touched my elbow with those soft fingertips when he showed me where the microfilm was kept — in small cardboard coffins lined up in a file cabinet with miles and miles of old newspaper in it. I told him the dates I wanted, and he clicked his long pink nails against one of the metal drawers. "Here," he said.

▼

"What do you mean?" I ask. He holds the doorknob tighter in his hand and doesn't look at me. He moves in front of the door, then, with his wide, weightlifter arms. "Why aren't you supposed to let me leave?"

He shrugs, as if he is embarrassed, and says, "This is Gary's business. I'm just doing what Gary says to do."

The voices outside grow closer, and there are more head-lights now in the driveway. The sound of bad brakes squealing to a stop. A man laughs. Another shouts, "Yeah!" Someone turns the doorknob from the other side of the door and pushes into it with his shoulder. When it opens, I smell cold air and whiskey, a stiff wind of it rushing past Gary's friend into the house.

The man who steps into the living room first has red hair, a quart of beer in his hand, a cigarette in his mouth. I recognize him from the Big City Bar. When he sees me, he doesn't smile. Half-open, the door is a crack into pure darkness now, and when it's opened all the way, Gary's friend turns his back to me with his arms out at his sides like a crossing guard — to keep me from running through that door, I suppose, though I haven't even thought of running, or why I would want or need to run, or where I'd go if I did, with no car, or money, wearing a thin summer dress on a cold night, lost and obvious as a white rat under thunderous wings and an owl's black nest.

▼

I sat on a hard wooden chair in front of the microfilm news-print, buzzing and glowing warm on my face, and I pressed a button which made the pages whir fast across the screen, like wind blowing evening papers out of the paperboy's hands — gray headlines and obituaries and comic strips whipping past a kitchen window while an old woman looked out, doing dishes, thinking of something else: whole years. Thin, fragile pages of them, too fast and light to catch, dragged with the rain, the leaves, the snow, through dusk, utterly lost.

But it was easier than I thought it would be to find my mother there. There she was, a familiar photo — her high school yearbook portrait, black V of her dress, and a strand of pale pearls. She was smiling, a smudge between her breasts.

And, in another, later snapshot on a page buried deeper in the paper, she stood with her back to a crowd. The faces behind her, small and gray, were smeared with motion. Was it a parade? Was that a float behind her, cluttered with tissue roses? Was a homely prom queen waving over my mother's shoulder, or was that a plaster Christ stretched out on the cross, hefted into grainy air?

Whatever it was behind her, my mother smiled widely, not seeing it, into the sun, her own hand at her waist. Her arms were long, bare, and her sleeveless top was scooped low on her chest, which was all white skin. Only her collarbone caught the shadows in front of her, and that was sexy. You could see why they printed that photo over and over in all the papers — Grand Rapids, Detroit, Kalamazoo. One of her shoulders was lifted slightly, a pose, as if she might be joking *Take me, I'm yours* — if this wasn't a photo. If she weren't dead. A glamour ghost.

And they were right, you'd buy this paper. If you were a man, you might sit in an armchair with a glass of wine or beer while someone fried chicken for you in the kitchen, and you'd look at her picture for a long time. If you were a woman, you might study the photo and wonder why she was beautiful, and whether or not you were. You might pin your hair loose to the back of your head that night after your bath, like her murdered hair in the news, not sure where you'd gotten the idea to do it. But you'd also think, no matter who you were, *This is what happens to women like Bonnie Murray.* No matter who you were, you'd know her name by now. By now her name belonged to the whole county, like the library, open to the public, like the name of a busy crossroad. *Meet me at the corner of blank and blank*, you'd say as easy as you'd say her name.

I looked at the photos but read nothing beyond the captions under them and the headlines, which I couldn't miss. SUSPICIOUS RIVER WOMAN STABBED TO DEATH BY LOVER/BROTHER-IN-LAW. *Bonnie Murray, 24, murdered.*

CRIME OF PASSION? *Suspicious River Murder Victim Was High-Priced Prostitute, Police Reveal. Sang every Sunday in church choir.*

After the news of October, there was the news of November. An earthquake somewhere. A pile of bodies in a ditch in another country, all of them boys in blue jeans and white tennis shoes, T-shirts with the names of American baseball teams in white block letters. *Militants, government sources say.* A plane crash somewhere. 47 bodies recovered. 87 missing. Scattered over 44 acres of harvested corn. *An unidentified woman told reporters, "It just burst into flames above my head. I heard the roar, then looked up. The sky was white. At first I thought it was the sun, that the sun had exploded in the sky."* Nearby, a closeup photo of a high heel and a child's stuffed rabbit near a huge, silver wing, fallen in the field.

Then, on another page, I found my uncle, stunned by flash-bulbs, stepping awkwardly out of the back seat of a black car with his ankles tethered.

I stopped.

Ladies'-man killer receives a hundred love letters a day from women all over the state, prison officials tell reporters.

I stopped and stared hard at the photograph of my uncle, who looked handsome even in his gray prison uniform, hands cuffed at his crotch. I could see why they wrote to him. His hair was long, though he must have tried to grease it back, even in his prison cell. It still fell damp into his eyes. I could imagine secretaries passing the newspaper between them in a lunch room, their pilled sweaters loose and pink around their shoulders, a cold November pressing down on the long, white bones of their necks — stretching, laughing, the pale fringe of a lettuce leaf left at the edge of someone's cellophane, a wet crust of Wonder Bread. Maybe they'd take turns reading the article out loud, looking over each other's shoulders to study his picture, interrupted when some short man in a blue poly-ester blazer said, *Time to get back to your desks, girls.*

In one photograph, my uncle's eyebrows looked darker than they were in real life, knitted together. He looked desperately tired, ill with desire, like a man who would stab you if you didn't love him enough. A man who would press your wrist against the wall and tear your blouse if you told him no. A man who could seduce you away from your ordinary husband — your ordinary husband who would never make enough money to take you on vacation somewhere warm, while November curled the edges of the horizon like frozen steam rising from an iron as it passes over a man's cotton shirt, pinned to the ironing board. Seven months of winter on the way.

▼

"You better get back in the bedroom," Gary's friend says, looking at my bare feet as he says it. A few more men are waiting on the front steps to come in. Quiet, but I can hear their boots on the stoop's wood planks. I can hear them breathe.

I turn off the light in the bedroom when I go back, and I get in the bed, roll onto my stomach, and press my face into the pillow. I close my eyes, and I don't open them when I hear someone open the bedroom door.

I don't open them when he sits at the edge of the bed.

I hear him kick off his shoes. "Take off your dress," he says, and I roll onto my back and unbutton it, fold it, put it at the foot of the bed, on the floor, so it won't get wrinkled, my eyes closed tight the whole time. Hovering above my body, ready to be born.

▼

Ladies'-Man Killer. There he was. *Pleads guilty to manslaughter.*

Killing was accidental, he claims.

High cheekbones. Boyish, murder-you eyes: He is the handsome, younger one, the spoiled and sexy one with a fast red car, the one who doesn't care that your husband is his brother. He wants you that bad. He's a man you will never meet, a man you can think about as you type, or cook dinner in a skillet, or drive your children to school in the dark, in the morning, in November, after another hard frost has finally killed everything.

Even I could see that, and why those women wrote to him in prison, why they probably sent him tins of oatmeal cookies that never made it past the prison guards. Even I could see that, and I was the one who'd also seen him sitting dull-eyed, with his mouth open, at the foot of a bed, my mother's blood on his chest.

I peered into the microfilm — a lost month, a decade earlier, projected and lit up in front of me while the librarian chewed his fingernails in the silence — and, in it, I could also see a hundred women a day sit down with ballpoint pens at their kitchen tables while their infant daughters slept and their husbands read damp newspapers in dens. *You don't know me,* they might begin, *but I read about you in the* Kalamazoo Gazette.

Those women thought they wanted a man like that, but what they really wanted was to die.

$\mathcal{T}$ HE LETTER was written on both sides of one piece of notebook paper with jagged edges. The printing was small and hard, all capitals, and black. It said: *Dear Leila, You probably will not remember me since you were just a little girl when I left. But I am your father's brother. I have just learned that my brother Jack died last week, and I wanted to send you this letter to tell you I'm sorry. He was a good man, and I'm sure you must be missing him. You probably know that I was in jail for eight and a half years. Manslaughter. But I have a new life now in Indianapolis. I am enclosing my phone number if you ever need anything I hope you will call. Despite all that has happened I am still your family. I will be thinking of you during these hard times. sincerely, Andy Murray.*

I folded the paper along the exact lines it had originally been folded along, and I put it back in the envelope, then I put the envelope in the pocket of my coat. I could hear snow melting off the roof, trickling down the clapboard. The sun was even higher by now, and the windows glistened, prismatic with old ice, daggers of it hanging and dripping off the eaves.

I went to their bedroom and opened the door.

In the dark, with the shades pulled and so much light behind them, the sheets on the bed looked faded and blue.

But nothing had changed.

I closed my eyes.

My mother's shadow still hovered over the bed — silk slip soaked with blood and black by now, but not a slip. Her eyes were open, and she was smiling. Legs long and white. I could hear my heart thud, underwater, in my chest, and the sound of my breath was like the hissing whine of wind through cracked walls. When I opened my eyes and turned, he was standing in the hall behind me.

Older now.

His hair had gone prison gray.

The same good trousers, though. A nice white shirt with a button-down collar. I could smell him. Powder, and the alcohol underneath his cologne. He looked surprised to see me when I screamed.

"Open your eyes," he says, and his breath is hot with vodka and something else like white fire over my face, but I can't open my eyes. Too much light. "What the hell's the matter with you? You a nut case or something?"

He rolls off of me, onto his side, and runs his hand up and down my body like a man polishing a counter. "Jesus Christ," he says. He slaps me lightly on the side of my face a few times. The sound of water clapping ripples in the river, but I can't move.

"Fine," he says and whips the sheet off me. To someone else, someone who must have been in the room with us all along, he says, "She's all yours, Bud. A fucking nut case."

The bedroom door opens and closes while a bare white weight presses down on me, spreads my legs. Wind outside. Something rattling leaves off the trees until they're skeletons again. Someone says, "Open your mouth," and he laughs when I do. "She can open her mouth, anyway." More laughter. Outside, more wind.

▼

Light from the kitchen window shimmered with ash ahead of me as I walked toward the back door, fast — past my Uncle Andy, past my own bedroom, straight out the door, breathing hard. I let the screen door slap shut behind me.

Outside, the air was sharp and chilled, too fresh, and so bright I couldn't lift my face as I walked. My eyes watered, making the world a strange, warped mirror, but, watching the white ground, I could see my own boot prints make ruins of the melting cat prints where my father had died, and I kept walking — past my own house and down the street. I unzipped my black coat and stuffed my mittens into the pockets of it while I walked, but the sun still felt too warm, like something dropped heavy, invisible but burning on my back. I kept walking until I'd gotten to the end of the block, to the front door of the only house on that block I'd ever been inside except my own — the only neighbor on that block I'd ever known. I rang the doorbell and waited, hands stuffed along with the soft suffocation of mittens into the deep pockets of my coat.

When he finally came to the door, Reverend Roberts was wearing a bathrobe, but he opened the screen door for me, looking worried, squinting behind me to the street as I stepped in.

"Leila," he said, "you shouldn't just come by here, you know. No one's home, but if my wife — " He lifted his hands to the ceiling as if the rest were too obvious to mention, as if it were written all over the beige above us. He looked annoyed when he saw the look on my face. "What's the matter with you?" he asked, impatient, and then, just remembering, "I'm sorry." He touched my shoulder and mumbled, "I'm sorry. Again. About your father."

I could smell his breath. Musty and yellow. His feet and shins were bare under the white bulky robe, and his house was warm, all off-white wallpaper and deep brown carpet that looked clean and soft — and every inch of every wall was covered with a photograph of someone framed in fake, sprayed gold, or a little oil painting of the ocean, a dopey cow, a young girl in a white dress on a swing in summer, a cross, or a sepia-tinted portrait of Jesus, looking authentic and old.

I looked up at him, and he looked afraid this time when he saw my face. He shrugged before I'd asked him anything, then said, "Leila, I don't think I can help you. What we've been doing is really a terrible mistake. I could lose my church, you know. You can't stop by here. I thought you understood that. If anyone found out about this, it would ruin my life."

I looked down at my boots and saw that the snow was melting off them onto the Robertses' nice carpet, pooling under me, and I started to cry.

Reverend Roberts stood up straighter when I put my arms around his neck and pressed myself into him, sobbing. He tried to push me away with his hands above my hips, shaking his head back and forth fast, but I held to him harder, kissing the side of his face, his neck. Finally he said, "Look, Leila, let me get dressed and we'll get out of here. You go down to your father's house and wait for me, O.K.? There's no one there, is there?"

I shook my head, wiped my eyes on the black wool sleeve of my coat and drew a breath that trembled. "O.K.," I said.

Walking back down the block, I felt cold again. The sun had tucked itself briefly behind a cloud, then peered out — the cloud moving fast and high across the pure blue sky. I couldn't go back into my father's house alone, so I stood in the back yard and looked up at all that sky. When I closed my eyes I saw black circles against a yellow backdrop, like faces in a snapshot taken on a too-bright day — ruined, blanked out, the camera aimed straight into too much light.

▼

"She won't open her eyes."

"I'll open her goddamn eyes. Get outta here."

I know it's him without opening them. I recognize his voice. The blond. From 31. The one who'd slapped me until I tasted blood. I can smell him. Soft leather and denim. I can hear him pull off his boots, unbuckle his belt, the cold clanging of an old bell.

The light is on in the bedroom again, and it burns yellow through my eyelids. The bedroom door is open behind him, and I hear voices at the end of the hallway. Laughter and tinny music on a radio. Water running in the bathroom sink. And, beyond that, the river, snaking past.

He straddles my chest. The flesh of his thighs presses against my naked breasts, and he hits me over and over again with a fist. The sound of his knuckles on the bones of my face. The dead drum of something solid on something solid, until I open my eyes. When I do, he smiles.

I can see water swollen over my cheekbones, around my open eyes.

▼

"Leila," Reverend Roberts said. He had stepped out of his long blue car, idling. My face was still turned toward the sky, but I looked over at him when he said my name. He looked angry, and in a hurry.

"Leila, we can't stay here." He looked toward the back door of the house. "Lock it up and we'll go get some lunch somewhere. Then we have to go straight to the church." He got back into his car.

I pulled the door to my father's house shut, not looking in when I did, and I locked it with a cold silver key on a loop of string, then put the key in my coat pocket.

When I got into the car next to him, Reverend Roberts wouldn't look at me, but it was warm there, and he had the radio on. The music came from behind us, all violin and flute. I could hear someone breathe into the flute, gasping before each note. I looked at Reverend Roberts. A short man with a round face, round hands, round thighs. He was wearing a nice black suit, red tie. Hair thin and white as a baby's. He didn't look back at me.

"Now it's very important that you not touch me in public, Leila, you understand, and that, now that you've come over to my house like this and any of the neighbors might have seen it — it's essential that we are seen in public together. As if we don't have anything to hide. We'll go to the Golden Dragon for lunch; then it's essential that we are seen together at the church, too — linking us to the church, so to speak — so it looks like I am helping you in your time of need as I would any other parishioner. Do you understand?"

I nodded — awed, wondering how he'd had so much time to think it all out while he was hurrying to get dressed. He sighed, then, shaking his head as if I'd said something childish. But I hadn't said anything at all.

We turned out of the block and he drove west, in the direction of the river. There were no other cars around. The snow was packed down so hard on the road, I could hardly tell if it was the road or field grass under snow and wheels. Only in a few patches had it begun to melt, and the red sand of the road bled up through it, damp. The trees overhead looked wet, clawing at the sky. Reverend Roberts looked behind him, over his left shoulder, but whatever he'd been looking for wasn't there, and he turned down the winding road to Riverside Park, which would be empty in the winter, during the week, in the middle of the day. I knew that.

"Take your coat off," he said, "we have to hurry," parking the car. The river ahead of us was jeweled with ice, glistening, as if it had been made more valuable by the first sun shining on it in so long.

*A*T THE GOLDEN DRAGON, Reverend Roberts waved to two old women he knew who were sitting in a red plastic booth adjacent to our own. The women smiled widely at him, nodding their twin white heads at me — suspiciously, I thought.

"Hello Reverend," our waitress said as she handed menus to us. She was a blonde, nearly six feet tall, the only waitress at the only Chinese restaurant for eighty miles. She had a southern accent, and people in Suspicious River joked that the Golden Dragon had been named for her.

"Oh, I know what I'll have," Reverend Roberts said, handing the menu back to her. "We're in a hurry this afternoon, Amanda. I'll just have a bowl of hot and sour soup. Leila, how about you? My treat." He said that, and my name, loud enough for the women behind us to hear.

"I'll have the same," I said, handing my menu to her, too. It was plastic red, like the booth we sat in, and there was a dragon engraved in gold on the front. The dragon looked like an evil dog with a long, spiked tail.

"Now, Leila," he said when we were alone again, in a tone that pretended to be worried and hushed, still loud enough for the women in the next booth to hear, "how have you been doing since your father's death?"

I touched my fork. It was cold. Then I put my hands in my lap and turned the palms up empty, shook my head. "I'm O.K.," I said, "except for the house."

"Oh yes of course, that must be very painful, and a lot of responsibility for you and your husband. Do you plan to sell the house?"

The women behind us were sliding out of their booth, putting their coats on over their shoulders. I heard them drop some coins into the plastic check tray. One of them looked hard at me when she turned, pushing her hands through the sleeves of her coat. Her eyes were nearly pink they were so clear and clean, and her whole face was dusted with powder, thick as flour. There was even powder on her lips, and I thought she looked thirsty, dried. Like the snow that day, her face was blinding.

"Good-bye, Reverend," the woman said.

"Yes, good-bye ladies." He smiled and waved to them.

The other one didn't look at us, but she said "Good-bye" into the dark leaves of a vinyl rubber tree near the door.

When they were gone, Reverend Roberts sighed. When I said "I don't know," he didn't seem to remember what we'd been talking about.

"You don't know what?" He looked at me, blank.

"I don't know what we'll do about the house. But what's wrong is — " I touched my lips with my fingertips before I said it. "I think, I mean, I imagine, my mother is in it. Dead. And I think I see my uncle." I felt myself blush — a saucepan of lukewarm blood splashed across my face and neck. But, I thought, if I couldn't tell him, the man who spoke for a living about holy ghosts, rising from the dead, who could I tell?

"That's ridiculous," Reverend Roberts said, and the waitress came then, slipping bowls of soup in front of each of us. He looked up at her and said, "Thank you, dear."

I looked into my soup. Steam crinolined out of the bowl — a

bowl of weather, smoothing and breaking in foggy ribbons as I breathed.

Reverend Roberts blew on his own soup and stirred it around and around with his spoon, then he looked up and said, "Leila, you need professional help. I've thought it for a long time. Ever since you were a little girl. There's always been something very wrong, and I certainly can't help you. I'll give you the name of a counselor when we get back to the church, O.K.?"

He inhaled the soup off his spoon with his lips barely parted, but he looked angry afterward, as if it had been too hot.

I nodded. I blew on my own spoon of soup. It was thick, and there were green onions floating on the top, mushrooms and thin strips of gray meat just under the surface. I realized, suddenly, how hungry I was, but when I sipped and tasted the soup, I couldn't swallow. I had to spit it back into my spoon fast. Then I dropped my spoon into the bowl.

Reverend Roberts looked up at me, startled. "What the hell is wrong with you?" he asked.

I put my hand over my mouth. I couldn't breathe.

"Leila, what's the matter with you?" He still held his own spoon at a hover above his bowl.

I started to cry, and I pushed the bowl away from me. I said, sobbing, "There's blood in it," and I held my hands hard against my mouth. "I tasted blood in it." I hadn't meant to cry.

He put his spoon back into his own bowl then, and he looked afraid, but he said sternly, "There's no blood in the soup, Leila."

I sipped from my water glass, but I could still taste it, rusty on my teeth. I was afraid I'd gag. I could taste the salt of it on my tongue.

The waitress came over slowly, looking worried. "Is everything O.K.?" she asked.

Reverend Roberts looked up at her and said, "Amanda, this will sound ridiculous, but there's no blood in the soup, is there?" He nodded toward me when he asked it, patient, conveying a message about me to her in his expression.

The waitress put her hand between her breasts then and said, quiet, watching me, "Well, yes. I'm afraid there is. Cook makes the soup with duck's blood. I'd be happy to bring you something else."

*O*KAY," he said, "I'll go in the house with you if it's that important, but after that we have to go to the church, as I've said, so this will look like a professional engagement. Those old ladies at the Golden Dragon could very well be telling the whole damn town about God knows what by now. Leila, it's essential that we appear perfectly comfortable being seen together." He wiped the damp corners of his mouth with two fingers. We were driving back down the dirt road along the river again.

Still, the sun was shining on the snow, a billion mirror slivers of it shattered in the banks at the side of the road, but there was one cloud in the middle of the blue sky — low, purple, thick as Brillo. Magnificent. A lodestone. Other clouds raced from the edges to meet it in the middle, planning a blizzard.

When we pulled up at the house, I saw that my father's shovel, which had been propped up against the fender of his car, had fallen into the driveway again. It glinted when we pulled up in Reverend Roberts's car. A shovelful of purple cloud — soon it would be full of snow again. We stepped out of the car, and I followed Reverend Roberts toward the back door.

From outside, the house looked dark and empty, but I could see something moving behind the black glass of the bedroom window as we passed. "Look," I said, touching Reverend Roberts's arm. It felt surprisingly bony under his thick coat.

I pointed to the bedroom window, but he looked at my face. My skin felt tight and dry across my cheekbones in the cold, like laundry on a line, freezing and moist at the same time, or the way an animal's hide dries out lifeless with life. I could feel tears itch at the corners of my eyes, and my nose had started to run. Finally he looked up at the bedroom window and said, "Blow your nose for god's sake. It's just our reflection," and he started to walk in a hurry ahead of me toward the back door.

I dug the house key out of the deep pocket of my winter coat — that pocket, like a linty cave of winter, a black tunnel to winter — but the key slipped and fell onto a thin layer of ice that had begun to melt, once, but had frozen over again before it did, gone dead cold again when the sun had moved and the shadow of the house had fallen across the back steps once more. That ice was smoother and thicker now for having melted. More determined than ever to be ice. Slicker. More dangerous. I picked the key up with my fingernails, and Reverend Roberts crossed his arms and exhaled. A shred of white chiffon trailed past my ear in his breath, briefly, then disappeared.

"The house looks perfectly normal," he said when he stepped into it, scanning the kitchen, which wore a veil of blue winter haze. The air smelled silvery. The two ordinary appliances with their blank faces. The stainless steel sink with only a coffee cup and a white plastic spoon like a stiff tongue in it. After I'd moved out, my father had only eaten off paper plates.

"I know," I said, apologizing, blowing my nose into a paper towel. I pressed it to my eyes, too. I said, "Here," and walked toward my parents' bedroom.

The door was open. I said, "This is where I saw her," and I pointed to the bed. Reverend Roberts looked over my shoulder while I leaned against the door and stared. Again, I tasted a bird's blood on the root of my tongue. And, after my eyes had adjusted to the dark, there my mother was.

Light, watery bubbles of blood on her lips and the sound of air escaping from a slashed tire.

Or a teapot starting to boil.

Or wheels spinning on ice until it hissed.

"Jesus," Reverend Roberts said, backing away from the bedroom. His teeth were set hard against his teeth, and he breathed fast through them. "There's nothing in there, Leila."

I followed him down the hallway to the living room with my arms open. "I know," I said, "I know," but my body could have flown into an explosion of feathers, a white funnel of spine and hair. *Hysterical*, I thought, I was going to *become* it. I swallowed and swallowed, covering my eyes with my hands and then my mouth, to keep the hysterical feathers in.

"Don't get hysterical," Reverend Roberts said and gripped my arms with his fingers hard, pushing them into my body, my body into itself, as if to keep it all, all of me, in one solid piece.

"It's where I found her," I said. Panting, I leaned into him. "I found her there." I stopped and looked at Reverend Roberts, choking it down again — fluff, tuft, molt in my dry throat. My lungs were naked and beating — two featherless squabs behind my ribs. "My uncle wrote me a letter," I said, "from Indianapolis," fumbling in my coat pocket to take it out for him.

But Reverend Roberts said, "Who cares, Leila? There's no one in there now, and you're acting like a lunatic. You need to get your husband to help you with this, not me. We absolutely have to go." He shook me, loosening the grip I had around his shoulders, but I leaned further into him. I wanted to put my head on his chest. I could smell old sweat like an animal's abandoned nest beneath his black suit coat. I remembered the taste of his come. Chemical and sweet as candied aspirin.

"I have to go, Leila. My car cannot be seen in your driveway for more than ten minutes. I told you that." But as he spoke, I slipped my arms into his coat, which was unbuttoned, and I stood on tiptoes to kiss his neck. Desperate, the kiss sounded like a gasp.

"Jesus Christ," he said, backing me toward the couch, where my father's *TV Guide* was still folded open, upside down, like a bird with glossy, paper wings, spread.

Reverend Roberts was angry as he fumbled with my pants. He couldn't undo them fast, so I pulled them down for him and stepped out. He was grinding his teeth, and he threw his coat on the floor behind him and pushed my sweater up to my neck.

But the couch was too narrow, so he pulled me to the floor and tried to push himself into me, hard, but couldn't. "You're dry," he said, disgusted, then licked his fingers and rubbed the spit between my legs, pushing again until he was inside me, working at it, his hands on either side of my face, holding himself high above me. He wouldn't look down, kept his head upright and his face forward, a serious and winded expression on it as he stared ahead, starting to sweat, breathing hard. A man afraid of bridges riding an old bike over one.

I couldn't help but hear them. *Bonnie.* My mother laughed. Then it was muffled. They were suffocating something in the bedroom.

You're killing me. You're killing me. Leila?

Reverend Roberts stopped and pulled himself out, got on his knees between my legs and started to yank his pants up, frantic.

Leila?

He reached down and pulled the sweater back over my breasts, but the rest of my body was naked and spread under him on the old carpet like a beige feast, and when I opened my eyes I saw Rick's mother standing in dim kitchen light in the doorway.

Looking young again.

Her hair was pulled back in a ponytail and there was a white wool scarf around her neck.

In that light, hovering above us, Mrs. Schmidt looked beautiful and powerful. A lady aviator from the fifties. A ballerina, not yet past her prime, ready to dance Swan Lake in a snow jacket and boots in the middle of a dark blue blizzard.

Leila?

And then she saw us.

I closed my eyes and listened to her boots bleat across the linoleum with their rubber soles, the screen door slamming delicately behind her.

When I opened my eyes again, I saw Reverend Roberts scanning my father's living room — panicked, a caged cat. I'd seen one, once, in a live trap in the neighbor's back yard. They'd caught it, accidentally, instead of the groundhog who'd eaten away the foundation of their house. The cat must have been in the trap a long time. It's eyes were yellow, and there were strings of foam at its mouth, seeming to rope its throat.

I'd noticed that cat from the kitchen window while I was doing dishes. I'd pulled my father's raincoat on and run out into the early evening mud to rescue it — though my father muttered in the doorway behind me as I went, "You'd better just leave it alone, Leila. That's the neighbors' business, that trap."

When I opened the metal door to set it free, I expected screaming. I expected to be clawed bloody, bitten by its long teeth. But the cat just disappeared. I never saw or heard it go. The cage was simply empty when I looked again, and that's how it was with Reverend Roberts. I never even heard him start his car.

W HEN I LIVED WITH RICK and his parents, there was laughter every night like television static. In the summer, it rose out of that box of colored light like fireflies, canned, and sifted through the window screens into the street — electric snoring, while the curtains made a loose, seductive shadow dance in dusk. Rick's mother would put her feet in fuzzy red slippers up on the couch, and I would look at those slippers, not sure if I loved or hated them. My mother had never owned slippers.

Rick's father laughed whenever the television did, and Mrs. Schmidt would roll her eyes at him, as if he were an idiot, or a child, then she'd laugh, too.

I could never laugh with the television like that. It seemed so far away, and small. But I would sit with them in the living room those months, their house glowing blue and warm around me, strange waves of light from the TV rippling across our faces while it grew bluer, deeper, and more like river water outside. I could see night through the screen door all summer while the TV cackled and sputtered among us. Out there, a handful of bats. The blade of a half moon shredding the sky to ribbons or streamers of black crepe paper. But inside, the television shimmered. A boat of rhinestones. The Hope Diamond.

A whole world, like an afterlife, separated from us by an inch of glass in the Schmidts' cozy living room.

Though, one July night, it came in.

Rick's mother got up from the couch to open the door for the cat — white fur scratching and rattling at the screen door, then a flash of warm light as it ran in the house, past Mrs. Schmidt's ankles — purring, wet and loud, with something half alive and purple in its mouth: a scrap of night.

"Oh my God," Mrs. Schmidt said, but she didn't scream. Whatever it had been wriggled bloody on the carpet near her feet.

Mr. Schmidt jumped up then and scooped the thing into his hand. It was no larger than a child's severed thumb. He opened the screen door and threw it hard and fast back into the dark.

"What was that?" Mrs. Schmidt was breathing hard. The cat licked her shin, still purring, as if it were in ecstasy, or heat.

"God," Mr. Schmidt said, "I don't know, but that cat sure chewed the hell out of it whatever it was." He leaned down to scratch the cat's hot, pink ears. "Didn't you, kitty?"

Mrs. Schmidt laughed and spoke to the cat in a high, child's voice, "You brought your mama a present, didn't you, kitty?"

They laughed.

Then the cat sat on Mrs. Schmidt's lap after she put her feet back up on the couch, and the TV show went on.

During the commercial, I looked past Rick, who'd fallen asleep long ago in an armchair and had never woken up. I looked out the screen door to the darkness, and I imagined that thing flying through the air with its bloody fur, dragging its mangled self into shadow on the other side of the street to die.

Mrs. Schmidt backed away from me when I stepped into their house. I'd already seen her in the kitchen, moving in circles behind a curtain that hung over the window on the back porch door. I'd opened that door slowly and stood on the threshold, holding my breath. Ready to be slapped. Or stabbed.

But Mrs. Schmidt just backed away, shaking her head. "I want you out of this house," she said. Her cheeks were flushed, though her lips were pale and dry. It looked as if she'd bitten them over and over again with chalk teeth. "I want you out of this house tonight."

Mrs. Schmidt sat then, exhausted, in a chair at the kitchen table. The kitchen looked too clean around her, too cheerful — a photo of me and Rick was stuck with a black magnet to the fridge. It was our wedding day. Mrs. Schmidt had snapped it herself in the back yard. Now, that black magnet pinned us, smiling, to the fridge, looking young and stiff. An elaborate cascade of lilacs hung limp behind us. We leaned forward a little, as if someone were saying something to us that we couldn't quite hear.

Mrs. Schmidt looked up at me, then she pointed toward Rick's bedroom. "Get your things," trembling, "get your things and get out of here."

I followed the finger she pointed to Rick's bedroom, though there was nothing I wanted to take with me. Still, I pulled my overnight bag out of the closet — cracked animal skin and a broken handle — and I threw handfuls of underwear and socks into it, folded a few sweaters, some skirts, a dark dress. Mrs. Schmidt stood in the doorway with her arms crossed, watching, before she said, "You had better believe I'm going to tell my son about this. Do you understand that, Leila?"

I turned to look at her. "Yes," I said quietly, "of course."

Mrs. Schmidt looked even more angry then, folded her hands into little fists and punched them toward her own hips. A cheerleader, still. "What is the *matter* with you, Leila? Are you out of your *mind?*"

When I didn't say anything and didn't move, Mrs. Schmidt continued, "I think you are, Leila. I'm sorry to say it, but I think you are. I wish I'd believed that before." Then she started to cry and put her hand over her mouth as she said the rest. "This is all my fault. I told Rick that a good man would

marry you, after what had happened, that he'd have to marry
you to be right with his conscience and God. And I believed it
would be all right. That you could adopt children someday,
and you'd be happy. I felt so bad for you, because of what
happened to your mother." Mrs. Schmidt moved her hand
down between her breasts when she said it. "I always felt so
bad about that, even before I met you. I used to think about
that horrible thing all the time. Just a little girl, finding her
mother like that, and what that must have done to you. We all
talked about that — all of us mothers. And I never listened to
anyone say a bad word about you. I thought it was all just more
rumors. Because of Bonnie, what she was like. I thought everyone just wanted to believe you were like your mother." She
made fists again. "And you are. God forgive me, but you are."
She shook the fists at me. "Damn you. *Damn* you. You are. I
trusted you. I *cared* about you. I went over to that house today
because I was worried about you. And there you were. You
whore. Get out of my house."

I closed the suitcase and carried it like a big infant in my
arms, out the door and through the snow, back toward my
father's house, block by block.

The sky had gone dark.

The cold air burned the back of my nose and dried my eyes
until I couldn't shut them anymore.

When I was back in my father's house, I put the suitcase
on the bed in my old bedroom, where nothing had changed.
The bedspread was choked with clover, and the curtains were
heavy and yellowed. A braided rug coiled on the floor, and a
layer of dust coated it all — the top of the dresser, the tennis
shoes I'd left at the foot of the bed. I sat next to the suitcase
and listened. Now, it was quiet on the other side of the wall.
All I could hear was snow laying itself on top of snow outside.

I sat like that for a long time. I kept my coat on and my
eyes closed.

*L*EILA? *Leila?*" Someone pounded on the back door with a club or a fist, and I stood up from the bed and went toward the sound of my name, shouted.

"Leila!"

I walked down the hallway to the kitchen and looked out at the night, which would have been utter darkness except for a huge, bald moon, crouching low in the sky. It hung just over Rick's head like an ax, and his face glowed.

I opened the door. A blast of winter followed him as he stepped in and said, "Look. Leila. My mother told me what happened."

"It isn't true," I said, the lie as flat as a tin knife.

"I don't care right now, Leila. If you think I give a shit, you're wrong. I'm just here because I'm not going to have my mother tell me what to do anymore. It's got nothing to do with you now. It's between me and her. I married you because she told me to. I'm not just going to get a divorce because she tells me to. It's none of my mother's business anymore."

I could feel my skeleton vibrate under its clothes as he spoke. A tuning fork. One pure and honest sound, and, behind it, the river, tires flattening stiff snow with the sheer weight of a truck.

That night we slept together in my childhood bed, though I never slept. It began that night, Rick's tossing and muttering in sleep. In the small bed, I couldn't roll away, except to the wall, which was cold, the old glossy white paint kissing my kneecaps and hands when I came too close. Morning came fast, pure white as a flat screen of light all over the sky at once, and Rick opened his eyes slowly, looked at me for a while blindly, as if he had to reorder a file in his mind before he knew where he was, what had happened, who we were.

"What are we going to do?" I asked him. And then I whispered, "I can't live here."

"Oh." He cleared his throat. "Everything will be fine. We'll stay here until we sell it, and then we'll get an apartment."

He'd thought about it.

He must have been thinking about it in his sleep — the turning, the talking. He blinked at the ceiling, and I propped myself up on an elbow and looked into his eyes. The pupils expanded and contracted in my shadow. All black, but in them I could see myself, my face warped like a face reflected in a spoon, my hair messy around my face. For a minute I thought I recognized my mother in Rick's eyes. I thought I looked exactly like my mother — and for a moment, the thought thrilled me. Then, the pupils contracted to only a pinprick in the brown, and I disappeared in them completely. Then, I could imagine, perfectly, sinking my teeth into his neck. Sucking the blood right out of him.

But Rick closed his eyes, and I knew his blood would already be frozen if I tried.

Freeze-dried.

His blood would taste like powder, or old ice. It might be poisoned, or ash, or white.

"Christ. What are you doing, man?"

"None of your goddamn business. Turn off the light."

Silence then. I stare up at the light until I can see the black filament of its bulb. A dark thread. A wingless dragonfly. He says, "You heard me. Turn off the goddamn light."

The bedroom door closes again.

Then it goes dark. An exploded star, still, in front of my swollen eyes. When he rolls off of me, I wipe my face and mouth with the edge of the bedspread, and the mask of bone that is my skull feels unfamiliar under my fingers. A new layer of fluid, shell-like, has grown over the one I'd known.

"Look," the voice says from the dark of the bedroom door, "there's no reason to beat on her. Lay off it, will you?" and the door closes.

He touches my leg then as if he's touching nothing. A railing on the deck of a ship. His breath sounds solid and close, and I think I'd be able to see it like smoke, in and out of his mouth, if the light were on. But it's not. I can smell my own body. Salt water. Like soup with a bone floating in it — an old bone, something the butcher would give you for free to add some flavor to the soft vegetables and watery broth, but not too much.

"You know Gary told me to beat you up bad that night at the motel, don't you? That's what he does. How he gets little bitches like you to whore for him." He touches my neck when he says that, and I hear the hound outside again, not howling, just dragging that chain through damp leaves in the dark. "Do you hear me?"

He puts his hand near my face again, and I wince. I say, "Yes," and cover my face with my forearm. Pure instinct. A bat folding itself up in an attic.

He laughs when I do that.

"Did you know it?" he asks.

"Yes," I say. I knew.

"You stupid cunt," he says.

Then the dark shimmers with ash, throbs scarlet as a liver. I remember my mother turning in the kitchen once with something that color in her hand. Slick-purple. Livid. She laughed when I gasped. "Sorry," she shrugged, "It's dinner."

I open my eyes.

I close them: My mother, holding something dead over the stove. Something unfamiliar dragged up from an animal. Frozen. Thawed.

Someone opens the bedroom door briefly but closes it again, and I hear a scrap of Gary's voice in the distance of the living room. Laughter. Dull, as if it's passing through thick glass. I keep my eyes closed, and I know the bruises around them are magenta, or midnight blue.

He lifts his weight from my body, and I hear him pull his pants back on, stuff his shirttails into them, pull on his boots. I don't move.

Silence, then he sits back down on the edge of the bed.

I can smell October on his clothes. Dark, wet fur. The smell of winter pushing up through the Michigan dirt. Twisted tree roots. Rusty water seeping under that.

Something cold passes between my breasts, and I remember the tang of metal in my mouth, once, when I drank a handful of that rusty water from the river.

The cold passes up my chest like a tin finger into the soft, empty, round place that pulses at the base of my throat. As if a small animal lived under there, in a throbbing nest. I can hear him. Growling, I think, deep in his chest, like a hungry dog. Rattling and damp. Famished. Ready to eat some other ruined animal alive.

The cold doesn't move, and I don't open my eyes. It's as if a small, chilled bird has settled there. A frozen bird.

A frozen diamond.

Or a sharp sliver of hail:

Some mirror fragment of the sky fallen onto my throat.

And when I finally realize it's the edge of a knife he's holding there, steady and pressing, just above my collarbone, that it's a sharp metal blade pressed firm and icy against my neck, and what that means, I sit up.

Suddenly frantic, I gasp straight into that knife with all the life I have and cut my own throat fast.

$\mathcal{U}$NCLE ANDY stood behind my mother, his shadow falling across her, but she was laughing. A hoe in her hand, it filled up with blue sky when she wiped it on the grass and let it fall beside her as she packed the dirt down around the rosebush he'd given her.

Pressing the earth.

Packing it down. She was wearing a halter-top, and her back was pure light, reflecting nothing. He ran his darker hand over the skin, dividing the light between her bare shoulders.

I looked at the rosebush, which was already heavy with dead, red petals — though the earth under it was wildly alive, being tunneled and torn up, turned by insects squirming, being born. My mother hummed low and hungry behind her lips, and I could hear it coming up from that black soil.

She stood and kissed him, and I picked up the hoe and stabbed it over and over into the soft ground my mother had broken and closed around the rose.

▼

"What the fuck" — the light snaps on, and I see his face above me. The blue eyes, the blond beard, a few inches from my own before the yellow room flashes off the knife in his hands and I close my eyes *(too beautiful, too bright)*. His lips are wet, but his eyes are stunned as something just born. Blood on his shirt — redder than you might imagine, redder, maybe, than he'd imagined. When he sees it on himself, he gasps.

And when I close my eyes, I see my mother planting a rosebush in the back yard in summer — the only time I've ever seen her garden. That velvet red. Her hands are full of dirt, and the dirt squirms with fat and steaky worms. She isn't wearing gloves. Her legs are smooth and white. I remember, that morning, how she'd shaved them, and a trickle of blood had run from her thigh down the drain, billowing in the bath water, luxurious as hair. "Leila, get me a Band-Aid," she'd said.

"What the fuck did you cut her for?"

When I open my eyes again, Rob is standing over me — pale in the yellow light, shaking, weak, familiar. His forehead flickers with sweat. Someone moves into the doorway behind him, and he turns fast. "Get the fuck out of here," he says, voice cracking. He goes to the bedroom door and slams it shut.

"Oh my god, oh god, oh god," muttering. He starts to search the dresser drawers for something, throwing handfuls of white socks and underwear to the floor as he searches. Finally he hauls out a woman's short bathrobe. Terrycloth, and he tears it in half fast with his bare hands. There is the sound of fur being slashed with a pocket knife as the cloth rips. Something small and sharp cutting a tough, dry hide, and I see that deer again. In the neighbors' yard. Swinging a bit in the October wind. Its eyes were open, or closed, and something ran black from its slack mouth.

"Sit up, sweetheart," he says, slipping a hand behind my back, between my shoulder blades, easing me up. I feel dizzy, and the room grows darker before it explodes again with light. Rob presses a torn square of the bathrobe to my chest.

"We've got to get you out of here, baby," he whispers in my ear. The message, as it tunnels through the canals, musty paths to my brain, is soft and warm, while the rest of the house comes alive with louder whispering now. Outside, I can hear clear sound. A raccoon screams cold and sharp. Something dragged, metal, across cement. And the dog is back, chained again, leaping at the emptiness before him in silence, clanging, just the sound of a woman dancing without music in metal shoes.

"Do you hear me, Leila? We've got to get you out of here. You've got to sit up, sweetheart. We've got to get your dress on."

Out there, I can hear the cluttered ruin of the vegetable garden, too, rustle. Then, silence, except for Rob's breath, like a bear's — except for the low whispers in the living room. I think of a field of pumpkins I've driven past in October. Just at dusk, all those heavy heads resting, nestled, in deep green vines like godheads or sleeping hoboes off the road: They were dreaming the future for me. My death. A white frenzy of feathers in the sky over Suspicious River. Their whispers grew louder and louder the further and faster I drove.

Rob leans over to pick the dress up off the floor, stands to slip it over my head. There's blood on his hands and on the dress when I look down. Oily, and bright. He buttons the pearl buttons over the blood, and they go dark and thick with it. Whispering again, "You've got to stand up, baby. Gary's back. You got to get out of here now."

Rob's sweat shimmers on his upper lip as he slips another woman's sweater up my arms, buttons it up over my dress. It is a black sweater, and it fits. I can smell my blood in the unfamiliar wool of it like a strange, new animal — something undiscovered, moving through the sewers while we sleep, something that's made a nest and given birth down there.

The yellow light becomes cold as Rob slides the bedroom window open. I hear him rip the screen with something sharp. I hear animal feet scurry through the grass outside. Small claws clicking in the branches overhead. I think there must be new species being born all the time — in the sewer, in the woods, crawling out of the forest to be mangled, unrecognizable, on the highway under tires.

Beyond recognition comes to mind. *Identified by dental records* comes to mind. I remember a headline, *Two Severed Female Legs Found in Muskegon Dumpster,* and another article, an inch long, about a hunter whose dog dug up the body of a girl I'd gone to high school with. *A runaway* they'd called her when she disappeared one Saturday after a football game. Maybe they'd imagined her leaping, white-hoofed, across the burnout of autumn fields, *running away.* But she'd been strangled with a belt and buried in a duffle bag instead.

That hunter hadn't wanted to look, but the dog *would not leave the site,* the paper said. It howled and tore at the earth. Frenzied.

He knew what was under there, the hunter said, shaking, when reporters asked him for details the next day.

The dog pawed up the grave, snuffling, until the hunter saw hair.

Rob helps me to the window, and I stand in front of it, leaning into him, looking at the slash in the screen that leads outside to nothing but a blue-black sky.

The air blowing through it tastes like a tarnished spoon in my mouth, and I gulp what's on it down.

Shadows.

Something moves out there, slips behind a high hedge of loose leaves like a ragged wall. Thin blade of a moon. A few cool stars. Bats, maybe, or something with wings tossed from the roof — bleating a bit, but flying.

There's blood on my teeth now, too. Blood on the back of my hands. I can see black roses on my cheekbones, still swelling. Rob doesn't look at my face. He touches my hair gently as I step through the ripped-open screen into darkness and wind, not sure how far down the earth will be as I feel myself fall through it, getting used to falling just before the earth stops me fast and hard in an exhausted garden, covered now in cold leaves and a few damp squares of burlap.

I'm lucky, I think when I touch my knees and elbows with the palms of my hands: Once, I saw a bald, wet baby bird, wings pink and useless as the lids of a child's eyes. It had fallen like that from a nest and landed on the windshield of the neighbor's car with no sound at all.

Rob leans out of the window as I stand up again slowly, tired, and he's still whispering. I can barely hear him. He seems to be suspended over my head like a hollow planet, an exposed god, by long white threads. "Go down to the river and start running in that direction," he points to the sky in front of him. "You're five miles from town. I'll come after you as soon as I can."

"*Go*," he says, making an arc in the air over me as if he's throwing something invisible into the wind. "*Run.*"

I can't feel the ground underneath my feet, though I know it's there, shocking up through the bones of my legs each time I hit it with my bare heel. The house is quiet and bright behind me, but even without it I can see in the dark. I see a swing set, red striped, ruined by weather, and it smells like rust. An old bicycle, a girl's, collapsed on its kickstand as if it's been tossed off another planet. A meteor with plastic streamers on its white handlebars. An oily chain. A silver garbage can of rain. A shiver of trees around the river, and the sound of water slipping, down there, through earth — very close, the river sounds like a body, bleeding, but alive.

I run toward that, through the back yard, until the mowed grass turns to long, dead weeds. I run until the light from the house flickers in branches behind me and goes out.

Then I slide down.

The river's there. Quiet, but it smooths over a few white stones, and I can hear those stones.

Mud, crossing the river.

Beneath my feet, the stones feel smooth, and they don't cut. The muck is sweet, and something with warm blood, greased fur, passes between my ankles, kisses them, and a tree reaches down to take my hand and help me up, out of the water, to the other side of the river:

Strange, I think, how all of it has become human since I was last here — when it had all gone by barren around me, dragging its dead deer away, along with its fish — suffering, winged, or tumored in the chemical dark. Its styrofoam cups and beer bottles.

I run along the other side of the river, stumbling but strong, leaving a bloody trail of footprints behind me in the mud.

As if the glass has cracked in my glass slippers.

As if the river were a mother I should have trusted.

*L*OOK UP.

  The moon is a clean sickle, and only now and then a shred of cloud passes through its claw. When you hold your hand out in front of you, it fills with silver, like something filched. You give it back to the darkness when you make a fist, and even the stars hiss. A few of them fall when you stare at the sky. A handful of planets slip into the river — too quick to catch, even with a net. Now, each breath you take is a fast stab between your ribs, and your heart pushes water up through your lungs, through the moon slice across your throat:

  This is what the river says as it gets wider.

  It gets wider, the farther I walk, but I can hear footsteps on the other side.

EILA?"

"Leila?"

When they aren't calling my name, they are whispering to each other.

Sticks snap under their feet.

On the other side of the river, something flashes, metal. A wristwatch, or a ring — something silver catching moonlight like a razor. Even the sharp little slivers of the river's fish glint under the shallow edges of water.

That's how bright the night sky is.

I move out of its white dust, then, and the river's mirror fills with stars.

I move into the trees, the shadows of trees, where the moon hangs over me with nothing on its butcher hook — only a few leaves still clinging to the very top of the trees, high up, waving down at me like the little hands of children from the sky — snagged in branches, trapped there until the first snow drags them down. "Hello?"

"Leila?"

"Are you there?"

"Leila?"

"Leila, wait."

I hear footsteps in the water, crossing or wading with or

without shoes, and I think I hear a car ease its solid weight over soft mud, no headlights, then the whispers again.

I get down on the earth, kneeling at first, looking up at the sky as I do. If you saw me now, you might think I was a woman praying, a woman knocked to her knees by the love of a god, but I'm not. I'm hiding from everything, especially God. I put my hands in the dirt, press my stomach to it, my chest, my bloody dress.

And, wearing another woman's sweater, I cross my arms over my head — wet wool to protect it — and I press my face into the mulch, close my eyes.

"Where is she?"

I try not to breathe, but when I do, I smell deep sleep down there. Ruined sheets left on a laundry line all summer in the rain — brought back in and spread across the bed: Sleep in those sheets and you will dream you are the weather itself. In your dream, you are all four corners of the flat land tucked under the world with wind.

The blood on my dress has gone stiff across my breasts, and it feels like a new, tougher skin.

An animal's hide.

I hear my heart knock dull against the ground.

Small gasps through a damp slash, and pale red clay against my mouth.

Until suddenly I'm dropped, bloody and crying, by white wings into the world.

There is the glare of forsythia against a purple sky and the early, miniature unfolding of leaves like green baby hands in the trees. They reach, screaming with life, toward the hot gas and atoms they came from — star food, photosynthesis — until the earth and everything in it is dusted with sun — branches, bird feathers, imagination, and dishes.

Creatures crawl out of the thawed river. They die or survive, give birth to new creatures whose moist eyes flutter open in the light. Languages are forgotten or invented. Fires die. And a million random events begin to make sense in what is no longer the void. All the while, the deafening roar of steam engines or jets, and a tinny piano pounding out *Happy Birthday* down the block.

I'm born, a girl without wings, and when I look up at my mother's face through a new prism of tears, she is the world without end, amen, and the sky beyond her is only a white backdrop of flimsy cloth — day stars, feathers, something wriggling, now, on the moon's hook in the bright air, breathing with new gills.

My life spins forward after that, only faster:

I am standing in the doorway of my parents' bedroom, and it's bright. The white pine headboard is a blank screen behind them. A pink towel is flung like a glove on the floor. A small, smooth bottle of violet water on the dresser. The sound of something that's been boiling, slowing now, rolling but still warm.

My uncle stands then, picks up the knife, which looks no different than any knife — smooth and steel, a black handle. The blood on it is slippery and technicolor red. He opens the top drawer of my mother's dresser and drops it into a bed of slips and hose, then he slides the drawer closed again and looks at me. He puts his hands over his face. Breathing hard, it seems his face has melted in such brilliant light in the middle of the night. His face turns to water in his hands as he sobs.

Then he swallows. He takes his hands from his face, and I see that it is ruined. He turns his palms toward the ceiling, as if to show me they are clean. Washed in her blood, two handfuls of absolutely nothing. Behind him, light blazes white on my mother.

My own hands are small, white leaves. I put them near my mouth before I scream, but there's only silence inside me. Bright as the steam off a block of ice.

I look at my hands again. They are brittle as broken white

wings in the cold hand of a man on his knees in the slick-wet clinic parking lot:

Don't kill your baby, he says.

A rubber glove of blood: I am at the Golden Dragon, spooning up blood soup. And then I am in a hot room at the Swan Motel. Dust stuffs my throat. On my knees. He leans with his whole weight into my face to slap me, but it knocks me even further forward, into him.

He knew, when he slapped me, that my body would defy gravity.

His arms were already open to catch it.

He knew it when he saw me standing behind the counter, opening the guest book, looking for his name. Before he even heard me speak.

I look up.

Here she is, he says.

Shadows pass over me. Breathing, I press my ear closer to the ground, and finally, after all this time, my mother speaks to me, in a voice of water. She says:

He'll have a gun, Leila, and he'll push you down on your knees, stand behind you, and he'll fire it once into the back of your head. The sun will just be coming up, and a pink fog will rise off the river. You'll think you can smell that fog, like smoke from a cherry bomb, but it will just be gun. Then, he'll put your body in the trunk of your car. He'll drive it to the Leelanau Peninsula while the blond one follows in the silver Thunderbird. They'll drive to the end of a dirt road, and they'll set your car on fire.

Somewhere, already, a headline is being typed.

*O*NE OF THEM CROUCHES down next to me, touching the wet sleeve of my sweater with a light hand, and the other one stands behind me, face outside the shadows. He is the one I see most clearly when I look up.

"We were afraid you'd bleed to death," he says.

I roll to my side, and the night feels cold in the black nest of this other woman's sweater over my chest — cold now with my fresh blood.

Gary strikes a match under that one's face, and the blond beard and the cigarette glow orange, suspended for a moment in the dark, making a jack-o'-lantern of his skull.

There is movement all around us. Paws, claws, the cold slap of a fish in the river, beer bottles buoying, knocking empty against the stones as they wash away from town — wash down to bigger water.

I try to sit up, but can't. There is a rush of wind in my ears. A speeding train. I see myself for a moment as a passenger on it. *Chicago*, it says on my ticket. I might be wearing a raincoat. Beige. It is the future, charging ahead with clattering wheels with or without me. I ease back into the ground, slow motion. Settling.

"We didn't want you to die out here by yourself," he says.

I close my eyes.

The air smells like iron, and I roll onto my back and look up at the sky. Clouds of dust-light blow back and forth across it like chiffon.

Dance of a thousand scarves.

White sailboats, diffused as feathers — the Northern Lights: I recognize those. I remember dreaming those. I remember sitting at the edge of my bed, that jewelry box open — handfuls and handfuls of cash.

Maybe *this* is what I'd wanted.

I close my eyes again. The sound of lungs above me. I smell their smoke, their sweat, the way something smolders before it explodes. I remember the smell of meat roasting over coals in Vets Park on the Fourth of July. Animal sacrifice, it seemed. Bombs exploding beautiful and more elaborate than death in the sky, while the old soldiers in the cemetery slept under small, snapping flags — the grass above their dreams as short and burned back as crew-cut boys, as the fur on a pit bull's back.

When I open my eyes again, those lights blink and weave around the trees. The sky is a flat sheet — a huge white rug shaken into wind, dust and ashes flying. I whisper, "What are you going to do?"

Gary laughs, or coughs.

"We're going to kill you," the blond one says.

I open my mouth and feel the solar ash of those exploded stars fall onto my teeth from the sky. This is enough, I think: I've tasted space.

If you want to live, you should run, she whispers.

If you don't, close your eyes, and it's over.

Time passes.

Whole lives.

But then, unlikely as it seems, I stand up, slow. The sun in front of me has begun to push up into the distance like a thin curl of bleached hair. I stare at that for a moment, but I can hear their teeth — small circles grinding smaller circles. Gary says, "Kneel down."

I could kneel now, I know.

I could return my hands and knees to the mud, without hope — a woman drawing the forest around her like a grave, utterly lost, the East in every direction. Trees moving in around me. But, instead, something rises up, suddenly and in total silence, over a line of trees in front of me. It seems to rise *from* me. A tangible scream. All feathers. I don't even have to look to know what's there:

On the ground, their shadows could be children, or planes, monkeys, angels, dogs, crossing the sky with wings. They are rising, flustering, beating the air, ready to leave the only home they have. Hovercraft — the whir of those birds like celestial machines, and I know what this means. I have watched them every October for years from the office of the Swan Motel — this gathering of motion, migration. These hundreds of sweet beasts churning the air to ocean. I know, now, where I am — how close I am again to where I'm from.

So, I run.

Those massive birds. Bulky angels. I run in the opposite direction.

Behind me, their breathing, their feet hitting the ground hard, like mine, but I don't look back. The future, like the past, is only a few steps ahead of me, and when I stumble through the archway of trees into a clearing near the river, I see it. Sunrise. In it, three huge swans are waiting, pink-feathered in this new light, wading and shuddering at the edge of the river, making low, reedy sounds in their throats. When they see me, they honk, hunker, then all three beat their feathers together and fly into the sky, following the others. The three crucifixes of their shadows waver across the ground, then disappear.

In front of me, a thin fog rises off the water, and through it I can see the pastel sign of the Swan Motel as it brands the bright morning weakly with neon on the river's other side.

"Leila?"

A woman shouts. I see the arc of a cigarette tossed through air into water.

"Leila?"

I open my arms to her, and then I hold them above my head as I wade into the river.

It's deep here.

The black water rises over my waist, oily, and then my body goes numb with the cold. The mud at the bottom of the river sucks at my bare heels, but it can't hold me back. I'm stronger than the mud.

And at the edge of the water, wading toward me, Millie glows, rose-flushed in the sun coming up. Her hair is wild around her face. She has her hands cupped around her heart as if to keep it in her chest, and her eyes are wide with colored light. I stumble up.

"Leila. My god. You're bleeding to death," she says. She is sobbing then, "They've been looking everywhere for you."

Again, I am on my knees.

This time, I put my face down at Millie's feet, and I can smell the rubber soles of her shoes, the grass and mud under those. I can hear the buttons on her jean jacket rattle as she trembles over me, and then she bends down to touch my hair. I remember hands. I remember being touched, turned, in blinding light with rubber gloves. My eyes opening for the first time. The sound of my own first scream, my mother choking on still wind and her own sobs. Millie's fingers are warm and bony on the back of my neck.

"We have to get some help," she says, but she doesn't move. I see us from the sky.

Frozen.

A lime-green scarf of frost wreathes us while the sun continues to rise like beautiful red and yellow tropical fruit smashed and smeared low over the edge of the earth. Fog ripples the river like pink smoke skirts, and Millie just stares straight ahead, not blinking, crying, watching the weak trembling of branches across the river, something creeping through the trees. Snaking its way to us. The sound of strong wings receding.

Don't look, I want to say to her. *There's nothing on the other side.*

But she still stares, lips pale and parted, and even the small blond hairs on her arms shiver with life as she breathes the musty feathers they've left behind and the sweet, weedy air.